THE COTTAGE BY CONISTON

THE COTTAGE BY CONISTON

DEBORAH M. HATHAWAY

BOOKS BY DEBORAH M. HATHAWAY

Stand Alone Novels
A Secret Fire
When Two Rivers Meet
To Warm a Wintered Heart

A Cornish Romance Series
On the Shores of Tregalwen, a Novella
Behind the Light of Golowduyn, Book One
For the Lady of Lowena, Book Two
Near the Ruins of Penharrow, Book Three

Belles of Christmas Multi-Series
Nine Ladies Dancing, Book Four
On the Second Day of Christmas, Book Four

Seasons of Change Multi-Author Series
The Cottage by Coniston, Book Five

For my husband—

The first book I dedicated to you wasn't very good.
I thought I'd make it up to you by dedicating
a better one to you.

Well, hopefully it's better.
You'll have to let me know.

CHAPTER ONE

*B*ath, August 1816

This could not be happening. Not again. There was no possible way that Miss Amy Paxton could be rejected for the second time in under a year.

But she knew the signs. His flitting gaze, shuffling boots, reddened cheeks. And the utter dread sinking onto the gentleman's features as he opened his mouth yet again to express in the gentlest way that he, regrettably, did not return her feelings. Not in the slightest.

Unfortunately, Mr. Dominic Roberts was displaying all of the signs. "I truly am sorry, Miss Paxton."

Amy barely registered his apologetic tone, embarrassment cascading down on her like the pouring fountain they stood beside in her family's garden. Water spilled to the pool below, falling past stone swans, their necks slender and dramatically curved as they stood side by side. The tips of their wings merged at the bottom as if holding hands.

She stared at them listlessly. Even statuary birds were more fortunate in love than she was. Perhaps if she gawked at them and held her tongue long enough, Mr. Roberts would leave

1

without another word, then Amy could pretend this whole disaster hadn't even occurred.

"Miss Paxton? Did you hear me?"

Blast.

Her cheeks stung with bitter humiliation. Why had she ever invited him to Roseley House? Well, she knew why. But that plan had ricocheted to hit her squarely in the heart.

She drew in a deep breath. She couldn't remain quiet forever. Nor could she behave like she had the last time this happened with a gentleman—losing all dignity and running through his town, all while sobbing uncontrollably.

She grimaced. That was not her best moment. Nor was *this*. Her best choice now would be to maintain her self-respect by feigning confident indifference.

Strapping a smile to her lips, she faced the man directly. "Oh, there is no need to apologize, sir. I assure you. I simply ask that you forget I ever mentioned a word."

He blew out a disbelieving breath. "That may be difficult to do, as I'm certain you can understand. After all, one does not often hear a lady declare such things to a gentleman. Especially when unsolicited."

She blinked. Receiving compliments from and spending time with a gentleman was not good enough reason for her to express her feelings for him? She knew more than anyone how forward she could be at times, but what was the reasoning behind mincing words in regard to one's feelings? Especially when Mr. Roberts had clearly felt enough for her to *kiss* her. Of course it had only been on her hand...

"You really are a lovely woman, Miss Paxton," Mr. Roberts said.

Lovely? Ah, yes. There was nothing so flattering as being described by the same word one uses to illustrate the weather. Or food. This man was squeezing lemon juice into her already gaping wound. Perhaps she'd been wrong to assume he was a gentleman, after all.

His voice softened, no doubt to lessen the cruelty of his coming words. "But I believe our relationship is better suited for friendship."

Friendship. There it was. The ultimate blow.

She pumped her head up and down in what she wanted to be a nod, though she feared she looked more like a helpless duckling treading water against a river's flow. That wasn't too far from how she felt.

"Oh, that will be fine, of course. I am more than happy to remain friends." If friends meant she'd never have to see him again. "Yes, friends would be...lovely. That's what I would prefer more than anything."

He gave her an odd look. "If you are so content with being friends, why ever were you hinting at marriage?"

"Hinting at marriage?" She released a stinted laugh. "Sir, I was not hinting at marriage. I was simply complimenting your qualities as a gentleman."

"But you said you desired to spend the rest of your—"

"Very good, sir!" Her shout muffled his words. Thank heavens. She couldn't bear to hear them repeated. "I think I must return indoors now. Mama will be missing me. Thank you for calling today."

She took a step back, bumping against the edge of the fountain and teetering back and forth before managing to steady her footing. That would be just the thing to seal the coffin over her proverbial social death—falling into a water feature.

Mr. Roberts reached out to help her. "Are you well?"

"Of course!" Why was she still shouting? She waved him away, rounding the fountain. "All is well. I am well. Everything is wonderfully and perfectly well. Good day, Mr. Roberts."

After delivering the fastest curtsy of her life, Amy turned on the heel of her half-boot and fled toward her home. The clang of the iron gate signaled the departure of Mr. Roberts behind her, but she did not stop her quickened strides until she entered the safety of Roseley House and approached the sitting room. She paused in the doorway, her parents seated exactly where she'd left them before she'd taken her misguided walk in the gardens with Mr. Roberts.

"Good morning, my dear. I was…" Mama's voice faltered, her brow pursed as she took in the sight of her daughter. "Amy? Whatever is the matter?"

Papa lowered his book with the same look of concern.

"It happened again," Amy mumbled.

"What happened again?" Mama's brow wrinkled with worry. "You mean…"

Amy nodded. "Yes. Again."

"To what are you referring?" Papa asked.

Mama's indistinguishable whisper rippled across the room.

"What was that?" he questioned.

Amy closed her eyes with a stifled sigh as Mama's whisper sounded louder. "She's been rejected again."

"Again?" Papa's blunt question cut through the heavy silence.

Amy groaned, holding her hands to her face to hide the red flames of embarrassment that had yet to diminish from her time in the garden.

"Mr. Paxton!" Mother reprimanded. "Can you not see how heartbroken our daughter is?"

Heartbroken? Amy wasn't sure that was the right word. Sad, yes. Embarrassed, absolutely. But she wasn't heartbroken. Heavens, she wasn't even crying. But then, why wasn't she?

Mama stood with arms outstretched toward Amy. "Come. Sit, my dear."

Amy dropped her hands and followed Mama's entreaty.

"Again," Papa muttered to himself, fingers rubbing against his eyes as if he attempted to ward off a headache.

Amy would have a headache, too, if she had such a daughter.

One who was incapable of obtaining the love of a gentleman. Her parents had always encouraged her to marry for love, but Papa was no doubt dreading the prospect of having to provide for a nonsensical daughter for the rest of his life.

Amy sat on the settee nearest the soft, crackling fire, and Mama pulled up a chair to sit before her. "Now, tell us what has happened, my dear."

Amy shrugged. "I haven't the faintest idea, Mama. Really, I don't. I told myself to be more careful. I *was* more careful. Because of the last disaster."

She gave them a heavy glance. Mama and Papa nodded simultaneously, though they remained silent, much to Amy's relief. A year ago, Amy had thought a distant cousin had loved her. Foolishly, she'd attempted to share her own feelings by offering a kiss first, only to be set gently aside with another "I wish to remain friends" declaration.

Fortunately, she'd moved forward and dared to find love again. *Unfortunately*, she'd chosen Mr. Roberts with whom to do so.

"You both know the time I've spent with Mr. Roberts," she continued. "Horse rides, balls at the Assembly Rooms, picnics, walks. I've been very patient through the whole process. Then today, I waited until he…" She eyed Papa. "He kissed me."

Papa's inquisitive gaze instantly hardened. "He did *what?*"

"Do not be angry with him, Papa. I permitted him to do so. Besides, it was only—"

"The nerve of that man," Papa interrupted, his jaw tight and lips in a taut line. "I ought to—"

"For heaven's sake, Mr. Paxton, please allow Amy to finish her story." Mama's exasperated eyes met her husband's. "Then you may go on and on about all the things you wish to do to Mr. Roberts but never shall because you are a respectable gentleman."

Papa scowled, but he kept his mouth closed.

"Now, go on, dear Amy."

"It was only a kiss to my hand, I assure you, Papa."

Papa's shoulders lowered, though his frown remained. "Well, that is better than I assumed."

"Go on, Amy," Mama encouraged again with another fleeting look of impatience at Papa.

Amy nodded. "After Mr. Roberts's affection and his compliments on my nature and appearance, I thought for certain that was a clear indication that he held some regard for me. As such, I told him that I would not mind spending the rest of my life with him. But once the words left my lips, his entire demeanor changed, and he claimed a desire to remain friends and only friends." She finished with a confused huff.

Her parents exchanged looks.

"Perhaps he was simply not ready to hear your declaration," Mama suggested.

Amy tucked in her chin in disbelief. "How could he not be? He kissed my hand, for heaven's sake!" She leaned toward Mama, lowering her voice with a furtive glance at Papa. "And I assure you, Mother, his compliments about my appearance were very favorable, enough to make any woman blush tenfold."

Papa's eyes hardened further, and Mama looked away, flustered. "Many a man might flatter a woman without any intention of marrying her. But either way, a lady does not typically declare herself to a gentleman."

Amy pursed her lips. Yes, she was aware of the fact, and she was adamantly opposed to it.

She threw up her hands in surrender. "I will never understand men, nor why I must wait for one to declare his intentions when I am more than ready to proclaim my own." Her brow deepened. "And why would he say such things, spend such a great deal of time with me, and share his affection if he had no intention of marrying me?"

"Well," Mother began, "perhaps—"

"Because all men are repugnant," Father interjected. Their eyes fell on him, but he shrugged. "It's true. You must simply find the one least repugnant of them all."

"Oh, honestly, Mr. Paxton," Mama said, pursing her lips with displeasure. "Why would you say such a thing? We women wish to believe the man we choose to marry is honorable and amiable." She gave him a pointed look.

Papa leaned forward, closing his book and placing it on the table beside him. "I only say such a thing because our Amy must know the truth about men if she is ever to succeed in her many attempts to marry. Perhaps if she'd known such a fact before, she would not have been rejected."

Amy had inherited her bluntness from Papa, though she knew his words were not meant to harm her.

"Never mind your father," Mama said. "You know there are good men out in the world. You must work harder at finding the better ones amidst all the *repugnant* ones, as your father so aptly puts it." She softened her voice. "Perhaps next time, you might choose to disregard the attention from one of Hugh's friends. Mr. Roberts does stand out better than most of them, but you know your brother does not keep with the best company."

"Nor is *Hugh* the best company," Amy mumbled.

A cough sounded from Papa that sounded suspiciously like a stifled laugh, but he pulled up his book and focused harder on the pages.

Mama ignored him, giving the warning look to Amy instead. "Regardless of Hugh's choices, and no matter how we disapprove of his less than favorable behavior, he is still your brother. And you know he will wish to speak with you tonight about all that has occurred."

Dread trickled into Amy's stomach. She was not in the right frame of mind to manage her brother's teasing. "I cannot bear seeing him yet. Might I have dinner sent to my room this evening? Papa?"

Mama sighed, glancing to Papa, who gave a subtle nod with a twitch of his mouth.

Amy's lips curved in a smile. Papa had always had a soft spot for her.

"Very well," Mama relented. "Perhaps being kept from your brother's teasing for an evening will give you the fortitude to see to it in the morning."

Amy nodded, pressing a kiss to Mama's cheek then moving to embrace her father, who stood as she departed.

"Take heart, little cricket," he said with a wink, using his endearment from when she was younger. "You'll find love yet."

Amy's heart warmed for but a moment as she strolled toward her room. As much as Papa loved his "little cricket," the truth was evident. He wished her to marry as much as Mama did. For what parents would want to financially support their daughter forever? At nearly twenty-three and with two rejections already listed under her life experiences, the likelihood of her becoming less of a burden on her parents was becoming more and more unlikely—which was why she'd attempted to take control of the reins tied between her and Mr. Roberts.

She entered her room, standing mutely in the center of it. As much as she wished to be a recluse for the rest of her life—or at least until news of her folly made its way in, around, and out of Bath—she couldn't do such a thing to her parents.

But then, how was she to ever fall in love while rumors of her and Mr. Roberts abounded? For surely the man would not hesitate to share his experience about the woman who was so desperate for love that she created a relationship out of compliments and hand-kisses.

Her discouraging thoughts pressed heavily on her mind far into the night. She lay awake, staring up at the dark blue bed hangings until a knock sounded at her door.

She recognized the quick raps instantly.

"Leave me be, Hugh."

Her elder brother's muffled chuckle slipped through the thick door. "Come now, Amy. Do allow your brother to speak with you."

"No. I don't wish to hear anything you have to say." She looked to the door when he didn't respond. Had she convinced him to leave? No, that would be far too easy. Hugh would never relinquish a moment to tease her.

"Not even if I express my condolences? Or perhaps tell you how penitent Mr. Roberts was for rejecting you?"

Now *that* was compelling.

With a sigh, and knowing full well that the disadvantages fully outweighed the positives, she rolled out of bed, donned her dressing gown, then tiptoed to the door.

She opened it just a crack, alerting Hugh with a firm frown that she would not be tolerating any of his teasing this evening.

He must have missed her warning as he grinned from ear to ear.

"Good evening, sister. I hear you've made quite the unfortunate mistake with our Mr. Roberts."

Her lips pulled down. "Yes, my mistake was befriending one of your friends."

"Befriending? I heard you were doing much more than that."

Her ears warmed. "You are incorrigible, Hugh."

She made to close the door, but Hugh's hand prevented it. "No, no, wait. I do apologize. I truly wish to speak with you. And I will do my very best not to tease you."

She peeked at him through the crack between the door and frame. The mischievous light in his eyes shone all the brighter with the candle in his hand. Hugh could not help himself when it came to teasing her, no matter what he said. Amy would be far safer to remain away from him until the whole incident was in the past.

But she could not help her curiosity. "You promise to tell me what Mr. Roberts has said about the encounter?"

Hugh nodded with a dramatic hand to his chest. "On pain of death, I swear to tell you everything."

With another wary glance, she pulled open the door and pushed past her brother to sit on the window seat situated down the corridor. "Very well, then. Tell me what he has to say about his shocking behavior."

"*His* shocking behavior? From what he told me, you are the one to be blamed."

He sat beside her, placing the candle between them. They had situated themselves in a similar fashion many times when they were children. Hugh would convince her to listen to his ghost stories, which inevitably ended with Amy rushing to Mama's room to sleep the remainder of the night away.

At least Amy knew now she could leave if Hugh's conversation turned in the slightest way to spirits, teasing, or how many women loved him—all of which she could not abide.

"And how am I to be blamed? *He* kissed me. Or did he forget to recount that fact?"

"He kissed your hand, Amy. That is hardly a proposal."

So Mr. Roberts hadn't neglected that part of the story either. She pursed her lips, the sting of betrayal burning her cheeks. "So he feels no remorse in his encouragement of me?"

She knew Mr. Roberts to be a flirt—he had to be if he considered Hugh a friend—but in the near month she'd spent with him, he'd never crossed the line of impropriety, which was why the compliments and kiss to her hand that morning had meant such a great deal to her.

"On the contrary," Hugh said. "He certainly was not intending to encourage you toward matrimony. He was simply having a bit of fun. Like many gentlemen, he would not have been opposed to a kiss free of consequences or attachments."

Amy scoffed in disgust. Papa was right. Men were repugnant.

"However," Hugh continued, his voice lowering, "when he saw where your thoughts were directed, he wished to make quick work of it so as not to hurt you further. He is fond of you. But he is not ready to attach himself fully to another, that is all there is to it."

Well. At least Mr. Roberts had some honor, though it did nothing to lessen her humiliation. She picked at the hardened wax burgeoning at the bottom of the candle holder. "I suppose he has already told my folly to half of Bath?"

"For someone who wished to marry the man, you certainly think very little of him. Mr. Roberts desires to keep what happened close to his chest. He said he has a—what was it—a *conscience?*" He said the word slowly, as if he'd never heard of it before, then winked devilishly at Amy.

She gave him an unamused glare. "Yes, you wouldn't know about anything of the kind, would you?"

His smile continued, but Amy hardly noticed, watching a small drop of the melted, opaque wax sliding down the rigid candle stick. As much as Mr. Roberts declared his good intentions, Amy had very little faith that he, or Hugh for that matter, could keep her ridiculous behavior from eventually spreading through Bath like an insuppressible disease. And once word was set free—either from a man's tongue loosened by drink or by a woman—the rumors would evolve, and Amy would be labeled a brazen tart. Then what would she do? What would her family do with her?

And why had she not considered the painful consequences beforehand?

Her shoulders sank in time with another droplet of wax. "It was so humiliating, Hugh. I'm sure I shall never live it down, nor face Society again. I ought to take my dowry and use it to fund the purchase of a cottage somewhere far away from here.

Then I can live out the rest of my days in resigned spinsterhood."

As the words left her mouth, she knew at once that such a life was not for her. She was fairly certain she'd drive herself to madness with her own company.

"Oh, heavens. Please tell me you are not serious," Hugh said, interrupting her thoughts. "If you are this miserable at two and twenty, I shudder to think what I shall have to endure when you are older, living without a soul to care for you in some forsaken cottage."

"You forget, I said I shall live far away from you."

"Yes, but you know Mother and Father will haunt me if I don't see that you are taken care of."

"Then I shall follow through with this plan for that reason alone."

Hugh chuckled, and she finally delivered a partially amused lift of her lips that lasted about as long as her relationship with Mr. Roberts.

"Come now. It is not as terrible as you are making it out to be."

"You only say that because you have never been rejected once in your life."

He smirked. "That is because women cannot help themselves around me."

Instead of what she knew he was expecting from her—feigned gagging noises—Amy nodded. "Precisely. Which is what is entirely wrong with me. Men do not love me as women love you. Even if Mr. Roberts did not wish to be attached to anyone, if I was good enough for him, or if I did not have some distinctive flaws I must be blinded to, he would not have hesitated to marry me."

Silence followed. Where was Hugh's responding quip? She pulled her dressing gown tighter around her shoulders and looked to her brother, surprised at the hesitancy in his expression.

"What is it?"

He shook his head. "Nothing."

Amy frowned. "If you do not tell me what you are withholding, I shall go straight to Papa and tell him you've been sharing ghost stories with me again."

Hugh raised his hands in retreat. "All right, all right. There is no need to threaten me."

Amy arched her eyebrows menacingly. As much as Hugh liked to toot his careless horn, he couldn't deny Papa's intimidating nature. Though their father held a special place in his heart for his daughter, he never hesitated to express his disapproval of Hugh's behavior, nor scold him because of it. And with Papa's height stretching a full-head taller than Hugh's, Hugh typically minded his manners around their father—or at least learned to hide his debauchery better.

Candlelight reflected against the window and flickered across Hugh's features as his teasing glimmer faded away.

"There was another reason for Mr. Roberts's departure from you. Something other than his lack of desire to marry."

Amy shot forward, pulling herself away from the window. "I knew it! I knew that could not have been the only reason!"

"Hush! You'll wake Father." Hugh glanced down the hallway with a wary expression.

"So what is it then? Am I unattractive? Unaccomplished?"

"No, of course not. I—"

"Did he think I wasn't talented with the pianoforte when I played for him at the Alans' dinner party?"

"No, I don't believe so—"

"Then he must have taken issue with my winning the race we had upon our horses. That has to be it. I knew I should have held back. I—"

"Heavens, Amy," Hugh interrupted. "It was no doubt your talking that sent him running."

Amy clamped her mouth shut, pulling back at the sting of his words. "Is that what he said?"

His jesting smile faded. He shifted in his seat. Was he experiencing remorse? He typically only squirmed when he felt the most despised of feelings.

"Forgive me," he whipped out. "I did not mean to offend you. No, that is not what Mr. Roberts said. He was merely frightened away by your acknowledgement of your feelings, expressing them before he even had the chance to consider his. You know you can be rather…blunt."

Amy stared. So she was right, he had not appreciated her forthrightness after all. Neither had her distant cousin. If all men didn't approve of such behavior—and Amy could not help but be forthright—she was done for.

She covered her face with her hands. "I'll never marry. This just proves it. If I cannot understand men, how can I have any hope of convincing one to marry me?"

Hugh remained silent.

She dropped her hands and stared at him. "I'm asking you a question, Hugh. How am I to marry a man for love if I cannot help but make poor decisions whenever I am around gentlemen?"

He stared, his mouth hanging open like the salmon they enjoyed eating by the sea last summer. "I suppose you must cease making *poor decisions*?"

She scoffed, turning to the light flickering in the window. "Would it could be so easy."

"It is unfortunate our parents are so good to us. Otherwise they might have made every decision for you like others are known to suffer."

He'd meant his words to be taken in jest, but Amy paused. Perhaps they *would* agree to deciding her every move? But, no.

They'd always encouraged her to have her own mind. They would not deprive her of the freedom of choice, even if she begged. Nor would any of her friends.

But her brother...

Slowly, her eyes roved toward him. Hugh had never hesitated to tell her when she was being foolish, and that was what she needed most. Guidance. Someone to help her on her journey to wedded bliss. Someone who understood men because he *was* a man.

Before she could think better of it, she blurted out her idea. "You must make my decisions for me."

Hugh sniffed a laugh. "I beg your pardon?"

CHAPTER TWO

"You must make my decisions for me," Amy repeated, bright hope flourishing past the darkness of dread inside her.

His humor slowly faded to a look of incredulity. "You can't be serious."

"I am. Completely. Don't you see? It is the perfect solution. Being a gentleman yourself, you can help me to understand the social cues of other men. You must teach me what to do, what to say, how to behave. Then I will no longer make a fool of myself, and I shall not be a burden on you or our parents any longer. You know we are to visit the Lake District with them soon. This shall be the perfect opportunity to escape my past and begin anew elsewhere—with you as my guide."

He shook his head. "Are you listening to yourself, Amy? You're asking me, Hugh, your brother—the person you've called a cad, libertine, flirt, and countless other names—to make your decisions for you."

She stared at him, unflinching. "Yes. There is no one else better for the task. And, if you help me find a husband I love, you won't have to care for me when I'm older."

"But why on earth would you trust *me* to aid you in the proper manner? What is to stop me from making a game of the whole thing?"

"Because I know, deep down in your heart, you want me to be happy." She produced a smile she hoped mimicked Hugh's most mischievous grin. "And because if you lead me astray, Papa will most certainly hear of it, and he will not be pleased."

Hugh narrowed his eyes, their dark depths not entirely void of pleasure. He was no doubt pleased to see his typically rule-adhering sister result to semi-blackmail. "You *do* make a compelling case." He rubbed the day's growth of facial hair spreading across his jaw. "You will do whatever I tell you to do if your actions concern a gentleman you desire to pursue?"

"Absolutely. Within the bounds of propriety, of course."

"Of course." His eyes twinkled. "And I assume this is going to stay between the two of us?"

"The four of us. Mama and Papa must be included, as well. You know I dislike keeping things from them."

He nodded, contemplating her offer once more before slapping his hands against his thighs with a loud clap. "Very well, I shall do it."

"Excellent. We shall begin the moment I enter Society again." She grinned, hopping down from the window seat and moving to her bedroom as she spoke over her shoulder. "That will be one month from now. In the Lake District."

He called after her. "You're not leaving the house for an entire month?"

Amy paused in her doorway. "No, I am not. I may trust you to make my decisions in finding a spouse, but when it comes to keeping your mouth shut about something embarrassing I've done, I doubt very much you are capable of doing such a thing."

He chuckled, and Amy stepped into her room with a grin.

"Amy?"

She leaned back out. "Yes?"

"I am sorry for what has occurred. And I'm sorry if he hurt you." He shifted anxiously in his seat again. Compassion. That was another feeling Hugh was always uncomfortable displaying.

Amy knew how much it took out of her brother to say such things, and suddenly, the hurt she had felt from Mr. Roberts's refusal, and the embarrassment from being rejected yet again, didn't seem so very insurmountable after all.

"Thank you, Hugh. And thank you for agreeing to help me."

"As if I had the choice." He winked, standing from the window seat with a nod. "Goodnight, Amy."

He disappeared down the hallway, his candle's light accentuating his departing shadow.

Amy let out a heavy sigh, closing the door behind her. Removing her dressing gown, she climbed back into bed and curled underneath the warm covers.

The humiliation she'd felt earlier threatened to crawl in beside her, but she pushed it aside. With Hugh dictating what she ought to do—and more importantly, what she ought *not* do —she wouldn't be a burden for much longer. Such a benefit merely required drastic measures, and following Hugh's advice was the most drastic action she could consider. Excepting, of course, essentially proposing to two gentlemen who did not love her.

Heaven knew *that* hadn't turned out well for her at all.

Coniston, Cumbria, August 1816

As the vicar began his oration, William dutifully bowed his head, staring at his boots dotted with raindrops. He stood within the drizzly churchyard, surrounded by grave markers ranging from carvings of cherubs to morbid skulls.

Water poured down from the brim of his black hat as rain pelted the back of his head, trailing down to seep through his jacket and cravat. This was not worth the misery, standing in such weather. But the rain made sense this morning. Grandfather would have wanted them to be miserable.

"'Man that is born of a woman,'" Mr. Morton read from the Book of Common Prayer, "'hath but a short time to live, and is full of misery. He cometh up and is cut down like a flower; he fleeth as it were a shadow and never continueth in one stay...'"

William clenched his hands together behind his back, fighting the urge to look at his pocket watch. The service couldn't go on for much longer. He simply needed patience. He'd waited twenty-seven years to be free. He could wait a few moments more.

"'In the midst of life we are in death. Of whom may we seek for succor but of thee, O Lord, who for our sins art justly displeased?'"

Had the vicar ever delivered the lines to someone so aptly deserving of them as Grandfather with his many sins? Everyone in attendance had to be thinking the very same thing. Arthur Eastwood's poor reputation and controlling nature stretched the length of Coniston Water.

William eyed the small gathering of men circled around the coffin. Mr. Stewart, Mr. Allen, Mr. Rutledge, Mr. Booth—not one had a glimmer of sorrow in his eyes. William was certain not a soul would be in attendance, either—including himself—were it not for their desire to support Father.

William's heart slumped low as he turned his attention to his father's red-rimmed eyes shining with moisture that rivalled the saturated graveyard grounds upon which they stood.

"I do not mourn for the man that was, Will," Father had told him just the night before, "rather for the man that could have been."

Emotion wedged in William's throat at the thought of his father's pain, but this was not the first time tears had been shed due to Grandfather's actions.

"'...Yet, O Lord God most holy, O Lord most mighty, O holy and most merciful Savior, deliver us not into the bitter pains of eternal death...'"

But Grandfather could not hurt them any longer. He couldn't keep Mother and Father in Coniston by sheer manipulation as he'd done over the past decade, nor could he keep them from improving the multiple properties they owned, or helping their tenants because Grandfather didn't think the lower class deserved their help.

And he could no longer keep William from marrying the woman he'd chosen long ago.

"'...Thou knowest, Lord, the secrets of our hearts. Shut not thy merciful ears to our prayers, but spare us, Lord most holy, O God most mighty, O holy and merciful Savior, though most worthy Judge eternal, suffer us not at our last hour for any pains of death to fall from thee.'"

Finally, the vicar paused, and the coffin was lowered into the ground. William watched the freshly cut dark pine disappear into the earth, the flourished carvings and shining brass handles emblazoned in his memory—just as Grandfather's face was, as gaunt in death as it was in life.

"'Forasmuch as it hath pleased Almighty God of his great mercy to take unto himself the soul of our dear brother here departed, we therefore commit his body to the ground...'"

The vicar's words faded from William's attention, the weight shifting off his chest and shoulders as the coffin disappeared out of sight. He drew in a deep breath of the fresh rain.

Grandfather was gone. Without his coffin in sight, without the man's constant, watchful eye on him, William was finally free.

When the vicar ended, and the condolences were delivered by the men in attendance, he and Father were left at the gravesite.

William stood by in silence as Father drew in a steadying breath, his tired eyes still staring at the dirt being piled atop the coffin.

"Would you mind, son, just for a moment, if…"

Nodding at once, William stepped away from his father to allow him privacy. Mr. Rutledge stood nearby, leaning heavily against his walking stick.

"How is he?" Mr. Rutledge whispered with a motion of his head to Father.

"Adjusting," William replied.

They stood for a moment in silence, rain tapping on the leaves behind them creating a calming ambience. Or perhaps it was merely being around Mr. Rutledge that prompted that peace inside William. He'd always felt that way around the gentleman.

"Mrs. Rutledge asked me to invite you to dinner tomorrow night. But if you wish to be with your family…"

"No, no. I would be more than happy to join you." William had always preferred dining and visiting with the Rutledges to remaining at home. The elderly couple had been better parent figures for William than his own mother and father had. Being with them was a nice change of pace to the gloom he'd always experienced at Birchwick Hall.

"Mrs. Rutledge will be pleased. I'm sure she'll make another apple pie to celebrate your coming."

William smiled. "Then I look forward to tomorrow even more so."

Mr. Rutledge shifted his feet with a wince, and William frowned. "You ought to go home, sir. You've been more than kind to venture out."

William had been witness to Mr. Rutledge's pains for years.

As a young boy, when he needed to escape Grandfather, he would go to the Rutledges, where he was always treated with respect and kindness. He'd seen the elderly man's health deteriorate year after year, though Mr. Rutledge's goodness remained.

William knew what a struggle it must have been to even come to the graveyard. Although, he wasn't surprised. Mr. Rutledge had always been selflessly kind.

Mr. Rutledge grimaced as he shifted again. "I think that will be for the best." He gingerly raised a hand to clasp William's shoulder. "Take care, William, of yourself and your parents. And we shall visit tomorrow."

William nodded as Mr. Rutledge hobbled away. How grateful William was for having the man as an example. Heaven knew he didn't have anyone else for that.

Intent on waiting by the carriages, William left the headstones behind, only then seeing a young woman standing just beyond the church, half-shrouded beneath grand yew trees.

Charity.

He changed his direction toward her as she stepped out from beneath the tree, her dark dress complementing the blackness of her curls, protected by a wide bonnet.

She nodded her head in greeting as he approached, her red lips void of any smile. "I do apologize for intruding. Mama advised me not to come, but after the procession, I wanted to ensure you were well."

"That is very kind of you, but I am well. It is Father I worry over."

He looked behind him, Father's shoulders sunken so far forward, his head nearly disappeared from William's viewpoint.

"I'm certain he merely needs time," Charity offered.

There was the logical answer for which he was hoping. He'd always admired Charity's intelligence and strength of mind. That was one of the reasons Grandfather had disapproved of her as a match—which was why William had been drawn to become her friend in the first place.

"Yes," he agreed. "I only hope his spirits will improve when he discovers all that life has to offer when one does not have one's every move dictated by another."

"And will you discover the same one day?" Charity stared up at him with that intent gaze she'd had ever since she was a little girl asking to play with him in his garden.

"You know I have already tasted more freedom than my parents ever have."

He may not have been able to prevent Grandfather from controlling every aspect of Mother and Father's lives—and even part of William's. But he'd done his best to keep the man's dictatorial hand from extending to others, which was why William had kept his distance from Charity.

Until now.

"At any rate, my life will be far better now." He paused, staring into the dark brown of her eyes. "*Our* lives will be better."

He hoped to make her smile, but her lips stretched into a solemn line. "You still wish to proceed, then?"

"Of course. I see no reason not to."

"Even with my departure?"

William paused. Departure? Departure. That was right. Charity was to leave for London with her mother that very week. Still, that was no reason to stop planning for what they both knew was to occur.

"Have you any objection?" he asked.

She shook her head. "Only...you recall my mother's stipulations, of course."

"Yes, I do."

How *could* he forget? Mrs. Winslow, Charity's widowed mother, was requiring Charity to spend a few months in

London to provide her with a little more "experience" before settling down and starting a family.

William didn't blame Mrs. Winslow. The woman had married at the young age of fifteen and often spoke of her regret in doing so. Though Charity was two and twenty now, Mrs. Winslow was simply behaving with caution. He couldn't fault her for that, nor Charity for thinking it wise to do, as well.

"So I shall go to London then," Charity said, "and if I return without having fallen in love with another and *you* have not fallen in love with another..."

A touch of insecurity lowered her gaze. William reached forth, taking one of Charity's gloved hands within his own. "That is not something you need to concern yourself over, surely. We *shall* wed."

Finally, a whisper of a smile brushed against her lips, but it vanished in a heartbeat. "I wish I did not have to go for so long. I shall miss you."

"And I, you. Your absence here will be felt keenly."

This time, her smile remained. Good. She didn't show it very often—yet another similarity between them. They didn't really have much to be joyful about.

"I fear I must depart now. Mama will be waiting for my return." She faced him again, holding out her hand to him. "I shall see you in three months' time, yes?"

"Yes." He reached forward, placing a kiss to the back of her glove. "I look forward to it."

And he would.

As Charity departed from the churchyard, disappearing amidst the yew trees once again, William blew out a deep breath.

Three months. He would miss his friend, their weekly horse rides by the lake, their philosophical conversations. Life was easy with Charity—and easy was what he needed for his future.

But not now. Now was the time for him to work. To set his

estates in order, to see to the tenants who were now his, and to convince his parents to take much-needed time away at the sea.

And in three months, he would marry Charity.

Because he would make his parents proud. Because his duty demanded it. Because he'd planned his whole life for it.

And because it's just what Grandfather *wouldn't* have wanted.

CHAPTER THREE

*C*oniston, *September 1816—One Month Later*
Papa peered out of the moving carriage's window. "I've been assured that Corcliffe Manor is the loveliest country house in all the Lake District. I'm sure it will become a quick favorite. We'll be certain to stay here every year from this point forward. Ah, here we are."

Amy leaned forward in the carriage seat, excitement stirring within her at his words. She was anxious to arrive at their new home—well, their home for the next two months—as well as to be rid of this jostling carriage. Her curls had nearly flattened out at her temples from all the bouncing.

But as the carriage stopped and she peered out of the window, she was met with the sight of faded white doors, overgrown ivy, cracked windows, and a garden in desperate need of a good trimming. Her smile vanished.

"Is that it?" she asked, her voice falling flat.

"Oh, dear," Mama murmured. "Mr. Paxton, are you certain we are at the right location?"

Papa frowned, leaning past his wife and moving up and

down to better see the derelict manor. "I'm certain Bryant followed the innkeeper's directions perfectly."

His thick brow pursed as their footman opened the carriage door. Father stepped down first, followed swiftly by Amy.

"Perhaps you ought to remain inside for a moment, Amy," Mama advised, still seated inside.

"No, Mama, please. My legs are desperate for a little stretch."

Mama relented with a sigh, focusing her attention instead on their second carriage pulling up behind with their help. The maids, valet, and footman stood there with whispered words to one another, unsure how to proceed about their duties.

"Mr. Bryant," Papa said. "Are you certain this is Corcliffe Manor?"

"Yes, sir." Mr. Bryant hopped down from his spot at the front of the carriage. "Says it right there."

He motioned to a crooked sign with a crack straight down the center, the piece of wood dangling from the fence with a single wire.

Sure enough, *Corcliffe Manor* was written across the sign.

"Perhaps this is why the innkeeper gave us such an odd look when we asked for directions here," Papa mumbled.

"Yes, sir. I would've driven up the rest of the drive, sir, but as you can see, it ain't fit for travel."

All eyes fell on the large holes littering the drive that stretched up to the side of the house.

"Oh, dear," Mama said again. "Clearly they are not ready for us. What are we to do, Mr. Paxton?"

Papa tapped nervous fingers to his lips. "I suppose we knock. Perhaps someone will be here who can help to guide us toward the next step."

He moved forward, and Amy instantly followed.

"No, Amy, you must stay with me."

"But, Mama, you do recall my legs." She motioned down with a theatrical gesture, and Mama relented with another sigh.

Amy scurried ahead to catch up with Papa while the rest of the household remained with Mama. Everyone apart from Hugh, of course, who had stayed behind at the Black Bull Inn for a drink and no doubt a few games—much to Papa's utter disapproval.

Amy was relieved to be away from her brother for a moment. For the past month, she'd been bracing herself to keep her agreement with Hugh. At times, she wished to go back on the deal, but as the rumors began to surface about what had occurred between Amy and Mr. Roberts, she was reminded yet again to continue with her decision to follow Hugh's advice in the Lake District—and to forget Mr. Roberts's rejection entirely.

The latter was proving rather easy. The former, however, she knew she would struggle with more.

As she approached the manor with Papa, the neglect of the house became more and more pronounced. Most of the windows were so dirty, one could not see within them if one tried, and the outside chairs and tables were overturned with only the barest of hints that the rusted furniture had once been white.

"What could cause such an abandonment of one's home?" she wondered aloud.

"Perhaps they could no longer afford the upkeep," Father suggested with a shrug. "Though, Mr. Chamberlain's last letter a mere month ago assured me the property was in a beautiful state."

Amy wrinkled her nose, stepping over a broken stone vase, spilled dirt, and dead flowers strewn across the pathway. This manor was one of the first stately homes visible outside the center of Coniston. How poorly it reflected on the town as a whole. "Well, whatever has occurred to allow such negligence, it is a tragedy. To think of the disrespect shown to what was once surely a beautiful home."

"Mmm. Indeed."

"Do they attempt to cheat us, do you think, in bringing us here?"

Father hesitated. "I'd like to believe that is not the case."

Amy's chest tightened at the idea of such dishonesty—especially to her kind and loving father. If they *did* find the owner, she wasn't certain she'd be able to keep her thoughts to herself.

They stood at the entrance together as Father knocked, waited, then knocked again.

"Just as I feared. Not a soul to be seen."

Amy leaned to one side, peering through the window from where she stood before Father knocked one last time.

"No, we shall have to return to town and ask for aid there," he said.

The thought of willingly riding in that rumbling contraption again was almost too much for Amy to bear. Just a moment longer was all she needed to stretch her legs. Then she'd be more than fine to return.

With quick steps, she moved to the window and cupped her hands against the glass, pressing her face close to the window.

"Amy…"

"I'll be but a moment." She scrunched up her nose to see better through the dust grasping onto the glass.

The inside was just as filthy as the out, though white cloths were draped over the furniture in the main entryway. Rugs were rolled and propped up on the sides of the walls, and a thick layer of dust coated the banister. It appeared as if no one had set foot inside the manor in years—apart from the freshly swept section of the floor and a small wooden bucket filled with water. A rag hung over the edge of it, and water dripped down from the fabric to the floor.

Amy pulled back with satisfaction. "There *is* someone here."

"You saw someone?"

"No, but I saw evidence of someone. See for yourself."

Papa took a few hesitant steps forward, glancing around him

as if to avoid being spotted spying, then took her place at the window.

"Ah, you are right. The water." He pulled away, looking around the grounds. "Perhaps they are outside?"

They wandered away from the door onto the overgrown grass.

"Excuse me?" Papa called out. "Is anyone there?"

No response.

"Perhaps they are behind the house," Father suggested. "I'll take a quick look while you return to Mama and the carriages."

"But, Papa—"

"We've already upset your mother enough, I think. Go on."

With a stifled sigh, Amy nodded. It was just as well. She'd have to get back in the carriage sooner or later, as they could not stay here.

Grumbling internally, she stomped along the pathway to the main drive near the stables as Papa went in the opposite direction.

Amy was not typically grumpy, but knowing her father might have been swindled—and knowing she and her family could very well be spending the night at the Black Bull Inn instead of what could've been a lovely stay in this manor—her patience was thinning.

How irresponsible of the gentleman who owned such a property and allowed them to lease the home. If Papa found him, he'd be courteous, as usual. Even *if* the gentleman needed a good talking to. Now Amy, on the other hand...If only she had the chance to speak with him. Tell him how unkind, how disruptive his decision was to...

She paused along the drive, turning to the shrill sound of a chicken's squawking, followed by more clucking behind the stables.

Chickens? That had to mean *someone* was here. Unless her father was the one disrupting the hens.

Still, she'd better be sure.

"Amy?"

She paused, looking over her shoulder to where Mama called from the just-visible carriage.

Amy nodded, though she held up a forefinger, signaling for her mother to wait just a moment. Swiftly, she turned and headed for the stables that were rather fortunately placed just out of sight from the carriages and Mama's disapproving gaze.

She poked her head into the stables first. Old, damp straw filled the ground to capacity, the stale scent accosting her nostrils. She wrinkled her nose and backed out of the edifice. No one had been inside there that day, or that year, by the look of it.

She rounded the stables next, and the clucking grew louder until she turned the corner and reached the back of the building, coming upon a small henhouse with three chickens wandering within. Their heads tipped to the side in a jerking motion as she approached, as if they wondered what this strange woman was doing on their property.

Smiling, she bent down toward them on the outside of the henhouse. "Good morning, ladies."

They clucked in response. Their lush golden feathers shone in the warm sunlight, their bodies full and plump.

"You certainly seem well-taken care of, eh? But where is your master?"

More squawking.

"You aren't being of much help, you know." She smiled at her own joke. "Well, whatever happens, I shall seek after your well-being. Will that suffice?"

Cluck, cluck, cluck.

"Excellent." She stood from her hunched position and looked around her, dusting off her skirts in the process.

There was no one in sight back here, either. She blew out a breath. The hens were clearly fed and watered, what with their glossy feathers and swelling chests. But if the owner could allow his manor to become derelict, who knew what he'd allow to happen to these hens.

Indignation rose within her. Even the mere *idea* of anyone neglecting the animals made her ill. Turning on her heel, she made for the front drive. Mama was typically just as defensive of animals. Once she heard of the chickens on the property, surely she'd be as defensive as Amy.

But Amy did not return to the carriage, for just as she rounded the corner of the stables, she came face-to-face with a cream, pointed beak and small, beady eyes.

Yelping, she lifted her hands and jumped back in surprise. The chicken, frightened by Amy's shriek, frantically flapped her wings, sending the pungent scent of poultry and golden feathers flying toward her.

In all the commotion, Amy barely registered the hands holding onto the chicken as the hen attempted to escape—the feathered body preventing any view of the person behind it.

Finally, the bird was let loose and sailed toward Amy, who waved her hands in front of her to stop the assault, backing farther away with another yelp.

Finally, the chicken landed on the ground and scurried away on her thin, scaly legs. The red, fleshy comb on top of her head quivered as she clucked toward her friends on the other side of the henhouse.

"Blast! Now she's got away again!"

Amy pressed a hand to her chest, her heart racing fiercely as she whirled toward the culprit who had managed to accost her with a hen. A *hen*, of all things.

"What in heaven's name are you doing?" she shrieked.

The man scowled, his lips parting in disbelief. "What in heaven's name are *you* doing? This is private property, ma'am. And you've just cost me a quarter of an hour's work."

She pulled back, raising her chin with indignation. He was

blaming her for losing the chicken? She scanned him from his black boots to his thick, dark brown hair. She could not deny his handsome features, though dirt and sweat tainted his brow. He wore no jacket, cravat, or waistcoat, and his braces stretched from his buckskin breeches over his broad shoulders.

Clearly, he was tasked to maintain the manor.

Clearly, he was doing a very poor job of it.

"Well, forgive me for costing you such precious time," she spat back with sarcasm. "However, I must say, it was your own doing that the chicken escaped your mannish clutches."

He propped his hands on his hips, causing the front of his shirt to open farther, revealing the top of his muscular chest.

She kept her gaze steady on his face. For the most part.

"My fault?" he questioned. "It was your screaming that sent the hen flying."

"Well what am I to do when an animal is thrown into my face? At any rate, it *was* your doing. You ought to have known better than to hold her so far away from you. You were frightening her."

He scanned her person, and she shifted to the side uncomfortably as he lifted a dubious brow. "Forgive me if I choose not to trust you. I find it difficult to believe a lady such as yourself knows the proper way to hold a hen."

She pursed her lips. Mama always advised her she need not prove others wrong just on principle. But this man needed a firm dressing down. Especially if he was the one who would be caring for the hens. The poor creatures would be injured if he carried on in such a manner.

Without another thought, she turned toward the chickens, slowing her pace as she approached the one who had unwittingly scared her half to death.

As she'd done a hundred times before, she clicked her tongue and bent toward the ground. The hen strode directly up to her. With a soft grasp, Amy reached out to her, holding her close between her side and upper arm. Securing the clawed feet with one hand, Amy used her free fingers to stroke the hen smoothly along her feathers.

She delivered a pointed look to the gentleman then deposited the hen with her friends in the henhouse and secured the latch on the door.

She turned back to the man, brushing off her gloved hands and dress. "There, you see? That is the *proper* way to hold a chicken."

He remained silent, studying her.

"And now that I have done your work for you," she continued, "I would be most appreciative if you would inform me as to where your master is."

"My master? Ma'am, you—"

"Yes. I should very much like to express how displeased I am with our encounter, as well as the state of this house and what might occur to these hens. How would we ever be content living here?"

"Living here?" he repeated her words again, narrowing his eyes. "Forgive me, ma'am, but are you confused, lost? Did you wander too far from home, perhaps, and are now turned round? I can help you find your way back, if you know where you are even supposed to be."

How dare the man be so insolent as to assume she had wandered there by mistake? He clearly thought her a simpleton, a weakened, female waif. "Of course not. My family and I are —*were*—to lease this property."

He shook his head, obviously still baffled. "I fear the more answers you provide, the more questions arise within me. Why—"

"I could say the same for myself, sir." She propped her fisted hands on her hips, only vaguely aware of interrupting him. She was far too preoccupied with her rapidly rising defenses. Who did this man think he was? "I should like to ask after your employer's choice in servants, as well as his ineptitude in keeping up with the deplorable state of this house."

His scowl returned, and his jaw twitched. "Deplorable? You—"

"Indeed, deplorable. I don't believe I've ever been so disappointed. He ought to be ashamed with the state of his property."

His eyes hardened, and silence pulsed between them before his slow, deep voice filled the air. "Tell me, ma'am, were you taught to be so blunt and disagreeable, or does behaving in such a way come naturally to you?"

She pulled back, pained as if struck with a switch at school.

Blunt. The word seemed to follow her around like a dark specter, made even worse by the accompanying word, *disagreeable.*

The man was right, of course. She'd interrupted him countless times and accused him and his employer of neglect and incompetence. *And* she'd held a chicken in front of him. She was behaving exactly as Hugh had told her not to, and now this man had seen her at her very worst.

Instead of humility lowering her defenses, or common sense reminding her to be kind and silent as Hugh had suggested, strong barriers fortified round her heart.

After all, she hardly needed to impress *this* man, as she would never pursue him. And if he had the audacity to critique her for the faults she already knew she possessed, he hardly deserved any kindness at all.

She leaned forward, setting her lips in a determined line. "How do you even—"

"Amy? Amy!" Father appeared at the side of the stables at a quick walk, relief sweeping across his features. "There you are." His eyes flickered to the man then back to Amy. "What has happened? I returned to the carriages when your mother told me she thought she heard you scream."

His accusatory eyes settled on the half-clothed man.

"I'm sorry to have worried you both," Amy said, a soothing hand on Papa's arm. "I assure you, I am well. Merely startled by the sudden appearance of this man and his chicken."

"His chicken?"

Amy motioned to the henhouse, and Papa looked from the hens to Amy to the man. "Do you work here, sir?"

"I—"

"His employer owns this property," Amy interjected. "Though he will not tell me where he is."

The man huffed a disbelieving laugh. "I beg your pardon?"

"All right, then," Papa said in his no-nonsense tone. "Tell us at once where we may find Mr. Eastwood."

CHAPTER FOUR

*W*illiam blinked as the father and daughter finally quieted down, their critical eyes honing in as he shifted his feet. What on earth was going on? How had he not heard these people come onto his property? And more importantly, *why* had these people come onto his property to seek him?

He clasped his hands behind his back. "I am Mr. Eastwood."

The woman's disbelieving gaze skimmed the length of him again. If he hadn't removed half his clothing upon arriving at Corcliffe Manor, perhaps she would have treated him with greater respect.

"You are Mr. *Arthur* Eastwood," the gentleman clarified, his disbelief as apparent as his daughter's.

William stared. Now they asked after his grandfather? What in heaven's name was going on? "My apologies. I am Mr. William Eastwood. Arthur was my grandfather."

"Was?"

"Indeed, he passed a little over a month ago."

The gentleman huffed out a sigh. "Heavens. My apologies, Mr. Eastwood."

William delivered the customary nod expected when someone expressed their condolences, though the past month had been one of the best of his life.

"Thank you, Mr...."

"Ah, yes. Mr. John Paxton. And this is my delightful daughter, Miss Amy Paxton."

Delightful? Perhaps when she wasn't scowling so fiercely, or criticizing his home, or correcting his holding of a chicken. Though in that regard, she'd been correct. How the devil did she know how to hold one, though?

He bowed. "It's a pleasure."

Miss Paxton returned the gesture with a begrudging curtsy.

"I do apologize for my state of undress," he continued. "But I assure you, I am now master of this estate."

A small degree of satisfaction tickled William's pride as the young woman's expression fell, a blush creeping across her cheeks. *Now* she believed who he was. Would she also regret her short behavior?

He pulled his eyes from her pink, pouting lips. "Forgive me, but I fear I am still at a loss as to what the two of you are doing here on my property."

Miss Paxton clasped her hands together, her blue eyes seething. She must still be upset about his words. Perhaps he shouldn't have been so harsh, no matter how truthful he'd been.

Mr. Paxton reached into his waistcoat and procured a correspondence. "Ah, yes. I do apologize. I can only imagine how we must look to you. Allow me to explain. We have been in contact with a Mr. Chamberlain for the past four months now in regards to renting out your grandfather's property through the months of September and October." He extended the letter to William. "I take it you had no knowledge of this transaction?"

William retrieved the paper, skimming over the letter with a knotted stomach. Sure enough, Grandfather's and Mr. Chamberlain's signatures were both signed at the bottom of the agreement to lease Corcliffe Manor to the Paxtons. But why in heaven's name had Grandfather agreed to such a thing? He'd always despised the idea of leasing out an inch of his property to anyone.

"I'm afraid I have never heard a word about this business," he reluctantly admitted.

Mr. Paxton sighed. "This is most disappointing. We were assured everything would be ready upon our arrival. Mr. Chamberlain even promised us the use of a few of Mr. Eastwood's servants."

William brushed a discouraged hand over his eyes. Of course Mr. Chamberlain would promise such a thing. And of course the man would not have told William a word about it.

"Forgive me," he said, his gaze flicking to Miss Paxton, who still frowned. No doubt she was from the city, Bath or London by the looks of her fine traveling dress. Even so, how did a lady of such high society know how to carry a chicken? He shook away the thought and focused on the matter at hand. "I am in the middle of shifting a great deal of information around after hiring another steward, as Mr. Chamberlain is no longer employed in my services."

"I see," Mr. Paxton said. "How dreadful."

Dreadful? Discharging Mr. Chamberlain from his work with the Eastwoods had been nothing but relieving. He and William had never liked each other. Mr. Chamberlain had been unreliable and unyieldingly loyal to Grandfather, so much so that he did nothing William asked of him. He'd omitted, if not destroyed, any information of renters at Corcliffe Manor, clearly desiring William to appear unprofessional.

Unfortunately, the steward's plan had worked. But William still could not understand the logic behind Grandfather leasing a property that was not fit to be lived in. Unless...

"I must ask, have you already provided my grandfather a deposit of some sort?"

"Indeed, we have. I have the agreement if you'd like to see it."

William shook his head. "No, there is no need." He did not need to see any evidence when he trusted this near-stranger's words more than Grandfather and his reprehensible plans to exploit whoever he could to gain more money. How many times had he done such a thing? And how many lives had the man ruined?

Extending the letter back to Mr. Paxton, William raised his brow with regret. "I am terribly sorry over all that has occurred. Of course you understand that I cannot allow you and your family to stay when the manor is in such a terrible state. But I am more than willing to return your deposit to you in full today."

Mr. Paxton merely nodded, and William's culpability increased tenfold. Would he ever stop running into the issues Grandfather left behind? Cleaning up derelict estates, allowing tenants back onto their properties, repaying strangers for dishonest deals. The deceit would never end.

But William would try his hardest to make the lies end.

"Furthermore," he said, "I'm more than happy to suggest a few places in the village where you might stay temporarily, until more permanent matters can be decided upon beyond Coniston. If you wish, you and your family would be most welcome to join me for a cup of tea at my main estate, Birchwick Hall, while this whole business is sorted."

Mr. Paxton nodded, though his expression had since fallen with disappointment. "That would be much appreciated, sir."

William motioned toward the drive. "It is only a short ride up the road."

Miss Paxton looped her arm through her father's as they moved past William.

"I had my heart set on Coniston," Mr. Paxton whispered. "As did your mother."

"Worry not, Father," Miss Paxton said, her voice in a loud

whisper, signaling her desire for William to overhear her words. "I'm certain we shall find somewhere much better to stay. A place with honorable people who treat their tenants and business associates with kindness and respect."

William clenched his jaw. How dare the woman accuse him of dishonesty, of showing a lack of respect? Clearly, he was not in the wrong here.

But he would let her words be. She was obviously highly favored by her father. Had she always received everything her little heart desired?

Thank heavens Charity wasn't like that. He couldn't abide a spoiled person, and Charity was the furthest thing from it. Having lost her father at a young age, she'd been forced to grow up too early—just like William.

This Miss Paxton needed a hearty dose of reality. Perhaps this experience would humble her.

But caring for the Paxtons was hardly his responsibility, and Mr. Paxton seemed more than capable of handling this mess himself.

William paused. He was beginning to sound an awfully lot like Grandfather—passing responsibility off to other people, refusing to help his tenants—exactly what Mr. Rutledge had taught William *not* to do. Grandfather never did a thing for anyone else.

William did.

"Wait a moment." He paused on the drive, and the Paxtons turned to face him. "I might have another solution."

Mr. Paxton's brow rose, but his daughter's lips thinned as she pressed them impatiently together.

"Thank you very much," she said, "but my father can—"

"Just a moment, my dear," Mr. Paxton gently interrupted. "Let us hear him out."

Amy looked away with impatience. Did William truly wish to help her when she wouldn't appreciate a thing he did?

Yes, because he was not simply helping. He was righting a wrong made by his grandfather. And he would never say no to that.

"I have another home that may satisfy your needs. You will have driven past it on your way here, the cottage set just by Coniston. Though, you may not have noticed it, as it is nestled within thick trees."

Mr. Paxton smiled, clearly intrigued. Miss Paxton covered her mouth with a gloved hand to stifle a yawn.

"The back of the house lets up to stunning views of the lake, and the gardens are lovely from the front. The cottage is also clean and comfortable and has four rooms, as well as housing for any help. If you do not mind close quarters, I think your family could be quite happy there."

Mr. Paxton nodded with excitement. "This sounds marvelous, Mr. Eastwood. But we wouldn't wish to encroach on your hospitality, as you must have had other tenants in mind for the cottage."

"No, not at all. In fact, I was looking for visitors to lease the property but assumed I would not find any until next spring or summer at the earliest. Really, you will be doing me the favor by staying."

That was only half a lie. He really hadn't wanted tenants until next year to allow him time to finish all of his work, but that was beside the point.

"And is this cottage overrun with dust, as well?" Miss Paxton's smooth voice dripped with feigned innocence.

"Amy..." Mr. Paxton whispered.

She kept her accusatory eyes on William, but he refused to cower.

"I assure you, the cottage has only recently been renovated to meet the standards of even the most fastidious of females."

"There, you see, my dear?" Mr. Paxton said. "Mr. Eastwood shall help us after all."

"Hmm." Miss Paxton turned away.

"I shall show you the way in just a moment," William said. "I must—"

"Make yourself decent?" she finished with arched brows, looking over her shoulder with a raised chin.

Mr. Paxton chuckled. "We shall wait for you by our carriages, Mr. Eastwood. Come, Amy, before that tongue of yours gets you into trouble."

"Of course, Papa. I wish you luck with your chickens, Mr. Eastwood. And do remember my advice. It may save any other unsuspecting visitors from your wrath."

Mr. Paxton gave her a quizzical look, but she merely smiled and walked away.

As they departed, William instantly regretted his offer of Flitfield Cottage.

That woman was trouble. And he was too busy to have any amount of trouble in his life right now.

"Why ever would you wish to leave the cottage, Amy? We've only been here two days."

Amy glanced around her, ensuring no one could overhear her and Mama's words, though her concern was unnecessary. The road through Coniston that they walked along was nearly empty, dotted only with the occasional passerby, carriage, or elderly couple seated outside the bakery.

She didn't mind the quaintness of the town. In fact, she was rather charmed by it. But she would never admit to such a thing.

"It is not that I have a strong desire to leave. Only that, well, it is too small for our needs, Mama."

"Too small? Nonsense. It is more than sufficient for our little family of four."

That was true. With four bedrooms, a dining area, and a sitting room, the Paxtons were in need of nothing else while on holiday. Still, Amy had to try again.

"But the windows do not close properly in nearly every room. I'm terribly chilly at night."

"We shall find you an extra cover then."

Amy frowned at Mama's response. "For two months? As the weather grows more and more chilly? The fireplaces are so small, there's hardly any warmth in the rooms at all!"

Mama laughed. "Come now. You exaggerate. If I didn't know any better, I would think you would wish to leave because you are still upset with Mr. Eastwood and are attempting to diminish any chance of happening upon him again."

She raised a knowing brow, but Amy looked away, unwilling to reveal her mother's accuracy. That was *precisely* why she wished to leave Coniston. The cottage, the lake, and the autumnal scenery were truly delightful. But the thought of residing in the same town as that pompous chicken-handler for two months was more than she could bear. They were sure to cross paths, and that she did not look forward to.

She didn't enjoy having her flaws being pointed out, nor did she like the idea of those hens being taken care of by a man who clearly did not know a thing about the animals.

"He is a charming gentleman, Amy, and so good to us, too."

Amy sniffed with derision. "I cannot understand why you tout Mr. Eastwood's praises when his actions are what any gentleman ought to do. He is not behaving valiantly. He is performing a duty."

"Now that isn't true. Why do you speak so harshly?"

They passed a modiste's shop, and Amy peered through the glass, exploring delicate, grey gloves and a silk green bonnet trimmed with lace and yellow ribbon—anything to distract her from Mama's impending words.

"Mr. Eastwood has done a great deal for us. Far more than any typical gentleman ever would."

Very well. Amy couldn't deny the man's kindness toward her family. Not only had he offered them the cottage free of charge —which Father, of course, had declined—he'd also allowed them the use of a few of his servants during their stay. Her parents had all but forgotten the elder Mr. Eastwood's deception and seemed to cling to Mr. William Eastwood as if he were their champion. They'd even laughed off Amy's encounter with him when she'd told them about the incident with the chicken.

"How humorous!" Hugh had said, guffawing uncontrollably.

Of course she would never rely on Hugh to take her side. Apparently, he'd spotted a few ladies in town while he was at the Black Bull Inn and was even more interested in remaining in Coniston now. Amy only hoped he would not be too occupied with females to remember his agreement to help her during their first social event—whenever the occasion arose.

Yes, her family had managed to set aside a number of things in regard to the Eastwoods. But Amy could not. Mr. Eastwood had shouted at her, accused her of getting in the way of his work, and then pointed out her greatest flaw. So she would use her humiliation to fuel her anger, hoping—praying—it would in turn lessen the embarrassment he'd caused her.

They continued traversing through the village, shops' window displays and open booths giving way to terraced houses boasting of half-timber work with wooden frames exposed and warped glass for windows. Rather than appearing neglected, the homes radiated a level of comfort that worked through the toughened knots in Amy's tight shoulders.

She sighed. Would that she could so easily find something terrible about this place as she could Mr. Eastwood.

"Oh, Amy, do cheer up," Mama said, having observed her dismay. "You must find it in your heart to forgive him and trust that he is a fine gentleman. After all, you know we are not the only ones to consider his goodness. Surely you recall Mrs. Morris's words. He is the best of men, according to her."

Amy suppressed a groan. Of course she recalled her words. The baker's wife had gone on and on about Mr. Eastwood's virtues for nearly ten minutes.

"Oh, charming, charming man," she'd said upon discovering they were Mr. Eastwood's new, temporary tenants. "He will do anything for anyone at a moment's notice. Remarkable coming from such an upbringing, really. He is the kindest man you shall ever meet. You will soon discover how attentive a landlord he can be. Though, even before he took charge of his estates, he always took great care to ensure all of the Eastwood's tenants were comfortable, secure, and at peace in their homes."

Amy boiled recalling the woman's words. Of course, she'd been intrigued when Mrs. Morris had mentioned his "upbringing," but Amy had promptly brushed the interest aside. His past mattered not to her, after all.

Pleasant chatter from open windows drifted across the street, and a few, early fallen leaves rolled alongside them noisily, as if racing Amy and her mother to the edge of town.

"Well," Amy began, "he may have fooled everyone in town, even all of you, but he will not fool me. No man can raise his voice to a lady and have her forget."

Nor could he potentially neglect hens. Or bring up a proven fault. But that was better to keep away from her family's knowledge. Hugh would give her an intolerable look of "I did say you were blunt, did I not?"

Mama shook her head in reproof, but Amy forged on before a word could be spoken. "Honestly, what sort of gentleman allows his estates to fall into such disrepair? The manor was unacceptable, but the cottage is in no way ideal either. Ivy crawling over the windows, chipped paint in the corners of the sitting room, and that wretched broken gate. I tore my best dress on it, as you know." She peered down at her skirt, holding it out to reveal the small tear in her hem she'd attained that morning. "If he cannot care for his estates, what *can* he do?"

"Amy, be kind."

"I am not being unkind, Mother. Simply truthful. I shudder to think what sort of gentleman refuses to take care of his property. Surely it is a reflection on how he treats his tenants. They must be neglected in the worst way."

"On the contrary, Miss Paxton."

Amy gasped, swinging around to face Mr. Eastwood himself. He stood with his arms behind his back, a tight-lipped expression across his face.

CHAPTER FIVE

*H*ow long had Mr. Eastwood been following them, listening to their conversation? Amy wanted to criticize him for eavesdropping, to scold his imposition, but she could not find the right words—because she was in the wrong. Her ears burned and her tongue buzzed after wagging it like a bitter gossip, criticizing a gentleman because her pride had been offended.

"Mr. Eastwood," Mama breathed in greeting, no doubt horrified at her daughter's hurtful words.

Curtsies and bows were extended, and as Mr. Eastwood straightened, his green eyes—Amy hadn't noticed they were green before—centered on her.

"Contrary to your belief, Miss Paxton, I always strive to take special care of my tenants."

His tone was not one of anger, as she'd expected. If Amy didn't know any better, she would have said she detected a hint of sorrow, instead.

"And I have done so since taking charge of my estates," he finished.

"Oh, Mr. Eastwood," Mama began when Amy said nothing, "of course you do. We would not think otherwise."

"Forgive me, but I believe your daughter does."

His eyes had yet to leave Amy's. Two days before, he'd taken the Paxtons straight from the manor to the cottage, dirt on his brow and hair falling forward with sweat from his day of work.

Now, he stood before them, clean and well-kempt, his cravat smartly tied and his silk green waistcoat reflected brightly in his eyes. Was he not mourning for his Grandfather, then? Or was his jacket black enough for that?

Blast, if he wasn't strikingly handsome—mourning or not. And blast, if he wasn't humiliating Amy again.

"Oh," Mama stammered, "that is due to my daughter being, well, she...she..."

"She was speaking her opinion," Mr. Eastwood finished, "which she is more than entitled to."

Mama nudged Amy with her elbow, but Amy could think of nothing to say. She knew she ought to apologize, but she'd never been caught speaking so uncharitably. Mostly because she'd never *spoken* of someone so uncharitably. At least not aloud. This man—or rather, being embarrassed by this man— truly brought out the worst in her.

"However, if I may defend myself..." Mr. Eastwood waited until Mama gave him an encouraging nod. He peered down at Amy, though he spoke as if to her mother. "Given the evidence, of course your daughter would assume the worst of my abilities to care for my property and tenants. And yet, I cannot help but think that, were she in full possession of the details surrounding my familial situation, she might change her opinion about my capabilities."

"Oh, of course, Mr. Eastwood. Of course," Mama cooed.

A second wave of blood rushed back to Amy's head, circling round her cheeks in a burning blush. He was humbling her in front of her mother now?

This man would be the death of her.

"At any rate, I am terribly sorry about your dress, Miss Paxton. Were I clever enough with a needle and thread, I'd offer to mend it myself."

Mama twittered a laugh at Mr. Eastwood's comment before he continued. "However, I will admit to being far more useful with a hammer and nails. So I should like to see to the—what was it?—the *wretched* broken gate, as well as any other issues you may take with my cottage."

"Oh, that is certainly not necessary," Mama said. "We are most pleased with the home you've leased to us. Aren't we, Amy?"

Amy opened her mouth, but not a word came to fruition.

"Worry not, Miss Paxton. You needn't attempt civility on my account."

She clamped her mouth shut, nostrils flaring at his thinly shrouded insult.

"I shall come with you directly, if you have no objection, Mrs. Paxton."

"We wouldn't wish to inconvenience you, sir," Mama said.

"It is no inconvenience at all, I assure you. It is the least I can do for the damage my neglect has caused poor Miss Paxton's dress."

Amy narrowed her eyes. The half-smile on his face hinted at sincerity, but his tone was unmistakable. He was poking fun at her. After a lifetime with Hugh, she could not bear to be teased.

"Shall we?" He motioned forward.

Mama turned with a look that was unmistakable to Amy. "Be kind," she mouthed.

Amy didn't know how she could be kind to this gentleman who had a keen propensity to call her out and humiliate her in front of her loved ones. At least Mr. Roberts had done so in private. Of course, he'd then gone on to share Amy's misguided words with half of Bath, but that was beside the point.

They set off down the street, Mama thankfully walking between Mr. Eastwood and Amy, until a call from behind stopped their progression.

"Mr. Eastwood? Oh, Mr. Eastwood? Do wait a moment!"

A short woman with a white cap atop her greying hair and a fichu tucked into her green floral gown rushed toward them, waiving a stick in the air.

"Mr. Eastwood, you've forgotten your walking stick!"

He reached out to accept his belonging. "Ah, thank you, Mrs. Rutledge. I don't know how I managed to forget it."

She chuckled. "You rushed so quickly from our house, it is no wonder you did."

Mr. Eastwood cleared his throat, averting his eyes from Amy with a motion of his hand. "Mrs. Rutledge, might I introduce Mrs. Paxton and her daughter. They will be staying at Flitfield Cottage for the next month or two."

Mrs. Rutledge's eyes brightened. "Oh, how delightful! I did not think you were to fill the home with tenants until well into the next year."

Mr. Eastwood shifted his footing, appearing flustered yet again. "Yes, it is quite fortunate how it all came together."

Mrs. Rutledge shifted toward Amy and Mama. "It truly is a pleasure to make your acquaintance. We do so enjoy visitors in Coniston. I hope your stay is most pleasant."

"Thank you," Mama said.

Amy managed to smile her gratitude at the woman, despite her continuous unease around Mr. Eastwood. Mrs. Rutledge was clearly from the middle class and poor, by the state and dated style of her clothing, but her infectious grin would pull anyone's attention away from her place in society.

"And to think you shall have the pleasure of being the tenants of Mr. Eastwood." Mrs. Rutledge rested a hand on his forearm. "He is the most attentive landlord for whom one could ever wish."

The irony of the situation brought about a fresh wave of embarrassment. Was this part of Mr. Eastwood's plan to retaliate for her unkindness? Bringing this woman out of nowhere to defend his capabilities?

The woman continued. "Just today, he called upon my Philip and me to bring a beautiful basket of fresh, green apples. I'm sure I shall make a lovely apple pie with such delectable fruit." She turned to Mr. Eastwood. "You had best expect an invitation to enjoy a slice soon. I know how you enjoy my pie."

"Of course. I would be delighted."

Amy avoided Mr. Eastwood's charming smile. Of course he'd be nice to Mrs. Rutledge. She'd just offered to make him a pie, for heaven's sake.

"Oh, it is the least I could do after you ordered us that lovely new spit-jack for our cooking oven." Mrs. Rutledge turned to Mama and Amy. "And this was after he'd removed a bird from our chimney. I do feel we take advantage of his hospitality at times."

"Nonsense, Mrs. Rutledge," Mr. Eastwood said. "You know I am always happy to help the both of you."

"He is rather helpful, isn't he?" Mama jumped in. "He is on the way with us right now to fix a broken gate at the cottage."

Mrs. Rutledge gave a warm look to the gentleman. "That doesn't surprise me one bit."

Mr. Eastwood looked away with an uncomfortable grimace. Feigned humility, no doubt.

"Well, as much as I should like to go on and on about Mr. Eastwood's many virtues—and you know that I could—I shan't keep you a moment longer. Mr. Rutledge will be wondering what has kept me. Thank you again for the apples, Mr. Eastwood." She turned to the Paxtons. "Lovely to meet you both. I should like to have you over for apple pie, as well. I live just there."

She pointed to the smallest, terraced home of the row with a proud gesture.

"That would be delightful," Mama said.

Amy nodded her gratitude for the woman's generosity, especially considering Mrs. Rutledge had so very little to offer. It really was unfortunate she had been duped by Mr. Eastwood, as well.

Of course, Amy didn't really believe such a thing. Her pride was still smarting. But she'd let everyone else in the village love the man.

Amy would not.

After bidding farewell to the woman who skittered quickly back to her home, Amy, Mama, and Mr. Eastwood continued, finally reaching the small dirt road leading out from the village.

Towering trees with orange and gold leaves lined both sides of the road, sunlight filtering through the foliage, speckling the pathway in dancing shadows.

The whole setting would have provided much peace for Amy —were it not for the fact that Mama had somehow managed to maneuver her way to the outside of their little party, pushing Amy to walk in the center between Mama and Mr. Eastwood.

"I trust you enjoyed your visit to town this morning, ladies," Mr. Eastwood said.

Amy kept her gaze forward, refusing to allow his deep, rumbling voice to coax her into speaking. Chatting openly about a gentleman in a place she could be overheard was yet another poor decision that reminded her that she needed Hugh's help. Not to capture Mr. Eastwood as a potential suitor, of course. Just to avoid another societal death.

When Amy's choice to remain silent became apparent, Mama finally responded for the both of them. "We did, thank you. Though, I must admit, the walk there and back amongst this delightful scenery has been my favorite part about it."

"Indeed," Mr. Eastwood agreed.

"Is Birchwick far from Coniston?"

"Not at all. A mere ten minutes west of the cottage."

"Do you prefer walking to riding, then?"

He nodded. "I was not allowed to walk—"

He stopped abruptly. So abruptly Amy did not have a moment to prevent herself from looking up at him. He blinked multiple times, as if searching for different words to say.

Had he said he was not allowed to walk? What gentleman was not allowed to go where he pleased? And who would prevent such a thing?

Amy studied him for a moment before their eyes met, but he looked away in an instant.

"That is to say, I was encouraged to ride more often, but I do prefer walking."

Mama hesitated. She must have sensed Mr. Eastwood's reluctance, as well. She gave a subtle shake of her head, warning Amy not to press the matter.

As if Amy would speak to the gentleman. Though, she had to admit, she was intrigued by what he was so obviously hiding. Had it something to do with his upbringing, too?

"I must agree with you, sir," Mama carried on naturally. "Walking is as fine an exercise as they come. My Amy agrees, too. Do you not, Amy?"

Was Mother not aware of her decision to remain quiet for the foreseeable future?

"Indeed," Amy mumbled.

Mr. Eastwood peered down at her. Amy walked slightly closer to Mama.

"What other exercise do you enjoy, Miss Paxton? Chasing chickens, perhaps?"

Amy frowned at the soft laughter coming from Mama. Why were both of her parents seemingly enamored by Mr. Eastwood's determination to constantly rain humiliation down upon their daughter?

Well, Amy would have to disregard her own decision to not speak with the gentleman. At least long enough to deliver a return to his mocking.

"You should know better than that, Mr. Eastwood. *I* do not have to resort to chasing chickens."

"Amy," Mama whispered.

Amy gave her an incredulous look. Why ever was Mr. Eastwood allowed to be unkind when Amy could not return the favor?

They continued in silence for a moment before Mama struck a conversation with Mr. Eastwood about the various trees in Coniston. Amy listened—not by choice—until they finally neared the cottage.

As the thatched roof peeked through the thick, orange leaves, Amy was struck again with the quaintness of the little house. The garden was a respectable size, enclosed with a short stone wall and a small, wooden gate. Beech trees towered around the cottage, mixing colors of sharp green and lemon yellow, while red and pink dahlias grew alongside the cream-colored walls.

A weak brooklet trickled in the front of the cottage with two bridges—one, a small, wooden curved crossing, and the other, large enough for carriages to pass on. Thick bracken grew alongside the creek bed, dipping long, reddish-brown fronds into the lazy water, as if testing the warmth of the creek before diving in for a lengthy swim.

The sight was a delicious feast for the eyes each time Amy viewed it, though she was loath to dote on anything in relation to Mr. Eastwood.

They crossed over the small bridge, their footsteps padding against the creaking wood, then approached the gate hanging on one hinge. Mr. Eastwood paused to examine it, pointing at a wayward nail sticking from the base of it.

"Is this the culprit who behaved so heinously toward you, Miss Paxton?"

Mama placed her hand to her mouth, no doubt hiding another amused grin.

Amy, however, did not appreciate the gentleman making light of her dress being torn. It would take her a good two hours to ensure the hole had been sewn correctly to avoid any notice of there being a tear in it at all.

She raised her chin. "Indeed, it is. If only it would have been taken care of *before* we settled here."

She ignored another whispered warning from Mother. It was not necessary. Mr. Eastwood did not appear to have heard her slight anyway.

"Well, it shan't take me long to fix this, as well as the hinge. If I may but allow myself into the stables for a few tools?"

Mother's eyes widened. "Oh, you hardly need permission on your own property, but are you..."

Mama was too polite to finish her words. Amy, however...

"Are you to mend the gate yourself?" she asked.

She'd truly thought he'd been jesting before about being handy with a hammer and nails.

He stood from his inspection with amusement. "Does this come as a surprise to you after witnessing me with that chicken?"

He certainly had a valid point. Still, she was sure any gentleman she knew would hire someone else to do this type of manual labor.

"So, if I may begin?" he asked with an expectant look.

"Oh, of course. Of course." Mama motioned him forward. "And thank you so much for your kindness, sir."

"Not at all."

He walked past them both, and Amy took a step back to avoid any accidental touch. The earthy scent of his cologne wafted under her nose, but she waved it aside. She'd had enough of the scent on their walk. That frustratingly tantalizing smell.

She followed Mama up the rest of the small pathway toward the cottage.

"I think we ought to invite him for tea after he fixes the gate," Mama said as they approached the door. "It is the least we could do for him."

"The least *we* could do?" Amy asked, ensuring her voice was as quiet as possible. She'd had enough of being overheard by the gentleman. "Mama, he is mending something that should have already been mended!"

"Hush, Amy!" Mama whispered, pausing at the front of the door with a stern look. "I don't see why you are so set to despise the gentleman. It is so unlike you and not at all becoming. He has been more than amenable. You know he did not have to offer this cottage to us, or his help."

Amy pulled a face. "Yes, yes, I know. But he is just so disagreeable. I cannot help but dislike the man."

"If you ask me, *he* is not the one being disagreeable."

Amy looked to her mother in dismay, though she spoke the truth. Amy was being terrible.

Mother's stern look softened. "Now, I wish you to invite him to tea as he sees to his task."

"Why must I do so?" Amy checked her tone, ensuring Mr. Eastwood had not yet emerged from the stables. "It was *your* idea!"

"Amy."

Amy frowned. "Very well, but I shall not be joining you for tea then."

"Yes, you will."

"No, I will not. I will—"

Mama shushed her as footsteps sounded, and they faced Mr. Eastwood, who now had a leather satchel and tools in hand. He gave them a smile, though it was tainted with a hint of uncertainty—no doubt due to Mama's innocent grin and Amy's recurrent frown.

"Go, Amy," Mama whispered as he turned away from them.

"No!" she whispered with vehemence.

"Yes."

Her word was firm, final, and she slipped into the house and closed the door before Amy could sneak inside, too.

With a stifled sigh of frustration, she turned toward the gate. Mr. Eastwood averted another odd look then dropped the satchel to the floor and hunched down to examine its contents.

Amy hesitated. She could simply return inside and inform Mama that Mr. Eastwood had declined their invitation. But Mama would undoubtedly see past her lies. She was as stubborn as Amy and would not relent until she received what she wished.

Begrudgingly, Amy trudged across the grass back to Mr. Eastwood's side.

He didn't look up as he pulled a hammer from the satchel. "Come to inspect my work, have you?"

Her eyes swept over his back as he turned. When had he removed his jacket? That waistcoat of his was doing wonderful things to his broad shoulders.

She blinked away the traitorous thought. "Well, after seeing how you handle chickens, I thought I might come to tell you that perhaps you're better off hiring someone else to do this work."

To her great surprise, the man chuckled. He maintained his actions, holding the gate closer so the hinge lined up alongside the wooden post near the stone wall.

"I was beginning to wonder if you were only so vicious in your comments while your parents were nearby. I can see now how wrong I was."

Her brow twitched, her anger drooping. Vicious? She'd

never been described as vicious in her life. Perhaps her comment had been a little harsh, but he *had* deserved it.

Her logic was as weak as the feeble stream trickling in the nearby brooklet.

"My mother wished to invite you to tea once you are finished here." There, that wasn't cruel, was it? That wasn't *vicious*.

He continued with his work, hammering a few nails before pausing to roll up his sleeves. "Thank you, I would enjoy that. Though, you needn't have informed me that your mother extended the invitation. I am well aware you would never offer such a thing."

She released a frustrated breath. Even when she said her words kindly, they were still taken offensively. Ah, well. She supposed there were people who would just never be happy with anything.

But was she not supposed to be ignoring him? Reminding herself of her resolve, she turned to leave, only to stop as he hammered into the post once more.

The angular muscles in his forearm flexed with each strike of his tool, and she moved her head to the side to obtain a better angle.

He stopped abruptly, catching her stare with a pursed brow. "What is it? Am I doing something wrong?"

Amy blinked, straightening her posture with deep breaths, though heat crept toward her cheeks in an instant. "No, I...I was wondering if you often mend broken items for your tenants."

Now, that was quick thinking on her part.

He gave her a look of suspicion then retrieved another nail. For a moment, she thought he might not respond. "If you must know, I *have* hired help before and still do on occasion. But sometimes, it is far easier—far quicker—to do the work myself."

"And how did you come by learning such a task?" she asked,

if only to distract herself. What with his forearms out for all the world to see, she could focus on very little else.

"Mr. Rutledge taught me." His answer was brief, as if he didn't wish to speak on the topic.

The husband of the woman they met in town had taught him? Now how had that come about? And why? She recalled his words from town, how she did not understand his familial situation. What could he have meant?

Before she could ask anything else, the door of the cottage creaked open behind them, and Hugh stepped into the warmth of the early autumn afternoon.

"So the dreaded gate will be fixed, I see," Hugh said with a grin, coming down the pathway and rubbing his hands together. "I must thank you, sir, as I've heard my sister complain of little else since we've arrived."

"I have not," she refuted with a wary glance at Mr. Eastwood. That was just what she needed—her brother giving more fodder which Mr. Eastwood would use to embarrass her further.

"Come now, Amy. You always have something to fuss about."

Mr. Eastwood straightened, and both he and Hugh looked to Amy for an introduction.

With a sigh, she relented. "Hugh, this is Mr. Eastwood, our landlord. Mr. Eastwood, my *charming* brother, Mr. Hugh Paxton."

"It is a pleasure to make your acquaintance," Hugh said. "I understand you are the gentleman who is responsible for preventing our stay at the Black Bull."

Yet another Mr. Eastwood admirer. Apparently, this list was never-ending.

"It would appear so."

"Lovely place to game. Not so lovely a place to sleep."

"No, indeed, Mr. Paxton."

"Please, call me Hugh. I'm not mature enough to desire my father's name quite yet."

"I couldn't agree more," Amy mumbled.

Hugh chuckled, wrapping his arm around Amy's shoulder in a light embrace. "My sister. Never one to keep her opinion to herself."

"I noticed."

Mr. Eastwood's eyes flicked between Amy and Hugh, and Amy thought she caught a hint of amusement in them.

Of course he would be amused. He had someone else to join in his mocking her.

"Well, do not let us stop your work, Mr. Eastwood," Hugh said. "I'm certain my sister was enjoying her observation of you."

CHAPTER SIX

*A*my's eyes widened. She glanced to Mr. Eastwood, who turned too slowly for her *not* to see his amusement over Hugh's words.

"Hugh," she mouthed out as Mr. Eastwood knelt before the gate with his back toward them.

He merely gave an innocent shrug, though his wicked grin spoke measures to his intent. He motioned to Mr. Eastwood with a nod. "Go on," he mouthed next.

She shook her head.

"You promised."

With sinking realization, Amy knew the time had come for their agreement to begin. But then, how could she explain to him that this man was certainly not in the running for a potential husband?

With a glance to Mr. Eastwood, whose back still faced them, she shook her head fiercely. "Not with this man. I refuse, Hugh. He is the most disagreeable gentleman I have ever beheld."

Confusion wrinkled his brow. Perhaps it was too much for him to have understood all of that without a sound. With a muffled sigh, she linked her arm through his.

"Do excuse us for a moment, Mr. Eastwood."

"Of course."

His eyes lingered on them for a moment before Amy fairly dragged Hugh across the garden.

"Amy, what the devil—"

"Shh!"

"We had an agreement to—"

She shushed him again, and this time, he kept quiet. Once they were far enough away, Amy whirled to face him with a vehement whisper. "I am aware of our agreement, brother, and that you are to help me find a husband. But I refuse to begin with Mr. Eastwood. That man..." She paused, peering over her shoulder at Mr. Eastwood's flexed arm as he hammered into the post once again, "will never be my husband."

"Heavens, Amy. I thought Mama was in jest about your resentment of him. You really do hold a grudge, don't you?"

"That is beyond the point."

He chuckled. "Very well. Although I would encourage you to pursue the man—he has wealth, after all. But I know of your desire to marry for love." He pulled a disinterested face. "At any rate, as we discussed earlier, you may choose whom to pursue, and I will help you. However, I must advise against your mistreatment of Mr. Eastwood either way."

Amy pulled back, ready to protest when he continued with a hurried glance at Mr. Eastwood.

"I have heard from both our parents now about the verbal contests between you and Mr. Eastwood. If the man—who is the foremost gentleman in Coniston, I believe—finds you disagreeable, you can be sure that the rest of the Lake District will be aware of your rude behavior before the end of this week."

Looking past her indignation over having a third person call her "disagreeable," Amy released a sigh. Disappointingly, Hugh was right. She couldn't risk having such a reputation in a new town. Not when she was hoping to find a match.

How she had not considered such a downside to her unkindness was beyond her. This was yet further proof that she, Amy Paxton, made poor decisions. Very poor decisions, indeed.

Still, she pouted at the thought of being kind to Mr. Eastwood. "Why do gentlemen feel it necessary to divulge every flaw a woman might have?"

"Why do women feel it necessary to have such shareable flaws?"

She reached out, swatting his arm for his chauvinistic views, but he merely chuckled.

"Just think of it as practice," Hugh suggested. "Even if you don't consider Mr. Eastwood a viable option, he is a gentleman. And you do need practice curbing your tongue."

She sniffed with derision.

"So will you agree to be kind to your Mr. Eastwood?"

"He is not *my* Mr. Eastwood. But I will be kind if I must."

"You must. Because I command you to do so."

With another swat of his arm—and another chuckle from Hugh—Amy sighed in surrender.

There were times she simply could not bear her brother.

Especially when he was right.

William tested the gate's movement again, swinging it back and forth as his eyes wandered again to Miss Paxton and her brother. Their muffled argument had drifted toward him, though he'd been unable to comprehend a single word. He had noted Miss Paxton swat her brother's arm a number of times, though, no doubt due to a smart comment he'd made. Apparently, mockery was a shared trait of the Paxton siblings.

William pulled his eyes away from them. He'd hate to have

Miss Paxton think he was eavesdropping again. Although, that afternoon had certainly been an accident.

He'd spotted the Paxtons from Mrs. Rutledge's window and departed swiftly to inquire after their stay at the cottage thus far. Little did he know he'd happen upon Miss Paxton criticizing his estates and his ability as a landlord.

He smiled to himself as he put away his tools. He was quite satisfied with the blush that had spread swiftly across Miss Paxton's cheeks at being discovered in her beratement of him.

At least the woman had some form of a conscience.

"Heavens, are you finished already?" Mrs. Paxton approached, motioning to the gate. "You certainly made quick work of that."

William eyed his handiwork with a gratified nod. Mr. Rutledge would be proud of that quick and easy fix. He'd taught William everything he knew, until Mr. Rutledge's hands could no longer grasp a tool. "Yes, it was a straightforward task, fortunately. I don't know how it managed to slip past my inspection earlier. I do apologize."

Mrs. Paxton waved an easy hand before her. "Nonsense. All it cost was a little snag of fabric." She leaned closer. "And as much as my daughter has lamented said tear, she will have no trouble stitching it up. She merely enjoys to suffer loudly at times, you see."

She winked, producing a genuine smile from William. He'd never heard a woman speak in such a way about her daughter. Not that she was criticizing her, but she did not boast of Miss Paxton's many talents, as was typical of many of the mothers with whom he'd come in contact.

"Are you ready for tea, sir?"

William nodded, returning the tools to the stables before making his way back to the side of the house where the entire Paxton family had assembled around the white, iron wrought tea table.

"Do join us, Mr. Eastwood," Mr. Paxton said, waving toward the empty seat remaining between Miss Paxton and her brother.

"Thank you." William pulled out the chair, iron scraping against the stone of the sitting area. He sidled in between the brother and sister, noting the subtle shift of Miss Paxton away from him. That was fine with him. The less he had to smell the lavender scent of her blonde curls blowing on the breeze in his direction, the better.

"My sister was just saying how grateful she is for your service today." Hugh leaned back on the chair beside William, propping his elbow on one armrest. "Weren't you, Amy?"

William readied himself for the biting comment in return. Would it be, "Yes, congratulations on doing the job you should have done before we arrived" or "I could have done it better myself"?

Miss Paxton looked to Hugh before proceeding with a lowered gaze. "Indeed, I was."

William's eyes darted toward her, narrowing faster than he'd flung the hen at her two days prior. "Were you?" He hoped his voice didn't sound as incredulous to them as it did to him.

Miss Paxton raised her cup to her lips, but when Hugh cleared his throat, she paused, swallowing hard. "Yes, I was. I am very grateful, Mr. Eastwood." She grimaced, as if the tea had scalded her tongue. "Now I shall only be required to stitch one dress instead of the countless others I might have torn."

Her tone was sincere enough, but William knew the woman enough already to feel the censure in her words. What he could not understand, however, was the reasoning behind her sudden willingness to feign politeness.

Perhaps something to do with the argument she'd had with her brother? Before he could decipher, Mrs. Paxton spoke to him from across the table.

"So, Mr. Eastwood, do tell us more about yourself."

He placed his teacup on his saucer, bracing himself for the barrage of questions that always followed such a statement.

"Have you any brothers or sisters?" she asked.

"No, ma'am. My family consists of myself and my parents, but we find it suits us well."

"Your parents?" Mr. Paxton's brow rose in surprise. "Forgive me. I assumed...You said Corcliffe fell under your care after your grandfather's passing. I assumed control went to you because your parents..."

His words ended in an uncomfortable silence, but William shook his head to ease the tension. "Not to worry. Of course that would be the natural assumption. My parents are alive, however, and are on holiday in the south, enjoying a bit of sun and sea."

Grandfather had forbidden Mother and Father to go to anywhere near the sea. Some rubbish excuse of the salty air making him ill, so he would not allow anyone to go since he could not. London was permitted occasionally, but for more than five years, they hadn't left Cumbria once. William had been the one to push his parents to Cornwall a fortnight after the funeral, otherwise he was sure they would have lived out the rest of their lives in Coniston.

The Paxtons—all but Miss Paxton—remained silent with heavy glances. Clearly, they wished to hear why exactly the control of the estates had passed over his father. William wished to keep the past where it belonged—in the past. It was one reason things were so easy with Charity and the Rutledges. They knew about his history, so he did not have to speak about it.

But a stranger's curiosity was insatiable unless he gave him or her just enough to thrive on.

He continued. "My father passed control to me when he did not consider himself well enough to do so."

That was true. Father never thought himself capable of managing such properties.

"You haven't the ability to see to such matters, son," Grandfather would say. "Leave it to me."

"And when you die, Father? What happens then?"

"I will do my best to outlive you, for then I shan't have to leave my property willingly in your hands."

Thank heavens the old man had been wrong. But his words had affected William's father to the point that he didn't think himself capable of anything—leaving the brunt of the work to William alone.

"Fortunately," William continued, "I've never minded a little hard labor."

"And fortunately, your hard labor has paid off," Mrs. Paxton said. "You are a most admirable landlord. Is he not, Amy?"

The words were meant to compensate for Miss Paxton's earlier slight, he was sure of it.

Miss Paxton blinked, as if coming out of a daze. With a quick look toward Hugh, she nodded. "Yes. Yes, of course. Very admirable, indeed."

William studied her for a moment, but she merely took another sip of tea and peered out over the garden. He had not understood her anger toward him, not when he'd returned the criticisms she'd lobbed at him first. But now her sudden kindness was even more baffling.

He hardly believed it had to do with anything her parents could have said. A sudden change of heart was even less believable. But the argument she'd had with her brother...

"Have you lived in Coniston your whole life, Mr. Eastwood?" Mrs. Paxton asked next.

He pulled his gaze away from Hugh, who stuffed a biscuit into his mouth.

"Yes, I have," William replied.

"What a lovely place to grow up. Mr. Paxton and I spent a

holiday in Ambleside when we were first married. Since then, we have made it a point to travel the Lake District nearly every year. Autumn is our favorite time to visit. Is it not, Mr. Paxton?"

"Indeed. The views cannot be matched. Nor the lack of crowds." He paused, a wink sent toward his wife. "And it is made especially delightful this time to have Hugh and Amy with us."

Miss Paxton's eyes twinkled at her father's words, though any trace of joy disappeared when she noted William looking at her.

"This is our first time staying in Coniston, though," Mr. Paxton continued. "We wouldn't mind a suggestion or two on which sights to see first."

"Oh, yes. That would be very helpful, indeed," Mrs. Paxton agreed.

William thought for a moment, acutely aware of Miss Paxton glancing over to Hugh, who was staring at the biscuit he'd bitten in two, nodding his head as if he was heartily enjoying the sweet.

"I would highly suggest taking the pathway around Coniston Water," William said, struggling to focus. "Or if you prefer a heartier walk, I would suggest the Old Man of Coniston."

"Oh, excellent suggestions," Mr. Paxton said.

"Yes, indeed. I've never seen the Old Man before," his wife said next with growing excitement.

Silence followed, and Miss Paxton's voice sprouted forth. "Who is the old man of Coniston?"

All eyes fell on her innocent expression. Mr. and Mrs. Paxton chuckled, and Hugh threw back his head with a chortle.

"Forgive me," William said with an amused grin. "I should have explained. The Old Man of Coniston is what we call the fell just west of here."

Miss Paxton's expression dropped, red tinting her cheeks. "I see. How silly of me."

More chuckling ensued, and, to William's utter chagrin, his heart reached out to her. "It is a simple mistake. No harm done."

Instead of the gratitude he'd foolishly expected, Miss Paxton glanced up at him, anger darkening the blue of her eyes.

He pulled back. Why was she not scowling at her family in such a way? They were the ones teasing her.

Her lips slipped into a firm line until Hugh cleared his throat, and her gaze shifted to her brother as she removed her frown.

"Well, such a fell sounds like a lovely thing to behold."

William stuck his tongue in his cheek, considering the woman for a moment as Mr. and Mrs. Paxton continued to speak with Hugh about the barren mountain range west of Coniston village.

Surely Miss Paxton had been about to critique William. And this time, he knew what had stopped her. Her brother had some sort of hold over her, he was sure of it.

His mind raced. He'd seen control evident in a relationship before. Mother and Father had cowered often around Grandfather. They'd hang their heads, never make eye contact, walked on protruding nails to avoid stepping a foot out of place.

Miss Paxton, however, had not only swatted her brother but was standing up to him before.

So why did it appear like she was relying so heavily upon him now?

"Mr. Eastwood," Mr. Paxton said, interrupting William's musings, "we are anxious for your opinion on the matter. Where would you recommend is the best place to see views of the Old Man?"

An idea sparked in his mind, like a candle glowing in the darkness. "As luck would have it, I do know the best place to see it. I know this is rather short notice, but I will be holding a little picnic on the grounds of Birchwick Hall this coming Thursday. We will be sure to take a walk to where we will have unbeatable views of the fell. I would be pleased to have you all there."

"Oh, how delightful!" Mrs. Paxton exclaimed.

Her husband nodded. "Indeed, we will be happy to attend, Mr. Eastwood."

"I look forward to it, as well," Hugh said, chewing through another biscuit, "as, I'm certain, does my sister."

He gave a significant look at Miss Paxton before she responded.

"Of course," she said with too much brightness. "I do enjoy parties."

"Excellent." William hid his suspicion. There would be time enough to decipher her behavior—and Hugh's sudden influence over his sister.

Though it was no business of his, he could not deny the inexplicable desire he had to decipher what secrecy was occurring between the siblings—and to ensure the same controlling relationship was not in place that he'd witnessed for so long between his parents and grandfather.

Heaven help Hugh Paxton if it was.

CHAPTER SEVEN

$\mathcal{T}$hursday came far too quickly for Amy. Hugh and their parents were of course more than thrilled to be finally stepping foot on the grounds of Mr. Eastwood's fine estate. Their eyes hungrily took in the tan stonework, rectangular windows, and bronzed chimneys of the three-storied home.

"How majestic," Mama breathed as they were shown to the back of the estate and Birchwick's immense gardens stretched out before them.

"I've never seen such meticulous work," Papa murmured.

Neither had Amy. Not a blade of grass reached over the pathway they walked upon, and every hedge was cut with perfect precision. Even the trees held onto their red and orange foliage, as if their branches feared dropping a single leaf, thereby ruining the exactness of the estate.

Instead of eying the scenery, Hugh walked backwards, still ogling the house with rounded eyes. "It's larger than Roseley, that's for certain."

Amy shook her head. Her family was besotted, clear as day. How was she the only one with any sense? They were focusing only on Mr. Eastwood's wealth and privileged birth. But Amy could not help but wonder, if this estate was so immaculately kept, why were the others left in tatters? Mr. Eastwood had admitted to Father that Flitfield Cottage had faired as poorly as Corcliffe Manor just a short month ago, but the man had given no explanation as to why.

Of course, he was allowed his privacy, but what naturally followed was Amy's belief that Mr. Eastwood only cared to improve the estate that revealed just how affluent he was. Perhaps he was not as wonderful as everyone assumed.

Or perhaps Amy was still bitter about his treatment of her upon their first meeting.

"Are you ready, Amy?" Hugh came up to walk beside her, interrupting her thoughts. "This will be the true test of your will to trust me."

He winked. This certainly *would* be a test. She'd never trusted Hugh—especially when it came to matters of the heart. But then, Hugh had more than proven himself by not pushing her toward Mr. Eastwood. Her brother had shown her a level of respect she wasn't sure he'd possessed until that moment.

At any rate, she didn't have much of a choice *but* to trust his advice. She certainly wasn't succeeding on her own, as was evident in her earlier pursuit of Mr. Roberts.

Nerves rustled in her stomach like brittle leaves trembling on a weak branch. "Are you certain I can do this, Hugh? I'm so worried I'll make a fool of myself again."

He nudged her with his elbow. "You needn't worry. I'm here to help. Unless, of course, another woman catches my fancy."

"You had better be teasing."

"Of course he is." Father came up beside them, offering his arm to Amy, which she readily accepted. "For he knows, should he do anything that hurts you, he'll answer to me."

Hugh feigned offense. "Have either of you any faith in me?"

"No," Amy and Papa declared simultaneously.

Hugh pulled his lips down, blinking mutely. "I shall simply have to prove myself then, won't I?"

He shook his head, as if unable to comprehend his family's lack of faith in him, then fell behind them to walk beside Mama, who gave him an encouraging pat on his arm.

As they neared the party, laughter and conversation sailed across the grounds toward them. Grass and trees of orange and yellow stretched as far as one could see. The sparse, white clouds sailed across the otherwise blue skies, casting dark, uneven shapes across the green fields and a large white tent set up on the open stretch of grass.

"Are you certain you wish to go through with this?"

Amy peered quizzically at her father, having to crane her neck back to see his face due to his tall stature. "With the party?"

"No, with Hugh advising you on how to find a husband."

"Oh," she said with a shake of her head. "No, I'm not certain. But I really have no choice, do I?"

"I wish..." He trailed off with a sigh.

"What, Papa?"

He hesitated, then with a touch of sorrow in his eyes, he smiled down at her. "I only wish you could see your value. Your goodness. Then you wouldn't feel the need to seek advice from your brother to capture a gentleman's attention. That is all."

The words sunk through her defenses, like water seeping through the cracks of a stone wall. She rested her head against his shoulder and arm in a brief embrace. "Oh, Papa. If only all men were like you, I wouldn't have to follow Hugh's advice on how to behave better."

He huffed. "*There's* something I never thought I'd hear. Hugh instructing someone else on how to behave."

They shared a look of amusement before Papa continued. "I suppose we must give him credit for your change of heart towards Mr. Eastwood, though. That gentleman deserves our full respect, I must say."

She didn't contest his words, even though she disagreed with him heartily.

Father rested his free hand on her fingers wrapped around his arm. "Just promise me, cricket, to never extinguish that vivacity within you to live life to its fullest. A true gentleman would never think to dim that brightness, only to help it increase in strength. That fire you have inside, that is what makes you, *you*."

She swallowed the swelling emotion in her throat. "Thank you, Papa," she whispered.

If she could but find a gentleman half as good to her as her father was, she'd be very happy, indeed.

Tucking his words into the folds of her heart, Amy walked toward the party with bravery and determination...until Mr. Eastwood stepped forward to greet them first.

"Welcome to Birchwick Hall. I'm so pleased to have you with us."

His eyes settled on each one of them, lingering a moment longer on Amy.

"Your home is stunning, Mr. Eastwood," Mama said. "And the gardens are simply immaculate."

His smile faltered. "Thank you. My grandfather took great pride in this property."

Amy narrowed her eyes. His grandfather? Was that where Mr. Eastwood had inherited his vanity? They must have shared a close bond, what with his spirits falling at the mention of his grandfather.

Mr. Eastwood cleared his throat. "Allow me to introduce you to the others."

He led the way forward, introducing the Paxtons to the three couples beneath the large tent. Mr. and Mrs. Booth were seated beside a young couple, the Shaws, who seemed incapable of removing their eyes from one another. Next to them was the older Mrs. Rutledge, who greeted them warmly after introducing them to her husband, Mr. Philip Rutledge, who sat beside her.

"It is so good to see you again, Miss Paxton, Mrs. Paxton." Mrs. Rutledge motioned to the chair beside her. "I trust you are enjoying your stay at the cottage."

"Indeed, we are," Mama said as she took the seat, Papa standing behind her. "Are we not, Mr. Paxton?"

As Father replied and the conversation continued, Amy's attention wavered to the small group of younger people playing Battledore and Shuttlecock nearby. They raised their rackets high overhead, struggling to keep the shuttlecock flying through the air. A young woman in a soft blue dress jumped to reach it, not seeing the tall, thin gentleman nearby, who was also attempting to strike the feathered cork. In the next moment, they landed atop each other, a tangled mess on the grass.

Scrambling apart, the young man and woman blushed from cheek to cheek, all while the rest of the group joyfully laughed at their discomfort.

Amy couldn't help but smile at the sight.

"Do you enjoy the sport, Miss Paxton?"

Amy turned to face Mrs. Rutledge. "Yes, I do."

"You ought to join in their game then. That is Mrs. Booth's daughter in the blue dress." Mrs. Booth nodded. "I'm certain they wouldn't mind extra players if you and your brother joined them."

Instantly, Amy shook her head. "Oh, thank you. But I wouldn't wish to impose."

"You are sure to be most welcome," Mr. Rutledge encouraged. "You seem as if you know the difference between the top end of the racket and the bottom. Mr. Eastwood here certainly doesn't."

The man winked at Amy, and her lips curled at his light-hearted teasing. Mr. Eastwood even seemed to have a spark in his eye.

"That's hardly true, sir. You've seen me play."

Mr. Rutledge nodded. "You play well enough, I suppose."

He shifted in his chair, wincing with a sudden grimace. Amy stared, pained wrinkles forming across his brow. Mr. and Mrs. Booth struck a conversation with Mama and Papa, but Amy stood by in silence as Mr. Eastwood leaned forward, whispering to Mr. Rutledge. "Would you be more comfortable inside?"

"Nonsense, Will," Mr. Rutledge whispered back. "The fresh air is making me feel more alive than I have in fifty years."

Will? He'd called Mr. Eastwood, Will? How close were these men? And what sort of pain was he feeling?

Mr. Eastwood hesitated, though he relented with a sigh, his watchful eye on the elderly gentleman who still winced.

Hugh's words nearby finally pulled her attention away from the intimate moment, and she looked toward him.

"I'm inclined to agree with them, sister." He tossed his head toward the group of players. "Come, let us join in their fun."

Her mind tried to revert to the previous conversation. She hadn't been lying when she'd said she enjoyed the game, but she didn't take to playing with strangers. Perhaps she might fall in the same manner as the woman in blue, Miss Booth? Amy would be humiliated in Coniston, just as she was in Bath.

She shook her head. "I think I should like to sit, Hugh," she said softly as the conversation picked up between the others.

"But *I* really think you would enjoy yourself given the chance."

Finally, Amy relented. After all, Hugh was merely attempting to draw her closer to the other gentlemen—the exact reason she'd enlisted his help. She must adhere to the plan. Besides, if she remained with the adults the entire time, she would have been put off the path of the other gentlemen and onto the path of Mr. Eastwood. Heavens, was she terrible at making decisions.

With an anxious flip of her stomach, she took her first step toward the others, not noticing until that moment that Mr.

Eastwood watched her every move. Had he been listening to her conversation with Hugh?

"You don't have to join in if you don't wish to," he whispered before she could pass him by.

Yes, he most certainly had been listening. But from where had these gentle words come? And where was his typical, snide comment to embarrass her?

"I-I do wish to," she stammered.

He peered down at her disbelievingly, his height as tall as Father's, but she moved past him before he could say another word.

"I would advise losing, Amy," Hugh whispered as she reached his side and they retrieved the extra rackets on the grass.

Amy nodded, only half-listening as she observed Mr. Eastwood from over her shoulder. He spoke once more with his own party, not a glance in her direction.

"If you do not try as hard to strike the shuttlecock, you will not fall as the other woman did," Hugh continued. "Do you understand?"

Amy pushed Mr. Eastwood from her mind one last time and focused on the task at hand. "Yes. I must lose."

She set aside her pride at the idea of throwing the game on purpose. For the sake of not embarrassing herself in front of her new peers, it would be well worth the sacrifice.

Following closely at Hugh's heels, they approached the group, who waved them over with broad smiles. Amy had never been so nervous. Typically, she could converse with others with relative ease, but after scaring away Mr. Roberts with her forward behavior, she feared doing the very same to another gentleman—to the point where she might never have the opportunity to marry.

She shook her head. She refused to lose hope. She might be two and twenty with a fair few Seasons in her reservoir, but negativity never helped anyone. She had Hugh's help now, and she was going to trust him.

The young woman in blue came forward first. "You must be the Paxtons. I am Miss Booth. It's such a pleasure to make your acquaintances."

"And yours," Amy returned.

Miss Booth then proceeded to introduce the others. Amy strived to remember their names, but with three new gentlemen and two women, she knew she was bound to make a mistake. As each of the gentlemen were introduced—Mr. Fisher, Mr. Payne, and Mr. Jones—Amy gave a subtle look to Hugh, who nodded just as furtively.

They'd discussed the process together earlier that morning. She would covertly inform Hugh as to the gentlemen who caught her fancy, and he would help her capture their attention. When she narrowed it down to one gentleman, Hugh would then serve as unofficial chaperone, mostly to ensure she did not humiliate herself and her family again.

Fortunately for her, there were three handsome gentlemen in the running with whom to start.

"Now we are all officially introduced." The slim man from before, Mr. Fisher, motioned to the grassy area. "Shall we begin our game again?"

The small party formed a circle in the grass, and the shuttle-cock was sent forth in the air. Amy held her racket with two hands in front of her, pointed down. She hoped her parents were enjoying their time more than she was going to be, losing. But losing hardly mattered when she was pursuing these gentlemen to be married and to avoid being a burden on her parents. She could lose a game for those worthy goals, surely.

She glanced to Mama and Papa, but instead of seeing them, she swiftly discovered a frowning Mr. Eastwood watching her. She tore her gaze away, only to observe him again a moment later from the corner of her eye.

His frown was not one of anger as he stared, but more contemplative. What was he attempting to discover?

"Miss Paxton?"

Amy turned to Mr. Payne, whose blond hair shone nearly white in the sunshine. "Pardon?"

He motioned to her feet, where lay the drooping shuttlecock. When had that been hit toward her?

"Oh, I do apologize." She reached down, retrieving it by one of its pigeon feathers.

Hugh gave her an encouraging nod before she pelted the shuttlecock into the air. A few calls of, "I have this one," "Oh, excellent shot," and "Marvelous volley!" rounded the large circle as the toy flew back and forth in the sky.

Instinctively, Amy struck the shuttlecock with ease as it sailed toward her next, but Hugh caught her eye with a shake of his head.

"Play poorly," he reminded her, mouthing out the words before flashing a grin at Miss Booth.

Right. Of course. Amy held the racket down, drawing in a deep breath until it came toward her once again. This time, she reached out apathetically, missing the shuttlecock by multiple feet.

"Oh, dear," she said as Mr. Payne retrieved it instead. "I fear I am not so very good at this game."

"Nonsense. You are playing wonderfully." He nodded kindly at her then set the shuttlecock flying once again, only to look back at Amy with another pleasant smile.

Heavens, Hugh's advice had actually worked. Feigning ineptitude at the game had endeared this gentleman to her.

Men were funny sorts of creatures.

Hugh gave her an "I told you so" look before directing the shuttlecock toward Miss Booth.

The game continued, and Amy took the time in between missing hits to observe the party around her—something Hugh told her was essential. Listening and watching how others act would tell her exactly how *she* ought to act.

A young woman with a bright yellow dress—Miss Cox, was it?—laughed as she swatted her racket through the air and missed the shuttlecock entirely.

"How silly I must look!" she cried out, flashing a grin at Hugh. "Perhaps you might give me a few suggestions, Mr. Paxton, on how to become better at the sport. As you appear to be quite adept."

"Of course I would be more than happy to," Hugh responded.

Amy pushed aside her concern over her brother paying attention to the woman. He'd promised to help her, and Amy would keep him to that promise.

"I will help you, too, Miss Cox," offered Mr. Jones, a gentleman who seemed to have a frown even more perpetual than Mr. Eastwood's. Even now, his brow creased down the middle as deep as Cheddar Gorge. "As you know, I'm just as talented in the sport."

Miss Cox gave him the required nod then returned her attention back to Hugh.

Mr. Jones's scowl grew, if that was possible, and his envious eyes remained on Miss Cox and Hugh.

Very well. Amy would not be pursuing three gentlemen after all, as Mr. Jones was clearly in love with Miss Cox.

Perhaps Amy ought to alert Hugh of their attachment so he might not pursue Miss Cox, either.

Amy turned to study the other two gentlemen—Mr. Payne, with hair blonder than hers, and Mr. Fisher, who seemed more interested in the trees nearby than the game. Both seemed to have easy temperaments and were quick to smile. They would do nicely as potential candidates for a match. Far more than Mr. Jones and Mr. Eastwood.

After missing yet another hit of the shuttlecock, Amy

glanced over her shoulder again. Mr. Eastwood stood beside Mama's chair, a small curve to his lips as he conversed. What did he speak of to engage his audience so fully?

With a shake of her head, Amy returned her attention to the men she *actually* cared about getting to know.

CHAPTER EIGHT

*B*y the end of the game, Amy had made great progress in discovering more about them, including Mr. Payne's keen ability as a hunter and Mr. Fisher's aptitude for naming birds—which she'd realized he'd been staring at instead of the trees.

She followed the group as they returned to the others, holding her head high after Hugh gave her an impressed nod.

Perhaps she could do this after all.

"I trust you enjoyed yourselves?" Mr. Eastwood asked upon their return.

Why did Amy feel as if the question was directed particularly at her? Either way, she said nothing as the others gave a collective sound of delight.

"And you, Miss Paxton?"

Amy started. So he was directing his question at her. But, why? Did he assume she did not enjoy it? Did he even care if she did not?

"Of course," she replied. "I always do, even if I am not very talented at the sport."

She'd added that last bit for good measure, earning another look of approval from Hugh.

Mr. Eastwood didn't respond.

A lively conversation ensued around the gathered group until Mr. Eastwood proposed the next activity. "Are we ready for our walk, do you think?"

The younger half of the group answered in the affirmative, though one voice rose above the others.

"Oh, yes!" Miss Cox sprang up, her yellow dress bouncing up past her ankles with enthusiasm that equaled her own. She skittered toward Hugh and linked her arm through his. "You must join us, Mr. Paxton. It is certain to be invigorating. You will surely come, as well, Miss Paxton, will you not?"

All eyes fell on Amy as they awaited her reply. The last thing she wanted to do was join the group when she was exhausted from *not* playing Battledore and Shuttlecock. The thought of continuing her charade of dull, unopinionated conversation was far too taxing. Especially when she was trying to avoid the very gentleman directing the journey—the gentleman with eyes as green as the emeralds in her mother's fine jewelry.

"Thank you, but I think I would like to rest here with the others."

"Come now, sister," Hugh said. "You will finally know what the Old Man is if you come with us."

He winked, and Amy was reminded once again of her folly. Well, two follies. One, thinking the fell had been a person. And two, imagining her brother might be kind to her for once in his life.

She had a mind to berate him for his teasing, but Mr. Fisher's approach stopped her.

"I do hope you will reconsider, Miss Paxton. It would be delightful to speak with you further. And the view truly is unmatched."

Amy swallowed a sigh. This was what she wanted, wasn't it? Attention from a gentleman?

With another encouraging nod from Hugh, she finally relented. "I suppose I ought to join you, then."

"You needn't come, Miss Paxton," Mr. Eastwood said abruptly as Mr. Fisher helped her to stand.

She paused. Her eyes, as well all the others, shifted to Mr. Eastwood. Was he disinviting her? Telling her not to come because he did not want her there?

A heavy tension nudged its way through the party, painting Amy's cheeks a bright red. Finally, the gentleman was revealing his cruelty in front of others.

However, all too swiftly, he recanted his words. "I only meant that, as your host, I would not wish for you to partake in any activity that makes you uncomfortable. Of course, we would all be very pleased to have you join us on the excursion."

The friction amidst the group instantly evaporated, but Amy's mortification over the encounter refused to dissipate. Even as their smaller party formed and set forth across the grass, her blush continued to burn.

Naturally, with Mr. Eastwood at the front of the group, Amy fell behind alone, contemplating slipping back to the others without notice, but Miss Booth soon joined her.

"I do hope you're enjoying your stay in Coniston, Miss Paxton."

"Thank you, I am."

Well, for the most part she was. If she could somehow find it in her power to keep herself from staring at a square-shouldered gentleman from his Hessian boots to his tight breeches and—

"Coniston is such a beautiful place," she said, interrupting her own thoughts. "I quite enjoy the peace and solitude it offers."

"Mmm, yes. You must enjoy the lake, as well. Especially from Flitfield Cottage. Your family is fortunate to stay there."

No doubt due to their being the tenants of the wonderful and admirable Mr. Eastwood. Amy would die if this conversation shifted into another praising session of the gentleman. Perhaps she could steer their discussion another direction.

"Yes, we heard the cottage had been in a dismal state of repair, much like Corcliffe Manor. That certainly was a shock, pulling up to see such a beautiful property treated so terribly."

"Oh, indeed. The manor had been beautiful in its prime. All of Coniston was thrilled when Mr. Eastwood was finally allowed control. We know he shall do wonders with the manor, just as he has done with the cottage."

Allowed control? Had he no say in the matter of the estates beforehand?

"Surely he had control when it came to Birchwick Hall," she said with a little laugh, hoping to sound indifferent. "Why else would it be so flawless in appearance?"

Miss Booth looked away. "Well, no. His grandfather made the decisions regarding all their property. He was…very proud of Birchwick."

They followed the curve of the lush land downward until the grass shifted gradually to a small dirt pathway, but Amy hardly noticed, chewing the inside of her lip as questions flooded her mind. So his grandfather had been the one to leave all estates but Birchwick to ruin? How did Mr. Eastwood feel about all of this?

Her pride longed to believe he boasted the same sort of conceit as his grandfather must have. But carrying chickens and fixing tenants' gates hardly spoke of vanity. Still, if Mr. Eastwood cared so passionately about his work, why could he not have pressed to do more earlier, before the neglect could occur?

If Hugh were here, he'd tell her to keep her lips closed and her questions to herself.

But seeing that he was more than occupied with the party ahead of them—particularly Miss Cox—Amy brushed aside his would-be warnings. After all, she was not trying to impress Miss Booth with her amiability, now was she?

"May I ask you a question, Miss Booth?"

"Of course."

Amy pushed away the rest of her hesitance—as well as the niggling thought that she ought not care about this discourteous gentleman at all—and pressed forward. "How is it the estates fell into such disrepair? Surely Mr. Eastwood could have requested his grandfather to do more for them."

Miss Booth wrung her gloved hands together with an averted gaze, clearly uneasy with the question.

Amy may not have been trying to impress Miss Booth, but she had no desire to make the woman uncomfortable. Perhaps she should have taken Hugh's imagined advice after all.

"Forgive my questioning. That was rather impertinent of me to ask."

"No, not at all. It is natural for visitors to have questions about what occurred. But, as it is, Mr. Eastwood does not like to speak of his past, and he values privacy above all else. He cannot abide gossip surrounding his name. I would hate to divulge any information he himself would not be comfortable speaking about."

Amy stiffened. Gossip. That's exactly what she was doing now—looking for information pertaining to Mr. Eastwood. Heat crawled up her neck, digging warm claws into her flesh.

In Bath, she'd been the victim of countless rumors and gossips. Now, here she was, treating Mr. Eastwood the same way she had been treated. No matter her opinion of the gentleman, he deserved more respect than that. As did Miss Booth, who was very loyal to Mr. Eastwood. Did she have an attachment to the gentleman?

Amy shook her head. No, that was more gossip.

"I do wish to clarify, though," Miss Booth said, drawing Amy from her battling thoughts. "Whatever has happened in the past, Mr. Eastwood is not to be blamed. And he is now doing his best to improve his properties, not only for his family, but for the image of Coniston as a whole. And we are most grateful for it."

Amy nodded, chewing the inside of her lip. This was not what she'd wanted to hear, more of Mr. Eastwood's goodness. But then, how long could she go on denying the evidence? Perhaps the gentleman was not whom she'd painted him out to be.

They walked in silence for a moment, stepping over errant puddles in the road and large strips of mud. Merriment drew their attention forward as Hugh and Miss Cox shared a laugh. Mr. Jones looked back from where he walked at the front of the group with Mr. Eastwood. Both men frowned.

"Miss Cox seems quite taken with your brother," Miss Booth said.

Amy cringed. Most women were. "Yes, it would appear so."

Miss Booth kept her eyes forward on the group. "We all grew up together, you know. Miss Cox and Mr. Eastwood. Mr. Jones, Fisher, and Payne. Miss Winslow. The Shaws."

Amy tried to keep up, recognizing all but one name. Before she could ask who Miss Winslow was, Miss Booth continued.

"We would often play together as young children, though Mr. Eastwood wasn't allowed to do so very often..." Her eyes rounded, flicking toward Amy with concern.

Amy stared forward, feigning nonchalance to avoid upsetting Miss Booth for her obvious slip of the tongue. Amy knew many children who hadn't been allowed to play often due to schooling or other familial commitments. So why did Miss Booth appear to have revealed some clandestine secret? Was it because Mr. Eastwood's grandfather had something to do with it?

Miss Booth continued as if she hadn't faltered in her words.

"At any rate, some of us have grown, matured, or even married. While others have remained utterly the same, like Miss Cox. She has always been an incorrigible flirt." Miss Booth paused, sending a heavy look to Amy. "I would hate to have her injure anyone."

Amy understood her meaning at once. Miss Booth was alerting her of Miss Cox's flippant flirtations.

Amy sighed. This was just what Hugh *didn't* need. Another noncommittal relationship. Another liaison for which he would not have to take responsibility. "Not to worry, Miss Booth. My brother is more than capable of taking care of himself."

And only himself—when it came to his relationship with women. But such behavior was not fair for Mr. Jones.

As the walk progressed, the pathway narrowed, and the party fell into single-file between thick underbrush and a stone wall covered in moss. Grass poked through the larger crevices between the grey stones, like facial hair making its first attempt to grow on a young man's chin.

As Miss Booth merged forward, Hugh fell back to walk behind Amy. Hugh had never been able to grow facial hair. Could Mr. Eastwood? No doubt.

"What on earth are you doing?" he hissed over her shoulder. "Speaking with Miss Booth is not going to find you a husband, Amy. You must converse with one of the gentlemen."

"Perhaps I would, had I your help like you promised I would."

He pulled back. "How am I not helping you?"

Amy slowed her pace, ensuring the others moved farther away so they might not overhear her conversation with her brother. "You are more interested in flirting with Miss Cox than helping me," she whispered over her shoulder. "Do not deny it, for you know that is true."

Hugh grinned from ear to ear. "Of course I am more interested in her."

Amy huffed a sigh, turning her back on him. When would she learn her lesson with her brother? "Well, you would be better off avoiding the young woman. Mr. Jones is clearly in love with her."

"I know." Amy didn't need to turn to hear the nonchalance in his tone. "That's what makes it all the better."

She scoffed, shaking her head. "You are despicable, Hugh."

"Come now, I've been helping you, though you claim otherwise. Tell me which gentleman you prefer."

Amy pressed her lips together, refusing to speak. But when she admitted to herself that Hugh had in fact helped her, she relented with another sigh. "I still cannot decide."

"Simply choose one," Hugh said, coming to stand beside her as the pathway widened.

She eyed the back of Mr. Payne's blond head and Mr. Fisher's tall stature. "I've been able to speak to them both with relative ease, and they both appear to be well-respected by those here. I suppose I ought to follow my instincts. But then, when have those ever been right? Whom do *you* think I ought to pursue?" He didn't respond. "Hugh?"

"What is it?" he replied distractedly.

Amy pursed her lips. She followed his gaze to where Miss Cox walked arm-in-arm with Mr. Jones. Miss Cox peered back at Hugh with a grin, which he readily returned.

"Hugh!" Amy whispered with vehemence.

He turned toward her in surprise. "Heavens, why do you feel the need to speak to me in such a way? No wonder Mr. Roberts was frightened of you."

She scowled. "You promised me you would not allow another woman to distract you from helping me."

"And I shall keep my promise. I swore to help you, and I will. Right now, as a matter of fact." He quickened his step. "Mr. Fisher, Mr. Payne. My sister has a most pressing question for you both."

Amy's mouth parted. What the devil did he think he was doing?

With an innocent look, he sauntered forward to walk beside Miss Cox and Mr. Jones, leaving Amy at a loss for words as Mr. Payne and Mr. Fisher stood on either side of her.

"Yes, what is your question, Miss Paxton?" Mr. Fisher asked.

"Well, I…" She swallowed, fighting the urge to pelt Hugh with a pebble atop his smug head as he looked back at her with another smirk.

She pulled her eyes away from him, desperate to find a question for these gentlemen, but her mind continued to draw blanks. That is, until a pheasant from somewhere in the nearby brush crowed out.

"I was wondering what color pheasants were," she blurted out.

What a perfectly horrid question. She knew what a pheasant looked like, and so did Hugh. What would these men think of her?

They shared a glance.

"You truly have never seen one before?" Mr. Fisher asked.

"Oh, of course I have. I was merely having a discussion with my brother. He claimed ring-necked pheasants were more green-feathered, but I disagreed. He really can be foolish at times." There, that would teach Hugh. "At any rate, I wanted a second or third opinion on the matter."

The gentlemen nodded with expressions of understanding. Thank heavens she'd managed to avoid them thinking she was an utter ninny.

Mr. Payne replied first. "Well, your brother was slightly misinformed, I believe. A pheasant has a head full of feathers that are far more blue than they are green, I would say."

"Mmm, yes, I agree," Mr. Fisher added. "Either way, they are far more colorful as a whole than their female counterparts."

Amy looked between them both, slightly more confident

now they weren't looking at her as if she'd gone mad. Hugh had told her gentlemen liked their ego to be stroked—much like a hound enjoyed a good petting. Hugh hadn't appreciated her adding that last part, but it was rather fitting. Perhaps it was time to try that.

"You appear to have a vast knowledge of pheasants, sir," she said to Mr. Fisher.

His chest puffed out like a robin's. "Indeed, I do."

"As do I," Mr. Payne piped in. "Were you aware, Miss Paxton, that they usually walk or run, as opposed to flying?"

"Indeed?" Amy gave a feigned look of fascination.

Pheasants were not her first choice in conversation topics, but at least the gentlemen seemed to be enjoying themselves.

Hugh and Miss Cox's laughter drifted toward her, chipping away at her raising spirits, but she focused all the harder on the gentlemen beside her.

Mr. Fisher was next to volley another fact. "When pheasants do fly, though, they are able to sail as quickly as a horse can run."

"Heavens!" she said with an exaggerated hand to her chest.

"Ah, they may fly hastily, but not so swiftly that I cannot shoot them from the sky." Mr. Payne imitated a gunshot in the air.

Amy's eyes widened. She hadn't expected that response. Nor had Mr. Fisher, by the color of his face that matched the red of a cardinal's feathers.

"Yes," he muttered stoically. "'Tis a marvel you are able to scare pheasants from their nesting grounds with hounds and still manage to capture them mid-flight."

Mr. Payne huffed a mirthless laugh. "Well, a gentleman must eat."

"And is said gentleman averse to fruits and vegetables? Cakes? Bread and cheese? There's a plethora of options aside from birds, Payne, as you well know."

Amy stared directly ahead of her, blinking mutely as their argument continued. Miss Booth had said they had all grown up together. Did that mean Mr. Payne and Mr. Fisher often argued in such a way?

"How you even call yourself a man is beyond me, Fisher."

"I don't believe skinning birds is a requirement of manhood, Payne."

Amy looked between the both of them. "Gentlemen, surely we can agree to disagree here."

Her attempt to ease the argument was weak, at best. How would Hugh have her handle the situation?

"Tell Mr. Fisher you love a good pheasant for dinner."

Well that certainly wouldn't help diffuse the situation.

"You are right, of course, Miss Paxton," Mr. Fisher said in an unaffected tone. "Payne and I will never see eye-to-eye when it comes to his barbarism."

"No, indeed," Mr. Payne agreed with a strained smile. "Nor will we ever agree over Mr. Fisher's judgmental comments."

Amy blew out a slow breath, looking between them both again as they stared daggers at one another.

"Fisher, Payne. Can you not see how terribly uncomfortable you are making Miss Paxton?"

Amy's heart thumped anxiously against her chest. Mr. Eastwood had slowed his progression to fall back to their small party and was now staring rather condemningly at his guests.

"Oh, dear," Mr. Fisher said with a contrite glance. "I do apologize, Miss Paxton."

"As do I, ma'am," Mr. Payne added.

"Oh, it is no trouble," she said hurriedly.

But both of them glanced away uncomfortably, tipping their heads in a bow and swiftly moving toward the others ahead of them.

Amy watched their departing figures, longing to call them

back, but she held her tongue. Her chance was lost. And now these men were scared away from her, too.

All because of Mr. Eastwood.

Indignation burned within her, and she stopped her progression to face him directly. "Just what do you think you are doing, sir?"

CHAPTER NINE

*W*illiam stopped. "Pardon me?"

Miss Paxton waved her hand toward the retreating gentlemen, remaining where she stood. Her voice was low, though it did not mask her frustration one bit. "You've run them both off now! Who knows when they shall return. This is all your doing."

He stared at her incredulously as she stormed off. She was upset with *him*? He could not make sense of the woman. He'd been watching her all day, but he was nowhere closer to discovering the truth about her behavior. She was all that was polite and amiable, only to turn caustic and biting in the very next moment—but only ever around William.

Was she truly still upset about the chicken incident, or was there something more? Either way, he was running out of patience.

Patience. Mr. Rutledge always said William needed more of it.

With an aggravated sigh, he jogged to catch up with her. "Miss Paxton, I assure you, I thought only to help, as I didn't think you were enjoying yourself in the midst of the argument.

Rest assured, I will not interfere in such a way again, unless you should wish it."

She blinked, anger fading away as her eyes rounded. They darted toward the group. "That is perfectly all right. You were trying to help, as you said. And of course I greatly appreciate the gesture."

William narrowed his eyes. Another switch of character. Was this the real Miss Paxton, or was she the angry one from before?

He glanced to where she stared, spotting Hugh, who had somehow managed to coax his way *between* Miss Cox and Mr. Jones and was now the one escorting the woman.

Whatever was going on with Miss Paxton, William was certain her brother had something to do with it. She constantly looked to Hugh for...approval? Permission? William couldn't be sure. But if control played even the smallest part in their relationship, he had to do something to help.

His parents had never been able to stand up to Grandfather, even with William taking the initiative to do so himself. But perhaps, if he befriended Miss Paxton, he might help her find courage of her own.

For now, it was time to swallow his pride. "Miss Paxton, forgive me if this is untoward, but I would like to begin our relationship anew."

She stared up at him warily, so he rushed forward.

"As friends," he clarified. "We did not meet on the best of terms, and I take full responsibility. You see, moments before I happened upon you, the hen I was carrying, well, she deposited her waste upon my waistcoat."

Her brow raised, but she made no further reaction.

William continued. "I was rather put out, as I'm sure you can imagine. I'd spent half the morning chasing after the indigent wretches, particularly that last stubborn hen, so when she escaped my clutches yet again, directly into your unsuspecting face, I fear I took out my frustrations on you, and for that, I truly apologize. As well as for the other ungentlemanly words I've expressed to you."

He ended his speech, barely aware that he held his breath as he waited to see if she would grant him forgiveness. If she did not, William would swear the woman off forever, and she would have to learn how to stand up to her brother on her own.

Much to William's relief—for he did not know if he could allow such an injustice to occur—Miss Paxton's lip twitched, and her features softened.

"Your apology is accepted, Mr. Eastwood. If only you will accept my own apology for my treatment of you that first day. And for my words in the village. And then by the gate after that. And a few moments ago concerning the other gentlemen. And the negative thoughts I've had about you every day from our first meeting up until this moment."

He stared at her, blanking as to what to say in response to such a confession. Her smile was hesitant and rather pained, and suddenly, the humor of her words percolated throughout him.

He laughed. It had been a long time since he'd genuinely laughed. Since long before Grandfather died. "Well, I do believe you are getting the better end of the deal. You are receiving my forgiveness for so many things."

His tone was light to ensure she knew he was in jest. "I am not unaware of your generosity, sir. But you *did* throw a chicken into my face."

He winced. "Ah, that I did. But only to keep my shirt and breeches clean from her...deposits."

Miss Paxton smiled fully this time, lips thinning and eyes squinting, creating small wrinkles at the sides. The reach of her grin was wide, though not too large to be displeasing or distracting. It was just enough to lighten the very air around her.

At the sight, William's heart forgot to keep its rhythm. He'd never seen anything so splendid, so bright, so infectious. And he wanted to keep it there for as long as he could.

"You've led us on a pathway with no end, sir!"

Blast her brother.

William looked forward, reluctantly tearing his eyes from Miss Paxton's cheery expression that vanished at Hugh's declaration.

The group had maneuvered around fallen stones swathed halfway in tall, overgrown grass and was now congregating near a wooden gate, where the pathway eventually disappeared.

"Worry not." He left Miss Paxton's side to open the gate for his guests. "I've already spoken with Mr. Smith, and he has agreed to allow us passage across his fields. At the other side, we will have reached the best view of the Old Man."

"Oh, wonderful," Miss Cox said, clasping onto Hugh's arm. "This has been such a delightful walk. I'll be loath to see it end."

William tipped his head to each of his guests who passed by, waiting until the last—Miss Paxton—had entered the gate before closing it.

After securing the latch, he turned to join the others, stopping short just before he would have barreled directly into Miss Paxton, who stood just beyond the gate.

Had she been waiting for him? No, that was ridiculous. She hardly seemed to notice him anyway, her eyes fixated on something at the opposite end of the field.

He walked around her, expecting her to join him, but she remained still. Following her gaze, he discovered two large Highland cows grazing in the corner of the field, their shaggy, orange coats and long, pointed horns standing out against the backdrop of the verdant grass and dark stone wall.

"Are you well, Miss Paxton?" he asked as she remained frozen to her spot.

"Yes."

She didn't move.

"Then would you like to continue?"

"Yes." She took one step forward, then another, her focus staying on the cows.

"Are you frightened of them?" he asked gingerly, not wishing to have her take offense and destroy the progress they'd made.

"No, no," she said a little too quickly. "I merely expected a field of sheep, not cows."

"Yes, the Smiths have a certain affinity for the creatures. They find them less cumbersome than sheep." He smiled, but Miss Paxton didn't respond. "You needn't worry about them. They're gentle creatures, and we are far enough away that we shan't bother them, and they shan't bother us."

That seemed to ease her worries to some degree, though her shoulders still raised tautly in her tan-colored spencer.

His brow pursed. Was she truly so terrified of them? Well, forcing her to do something she was afraid of would do nothing but injure her. He'd learned as much from Grandfather.

"If you wish, we do not have to cross the field at all. There is a way around the wall that merely adds a quarter of an hour. I wouldn't wish for you to be pressured into doing something you have no desire to do."

His pointed comment was a little heavy-handed, but Miss Paxton didn't seem to notice.

She shook her head. "Oh, no. I would hate to bring everyone back to walk elsewhere. No, I can do this." She took one final glance at the cows then faced forward with squared shoulders. "I *want* to do this."

They had not taken two steps together before one of the cows bellowed out a long call, and Miss Paxton started, her pace increasing. "You're sure they won't charge?"

"I'm absolutely certain."

He hid his grin, maneuvering to the other side of her so he stood between her and the cows. He'd never met anyone afraid of cows before, but he supposed growing up away from the country life had not done Miss Paxton any favors.

Charity was not afraid of cows. She was not afraid of anything.

She did not have so charming a smile as Miss Paxton, but—

He frowned, stopping his thoughts. Where the devil had that come from? A pretty smile mattered not to him in comparison to a strong mind, and Charity had a strong mind, even more so than Miss Booth or Miss Cox. Charity never did anything she didn't want to do. Admittedly, sometimes to a fault.

His brow furrowed, his thoughts muddling until he noted Miss Paxton fidgeting beside him, peering around him to keep her eye on the cows.

The woman was in need of a distraction. Perhaps a conversation would do nicely. After all, he still had a long way to go if he was going to befriend her enough to convince her she didn't need her brother's approval for every move she made.

"What is it about these cows that makes you so fearful?" he asked.

She peered up at him guardedly. "It is not just these cows. It is *all* cows. They can't be trusted, what with how large they loom."

Her lips pulled down. Why did he want to see them lift again so badly?

"So you are afraid of horses, too, then?"

"Horses don't have horns," she said with a grim expression.

He chewed his lip to prevent another grin. What was it about this woman being afraid of Highland cows that was just so...so *adorable*?

"So cows you dislike, horses, you fare well enough with."

She nodded.

"And I assume hens fall into the same category as horses?"

Finally, her eyes pulled to his, fear replaced with a bright twinkling. "Oh, heavens, no. Hens are at the very top of my adoration."

"Are they now?"

She opened her mouth to continue then paused, her brow wrinkling as if she regretted her confession. "That is to say, hens are fine enough creatures. I have no particular affinity for them. Having so would be quite unladylike, would it not?"

She looked ahead to where the others in the group still pushed forward, far enough away to not overhear their conversation. Was she seeking Hugh's help again?

William stifled a sigh. Her brother must have told her not to mention her love of hens. As unconventional as it was, such an admiration was innocuous. And William would help her see just that.

"On the contrary. Why would admiring any of God's creatures be considered unladylike, whether they be horses, hens, or hares?"

She peered up at him, as if studying to see if he was in earnest. Her eyes were a bright blue, made all the brighter when she bestowed upon him a warm smile.

His chest tightened, though from what, he couldn't tell. He cleared his throat, looking ahead to the group who'd nearly reached the other side of the field.

"So tell me, Miss Paxton. How is it you know how to hold a hen so well?"

"Common sense, sir."

He caught the teasing in her tone and clicked his tongue in feigned disapproval. "Mocking me again, even after asking for forgiveness? That hardly seems right."

"I do apologize." A faint dimple shone in her cheek. "The truth of the matter is, I had a few as pets."

His brow raised. "Indeed?"

"Yes. I begged my parents, and I was ever so grateful they obliged."

As William had suspected. She clearly received whatever she wished as a child. Although, if one appreciated what one was given—as Miss Paxton certainly appeared to do—there was nothing wrong with that, he supposed.

"Mind you, I did not know how to hold them in the beginning, and there may have been an accident or two similar to the disaster that occurred on your waistcoat."

"And did you have names for these hens?"

"Oh, of course."

"Go on then."

She drew a deep breath, pausing for what appeared to be dramatic effect. "My favorites were Miss Hen, Miss Clucky, and...Hugh."

"Hugh?" he chuckled.

"Believe you me, my brother was not pleased when I named a female chicken after him. Which, of course, was the reason I kept the name. My parents and I teased him mercilessly with it for years."

William laughed again, and their eyes connected in shared humor. From the warmth of her gaze, a stirring occurred deep inside his chest, as if he'd just sipped warm tea on a cold, November day.

He pulled his gaze away, rubbing at his chest to dispel the discomfiting feeling. He'd never experienced anything like it before. Not even with Charity.

And that alone was cause for concern.

Amy reached the far end of the field with Mr. Eastwood only moments behind the rest of the party, slipping past the gate with a furtive glance at the gentleman as he held it open for her.

"Thank you," she murmured, to which he replied with a touch to the brim of his hat.

Amy tried to talk down her fluttering heart, but she couldn't. That walk across the field had been the highlight of her day, by far.

After his heartfelt apology, her anger had collapsed like a weakened blancmange, and she knew she needed to seek his forgiveness, too. Their conversation had then flowed naturally, and he'd even defended her appreciation of hens when she'd thought he'd scorn her. And when their eyes had connected...

She ducked her head to hide her smile. A spark had occurred between them, she was certain of it.

She only had one concern now. How could she ever go back to speaking with Mr. Fisher and Mr. Payne after having such a delightful time with Mr. Eastwood?

"What think you of the view, Miss Paxton?"

Amy blinked, surprised to find Miss Cox at her side. "Oh, it is marvelous, to be sure."

"It is, isn't it?"

In truth, Amy hadn't even taken in the sight yet. She eyed the long fell, bare but for a few straggling grey stones and orange foliage at the bottom. It certainly was a unique sight, one to be admired.

Yet Amy could not get her eyes to obey as they instead admired Mr. Eastwood's profile.

How stupid she'd been before to hold onto her pride, trying to convince herself that he was a terrible person. Clearly, she'd allowed her embarrassment to cloud her vision.

This gentleman would certainly move onto her list of "possible men to pursue."

"He is charming, isn't he?"

Amy had nearly forgotten Miss Cox remained by her side. "I'm sorry, of whom do you speak?"

She knew very well who.

"Mr. Eastwood, of course. Shame he's been claimed by another, though."

Amy's heart sank back into the cold place in her chest where it normally resided. Miss Booth stood beside Mr. Eastwood, staring up at him with a smile. Of course. Amy had suspected it earlier. Miss Booth's loyalty now made perfect sense.

"Well, I hope he and Miss Booth will be happy together," she said.

This was silly of her to feel so disheartened. She'd liked the gentleman for what, a quarter of an hour?

Miss Cox twittered a soft laugh. "Oh, no, it is not Miss Booth who loves Mr. Eastwood. Miss Charity Winslow does."

Miss Winslow? That was the name she hadn't recognized with Miss Booth. "Oh, I'm afraid I don't know Miss Winslow."

"Of course not. She is in London for another few months." She lowered her voice. Miss Cox, unlike Miss Booth, certainly didn't have a problem sharing her knowledge of Mr. Eastwood. "Miss Winslow and Mr. Eastwood were the closest in our small group of friends as children, before Mr. Payne and Mr. Fisher went away to school. Miss Winslow wasn't allowed on the property, either, but Mr. Eastwood would often sneak away to meet with her."

Amy wasn't sure what to do with this wealth of information handed to her so freely. Part of her wished to plug her ears, to respect Mr. Eastwood's privacy. But then, Miss Cox's knowledge was intriguing.

"No one was allowed on the property?" she asked.

"Oh, no. Not us children, at any rate. Parties were held years ago, but for more than half a decade, the Eastwoods did not host one gathering at Birchwick. Until today, that is."

Amy's confusion merely grew with each piece of information she received. Had his grandfather prevented the gatherings as he'd prevented Mr. Eastwood from walking, playing with children, or altering his estates? She could hardly imagine such control.

"At any rate," Miss Cox continued, "we all suspect a formal

engagement between Mr. Eastwood and Miss Winslow when she returns in December. I assume you'll be long gone before the wedding."

Amy brushed a soothing hand to her churning stomach. "No doubt."

Amy looked back to Mr. Eastwood, who had since moved to speak with Mr. Jones. She should have maintained her early despising of the gentleman. It would have been far easier.

"Now, Miss Paxton," Miss Cox said, linking her arm through hers and pulling her closer. "It is your turn to tell me what your brother is like. He is quite a charmer, is he not?"

Amy suppressed a sigh. She was often treated this way by women—befriended only so she might share more about her brother.

Even with Miss Cox's less-than-sincere intentions, Amy was glad to have received the truth from the young woman. Now at least she knew not to pursue Mr. Eastwood, thereby avoiding future embarrassment.

Thank heavens she'd discovered the truth before she fell in too deep.

CHAPTER TEN

A few days later, Amy rushed through the back door of the cottage, closing it behind her with a heavy sigh as she leaned against the wood. Thunder rumbled above, and rain pelted against the only window in the small corridor. A grey light caused by the clouds outside shone dimly across the dark, wooden flooring.

The moodiness reflected Amy's feelings perfectly.

She blew out another breath, her chest rising and falling from her labored breathing. She should not have taken that last turn near Coniston Water. Of course she could not outrun a storm in the Lake District.

Pushing away from the door, she set off down the corridor, unbuttoning her spencer and sliding her sopping bonnet off of her wet, stringy hair. She'd have to change before speaking with Mama. If Amy was caught soaked through, she'd be forced to keep to her bed the rest of the day.

But she could not bear such a notion, especially after being confined in her speech while walking with Hugh, Mr. Fisher, and Miss Cox round the lake. All she'd done for an hour and a half was watch Hugh and Miss Cox flirt in front of her, all while

Mr. Fisher spoke, yet again, of birds. At least Mr. Payne had not been there to claim an ability to shoot each one stone dead from the trees in which they perched.

She'd reminded herself constantly of her intentions—to find a way to be happy and to no longer be a burden on her parents —and still, the afternoon had been unbearable. She'd listened intently to Mr. Fisher and responded with as much enthusiasm as she could muster, just as Hugh had suggested, but she would have died to converse of something—anything—other than robins and geese and starlings.

At one point, she'd brought up chickens, but the man claimed a dislike for the "essentially flightless" animals. Needless to say, she'd kept her mouth closed fairly tight after that comment.

Inching up the stairs to avoid any creaking, Amy pushed aside the continuous thought that had been popping into her mind all afternoon like the ducks on Coniston Water, incessantly bobbing their heads in and out of the water.

It would do her no good to dwell on the fact that—although Mr. Fisher did not like hens, and Mr. Payne no doubt only enjoyed them as food—Mr. Eastwood did not take an issue with her favoring the animal. Would he...No. The man was soon to be engaged to another, for heaven's sake. It didn't matter what he thought or what he did, at all.

Managing to peel her gloves off one by one, Amy reached the top of the stairs and rounded the corner to her room. Deep in thought, she did not realize her door was left open until she stepped within the small space and discovered Mr. Eastwood himself standing in her room with his head halfway out her window in the rain.

"Mr. Eastwood?" She took a quick step back in surprise.

He started, bumping his head against the side of the window as he turned to see her.

"Blast!" He rubbed his head with his free hand while holding onto the window with the other.

She winced. "Oh, I'm sorry. I didn't mean to startle you."

Mr. Eastwood straightened, water dripping from the strands of his hair down his temples. "That is quite all right. But I ought to be the one apologizing for being in your room."

As the words were said aloud, the realization of the situation finally dawned on her. He *was* in her room. Why was he in her room?

Tools lay scattered about his feet, as well as a puddle of water from the drops of rain slipping in through the open window. He wore no jacket, his waistcoat was unbuttoned nearly halfway, and his cravat hung loosely around his neck. Water droplets slid down the curve of his throat, disappearing into the white cloth below.

Amy managed to tear her eyes away from the angles of his jaw only to be captured instead by his green eyes.

As they trailed down the length of her, she became keenly aware of her state. Dress clinging to her legs, hair plastered against her face, spencer hanging half-open with a white day dress beneath, no doubt revealing her chemise.

She clasped the spencer together and swallowed. Mr. Eastwood certainly did not care how she appeared. He no doubt only had eyes for Miss Winslow. And yet, Amy's cheeks still burned.

"Yes, you are in my room. May I ask why?"

He stared at her legs for a moment longer before blinking and looking to the tools scattered around him. He dropped to the ground to place them in his satchel. "Forgive me. While at Birchwick Hall two days past, your mother mentioned that the windows did not close properly in a few of the rooms here. With so much rain today, and the temperature drop that is sure to happen this evening, I thought a little mending would be good."

He stood, brushing his eyes over her again. "Mrs. Paxton assured me the rooms would be empty, including yours. I hadn't any notion…"

His words trailed off as he shifted in place, and suddenly, a strange confidence boosted Amy's spirits. Mr. Eastwood was *embarrassed*. So often, she'd been the one to make a fool of herself. Now Mr. Eastwood was the one to be caught in an awkward situation, and she wanted to prolong it, to make him stew with discomfort for just a moment more.

Were the situation not so compromising, she might have. Funny how kindness came naturally to her when she did not think the gentleman was out to solely embarrass her.

She took a step back. "That is a viable response, Mr. Eastwood. So I shall leave you to your mending once again."

"No, please." He stopped her, slinging the satchel over his shoulder and heading toward the door. "I have only now just finished. Besides"—he eyed her up and down—"you appear to need your room far more than I do."

Just like that, her confidence dissipated. "I-I was caught in the rain during my walk, I'm afraid."

He nodded. Was that a hint of amusement in those emerald depths?

"I was walking with Miss Cox, Mr. Fisher, and my brother but decided to take an extra few minutes to myself when they left. That is when the rain set in."

Why did she feel the need to explain all of this to him? To prove she was not entirely reckless? Senseless? Foolish?

"I see." Mr. Eastwood moved to the corridor, standing outside of her room. "I hope you had a pleasant time."

"I did, thank you."

He took another step back, flicking his eyes at her dress once more before nodding his head. "Well, good day, Miss Paxton."

Hugh would have advised Amy to let the man leave, to focus

instead on tomorrow when they would meet with Mr. Payne for a ride across the countryside.

But Hugh was not there, was he? "Thank you for fixing my window."

Mr. Eastwood paused halfway down the corridor. "It was no trouble."

"But it is most appreciated. I find it rather difficult to sleep with irregular sounds at night, and an inconstant dripping from the leaking window into my porcelain wash bowl was rather distracting."

Was she truly speaking to this gentleman about her sleeping patterns? At least she didn't need to impress him now, what with his impending engagement.

"I'm glad I could be of service." He inched backward, buttoning his waistcoat.

He clearly wished to leave, and if Amy had any sense, she'd allow him to. But she was anxious for conversation about something other than Mr. Fisher's birds and Hugh's flirting with Miss Cox. And her tongue had a mind of its own. "Did Mr. Rutledge teach you how to mend windows, too?"

He stared at her for a moment, tipping his head in confusion.

"You told me he taught you how to fix the gate. I only assumed…"

"Ah, yes. He did. I'm surprised you remembered that."

Heat crept up her neck, but she drew in deep, cold breaths to fight it back. She was simply being a friend for remembering such a fact about him.

He looked away. "Mr. Rutledge has always had difficulty dealing with pains in his hands. He couldn't afford to hire help, so during my visits, he would teach me how to repair doors and windows, tables and hearths. Fortunately, I became more proficient than when I first started."

Could this man be any more selfless? "They must be grateful for your help."

"I assure you, I am more grateful for theirs."

Theirs? In what way could the Rutledges, a kind but clearly poor couple, have helped Mr. Eastwood?

As much as she longed to know the answer, Amy knew from Miss Booth's words that Mr. Eastwood valued his privacy, so she would not press him for more knowledge.

A moment of silence passed before he spoke again. "I do hope you and your family enjoyed yourselves at Birchwick."

Warmth settled around her middle as Mr. Eastwood was next to prolong their conversation. "We did, thank you."

"Good. I hope it helped you all to feel a little more at home during your stay in Coniston."

How had she ever managed to overlook his kindness? No wonder everyone in town fawned over him.

And no wonder Miss Winslow was in love with him.

Her smile faltered.

Should she ask…No. She shouldn't even consider it. But then, what if Miss Cox had stretched the truth? Surely Amy should validate the woman's words before taking them as gospel.

"Yes, we feel much more at home. Especially with making so many new friends. Miss Booth. Miss Cox. They also told me of another young woman I would like to meet. Miss Winslow, I believe her name was."

She watched him carefully, but he did not so much as flinch a muscle. "Indeed?"

His voice was flat. She really oughtn't continue. But then, she needed to know. "Yes. I was told that you and Miss Winslow are—"

"Friends?" Mr. Eastwood interrupted. "Yes, since childhood."

Amy's lips parted. She didn't know what to say. Miss Cox must have been lying. Why else would Mr. Eastwood say he and Miss Winslow were simply friends if they were truly in love with each other?

Unless, of course, he did not approve of her prying.

Oh, where the devil was Hugh when she needed him?

Anxious to return to their carefree conversation, Amy searched for something to change the subject, but Mr. Eastwood spoke instead, his tone short.

"Lovely to see you again, Miss Paxton. Good day."

After a brief bow, he disappeared down the stairs, leaving Amy with regret that dampened her spirits more than even her sodden clothing did.

William arrived back at Birchwick, shrugging out of his damp great coat with the help of the footman.

"A few letters have arrived for you, sir," the young man said. "Shall I fetch them for you?"

"I can retrieve them. Thank you, Henry."

The footman nodded then departed with the great coat in hand.

William walked to the silver tray resting on a small table nearby, pushing away all thought of Miss Paxton and her prying questions.

She was just like every other impertinent visitor to Coniston and just like every gossip in town. He should've known to expect her questions.

But he wasn't going to think about her now. Nor about his response to her questioning.

He retrieved the letters, shuffling through matters of business before settling on a correspondence in his mother's script. Setting the others aside for later, William broke the seal and unfolded the parchment, the paper crinkling loudly against the high ceilings of the front hall.

My dear William,

It has only been a little over a month since we left Coniston, yet it seems a lifetime since we saw you last. We have kept busy, as you've suggested, and as a result, we have fallen in love with Cornwall and the sea. We've toured a working copper mine, as well as a charming lighthouse, though the name escapes my memory now. I'm certain I wouldn't even be able to spell it should I recall it anyway.

At any rate, as much as we have enjoyed our time here, we feel a pull to come home.

William sighed, shaking his head. He knew his parents wouldn't be able to keep away for very long. He missed them. A great deal, in fact. But the moment they returned, Father would no doubt question every change William had made to each of the estates—still indoctrinated to do what Grandfather desired of him.

But at least Father was not a tyrant. If William explained his reasoning, Father would understand.

William continued reading the letter.

Now, William. I can feel your angst from nearly four hundred miles away. Worry not. We shan't return home just yet.

"Thank goodness," he whispered to himself.

Instead, we are to go to London. As much as we love Cornwall, I feel your father needs more of a distraction. Seeing the Thames and Vauxhall Gardens will be sure to provide him such, as he has not been to Town for many, many years. And, as you know, I have never been there myself.

Yet another thing for which they had Grandfather to thank.

I do hope you are well, as I have not received a letter from you yet. I will blame it on the post, though I have an inkling that you are responsible. Worry not. I'm certain you are busy with the estates.

We received word from Charity this morning that she is enjoying her time in London. (Of course we would delight in seeing her there.) You know how proud we are of your decision to be with her. It will do wonders for our familial relationships and will heal many wounds. You always do what is best for us.

As much as I'm certain she is enjoying her time in London, I know she must be missing you.

William winced. He'd been neglectful to both of the women in his life, completely consumed with matters of the estates. He needed to rectify that.

Of course, his letters to Charity would need to be accomplished in a covert manner, just like her letters were delivered to him. Mrs. Winslow wouldn't approve of their correspondence, as that would lead people to assume an official engagement was now between them. Since Charity was in London at her mother's wish to ensure Charity truly did want to marry William, they needed Mrs. Winslow to believe they took her request seriously.

Your father's spirits are improving daily. People often ask whom we mourn for, and though Mr. Eastwood is always gracious enough to respond, I believe it pains him each time he must do so. You and I will never understand the sorrow he feels in his own father's passing, but I pray you will try, as I continue to do so daily. All we must do is show patience and compassion—something your grandfather never could do.

Now, I think I shall end this letter before I must retrieve another sheet. Do take care, son. We speak often of our love for you, and our desire to see you happily settled.

Until then, I bid you farewell.

With love, your Mama

William refolded the letter, sliding it into his waistcoat pocket and climbing the stairs to his study. He would not put it off any longer. He would write to his parents and to Charity—if only to inform them that he was still alive and well.

Or to alleviate the curdling in his stomach.

How could he have been so heartless? Charity had written to him twice already, detailing the happenings of her day—balls, shopping, meeting new people. But never a mention of another gentleman.

He hadn't worried a great deal over her finding someone else in Town. She'd loved William since they were children. But of course she would need the same reassurance from him.

He'd been at a loss as to what to say in return, so he'd laid her letters aside and moved on with his progress with the cottage. Clearly, he was stupid.

He entered his study, sitting down behind the large desk and pulling out his quill and ink.

Dear Charity,

He paused. Such words seemed rather intimate written on the page. But he supposed if he was intent on marrying the girl, such an opening would suffice.

I trust you are enjoying your time in London. Your letters...

He pulled up his quill. What had she written about?

He shuffled around spare correspondences and loose pieces of paper on the desk before slouching forward with a sigh.

Perhaps he hadn't kept them.

He shook his head and continued the letter.

Your letters detailing the city were quite entertaining. Such a different life than the one we lead here, to be sure.

I'm sure you will receive word soon that my parents will be arriving in London shortly. Mother has expressed her desire to see you. I, of course, wish to, as well. But as you well know, my estates were left in a dismal manner. This is the reasoning behind my lack of correspondence, for which I beg your forgiveness, as I have spent my time doing little else.

The cottage was completed just last week. The manor will be next, and then I shall move on to Birchwick, where I shall make the grounds less stilted. Father is sure to disapprove at first, but all will be well in the end. At least, that is what I hope.

As for other matters, life has remained the same in Coniston. Still the same gossips, still the same simple life—with no one here to distract me from my thoughts of you and our ambition to wed.

A charming grin and a pair of shining blue eyes flashed in his mind's eye—as well as a pair of long legs clearly visible through a soaked-through dress.

He frowned, trying to push the image aside, but Miss Paxton continued to force her way into his thoughts—and the embarrassment he'd felt over being discovered in her room.

Of course, all discomfort fled at her mention of Charity. He'd known at once Miss Cox was the culprit behind such information—as per usual. The woman feasted on gossip and information about other people's lives like a weasel to a vole. Had she also told Miss Paxton how Grandfather had not only ruined his own family's life, but also the life of each member of the Winslow family?

Would Miss Paxton think less of him for coming from such a family?

Of course, her opinion hardly mattered. He was merely at wit's end with everyone in town discussing his life—his past and his future—as if they had some right to it. That was the main reason he'd kept his relationship with Charity quiet from Miss Paxton.

All of Coniston seemed to know everything about him. Why did this visitor require the same?

Then again, the regret in Miss Paxton's eyes, the hesitance in her expression as she'd asked him her questions, had hardly seemed like she was searching for gossip. She could have been making conversation, or perhaps she was attempting to set the matter straight between him and Charity to know if Miss Paxton might pursue...

He squeezed his eyes closed with a firm shake of his head. No. He would not travel down that road.

Opening his eyes, he peered down at the paper, forcing himself to focus on the task at hand. But all he could see was the large, black spot of ink feeding through the parchment in wild veins. It must have dropped as he'd thought of Miss Paxton—all while writing a letter to Charity, the woman he had to marry.

The woman he was *fortunate* enough to marry.

With a sigh of frustration, he dropped his quill and rubbed his hands across his face.

What the devil was wrong with him?

CHAPTER ELEVEN

*W*illiam would no longer go to the cottage. At least not while the Paxtons stayed there. He'd already hired Mr. Smith to fix any repairs needed. Short of the Paxtons inviting him over for a brief visit, he would avoid being there at all costs. That was what was best for Charity, Miss Paxton—and his own state of mind.

Now all he needed to do was take a different route to town. The main road placed him far too close to the cottage for comfort.

A few days had passed since Miss Paxton had discovered him in her bedroom. Though the mortification had long fled, his determination to forget the appealing way in which she stood before him—her sodden yet shapely form he hadn't been able to keep his eyes off of—was still fresh.

As such, when the cottage's thatched roof came into view, and laughter and conversation soon followed from outside of the small house, William lowered his head, reminding himself to not even offer a glance toward them.

But when a laugh he'd never heard before sounded out above the rest, light and lilting, he knew at once whom it belonged to because it was just like her smile. It illuminated the very air around her.

What was she doing to be laughing so heartily? Not that it mattered, of course. He cared more about what Charity was doing in London. Would she be eating luncheon now? Or shopping for a new gown?

He traveled along the road to where more of the cottage was visible, and movements appeared in the corner of his eye. A flash of a Pomona green dress. Blonde curls bouncing back and forth. No doubt a dazzling grin to accompany both.

Thoughts of Charity dissipated, and his will weakened as his desire to see Miss Paxton—just this once—won out.

He regretted his decision in an instant as his heart pushed against his chest with heavy thuds. Miss Paxton stood in the clear opening of the garden away from the house and hedges, playing Battledore and Shuttlecock with Hugh.

William watched with a raised brow as she continually hit back the shuttlecock strike after strike, laughing joyously while reaching her racket out time and time again with success. Where had this girl been at Birchwick? Rosy-cheeked and bright-eyed, she clearly excelled at the sport—and she was one of the prettiest girls he'd ever laid eyes on.

A pain shot through his chest. How could he think such a thing? Of course, Charity was beautiful, too, just in a different way. And was he not allowed to appreciate another woman when Charity herself was in London, no doubt admiring hundreds of gentlemen she found more handsome than William?

Indeed, that was the very reason she was *in* London—to ensure she loved no gentleman like she did William.

Even with his reassuring words, an uneasiness slid throughout him, coiling at the bottom of his chest, ready to strike without notice.

"Mr. Eastwood!"

His stomach hardened at Mrs. Paxton's voice. When had his horse stopped moving? He raised a hand in greeting to Mr. Paxton and his wife, who he hadn't noticed seated at the garden table near the house.

"You will join us, won't you?" Mrs. Paxton offered.

William skirted a glance toward Miss Paxton. The shuttle-cock sent from Hugh flew past her, her racket frozen in the air. With her free hand, she smoothed out her dress and blonde ringlets, though a few stray curls still draped down the length of her neck, fluttering against her skin in the cool autumn breeze.

No, joining them would not be wise. "Thank you for the invitation, but I wouldn't wish to impose. At any rate, I've a few letters to post in town this morning."

Letters to Mama and Charity, in fact.

Mrs. Paxton pressed on. "Oh, but you would not be an imposition, sir. I do hope you will reconsider."

The correspondences pressed heavily against his chest, but how could he, in good conscience as a gentleman, refuse the offer twice?

With a reluctant nod, he directed his horse toward the cottage, chewing the inside of his cheek as the hooves clopped rhythmically against the bridge.

He dismounted then approached their table, eyes flicking toward Hugh and Miss Paxton, who had since begun to miss every strike of the shuttlecock.

Was she playing poorly now on purpose, or was it nerves?

"We are so happy to see you again, Mr. Eastwood," Mrs. Paxton said when he reached them. "Would you care for a cup of tea?"

"Thank you, ma'am, but I fear I must decline. My letters are of business, so they must be posted without too much delay."

Business. He obviously didn't consider Charity and mother as "business." He only said as much to avoid the inference that they were something more. Although, his marriage to the woman could possibly be thought of as a business matter in all that it would do to benefit their families and their pasts...but that hardly mattered now.

"Well, we appreciate you taking time out of your busy schedule to speak with us for a moment. Do we not, Mr. Paxton?"

"Absolutely."

William gave a polite nod, his eyes wandering casually across the grass toward the Paxton siblings. Miss Paxton was bent over, rummaging around in a large bracken, no doubt attempting to find a missing shuttlecock.

"With the rain having finally departed, this weather is delightful."

William swiftly averted his eyes from Miss Paxton retrieving the shuttlecock, facing Mrs. Paxton instead. "I trust your windows fared well during the storm?"

"Oh, they were perfect, sir. Thank you again."

Miss Paxton missed another hit, due to her moving slower than William's mother ambling past shop windows.

"I do hope this weather will last for a few days." Mr. Paxton placed his cup of tea on the saucer. "We had the notion of renting a couple of boats to take out on the lake this morning, but it would appear that all of Coniston thought to do the same."

Mrs. Paxton nodded with a disappointed look. "Indeed. By the time we arrived this morning, all the boats had gone." Hugh's chuckling—no longer Miss Paxton's—sailed toward them. "At least Hugh and Amy seem to be enjoying themselves."

William didn't move his eyes from Mrs. Paxton's. "I wish I would've known your dilemma earlier. I've plenty of boats of my own that I would be more than happy for you to use during your stay here."

Mrs. Paxton's face brightened. "Oh, really? You are certain that would not be an inconvenience?"

"Not for me, I assure you."

Only for Grandfather. He'd never allowed anyone to take out his boats, even his own family.

"You'd find some way to break them, I'm sure of it," he'd told each of them.

William's parents eventually stopped asking to use them. But William resorted to sneaking out for a nightly row every now and again.

Now that the boats belonged to him, he would never hesitate to share them with others—not only to make Grandfather roll over in his grave, but to prove William was more of a gentleman than Grandfather ever was.

"That is very kind of you, Mr. Eastwood," Mr. Paxton said. "Though I'm sure we will only accept such an offer if you agree to join us out on the lake when the time comes."

William feigned gratitude before looking away. There was no possible way he could agree to such a thing, boating with the Paxtons, particularly Miss Paxton. But there was no need to say as much now.

"How fare the renovations of Corcliffe Manor?" Mr. Paxton asked next.

Hugh approached the table, Miss Paxton trailing behind as she picked at the wooden frame of her racket.

"We are still working to clean through the debris, but things are progressing rather nicely."

"Excellent," Mr. Paxton responded.

"Mr. Eastwood," Hugh said, standing at his side, "do tell me you play Battledore and Shuttlecock."

Miss Paxton deposited her racket in the grass then moved to the opposite side of the table, sitting rather rigidly beside her father. Was she thinking about the last time she and William had seen each other? *He* certainly wasn't.

"I do. Though, I don't claim expertise."

"A general knowledge will be just the thing." He motioned to

Miss Paxton. "My sister is abysmal at the sport, as I'm certain you've noticed. I've been trying to teach her for nigh on half an hour, and she still has not improved an ounce."

"Is that so?" William shifted his eyes around the family.

Miss Paxton stared at her fingers in her lap, and their parents exchanged unreadable glances.

Clearly, they had all seen Miss Paxton's talent at the sport. What sort of game were they playing?

Hugh continued. "It's true. Then again, it comes as no surprise she has not improved with me as her teacher." He lowered his voice, though everyone could still hear him. "She never was one to be taught by me. You, sir, on the other hand, will be the perfect instructor."

William gave a dry smile. Whatever this man's intentions—whether he was trying to annoy Miss Paxton or draw her closer to William—William would not be a pawn any longer. "I doubt I would be able to instruct Miss Paxton on anything. At any rate, I haven't the time."

"Ah, business, I assume?" Hugh clicked his tongue. "Surely letters can wait for the sake of a young woman in need of your help."

"Surely they cannot."

"Hugh." Mrs. Paxton's tone was light, but even William saw the warning in her eyes.

Hugh merely looked expectantly at William. Annoyed with the man's pushing, William opened his mouth to refuse again, but when Miss Paxton shifted uncomfortably in her chair, he cringed.

She was caught in the middle of all of this, and William had just made it worse by essentially rejecting her in front of her family. No matter what game Hugh was playing, William couldn't behave ungentlemanly, nor could he stand by and allow Hugh's control over his sister any longer.

"You are right, Hugh," William said. Miss Paxton's head

swung up. "Business can wait for such a cause as helping another." He reached for the racket and shuttlecock from Hugh then finally faced Miss Paxton. "Shall we?"

She stared up at him. "There is no need, sir. My brother may have forgotten his manners, but I haven't. You needn't linger when you have business to see to. You may leave at once, if you must."

William sniffed. And leave Hugh to berate her for standing up to him? He would not allow it. "I assure you, the letters can wait."

Neither Mother nor Charity would fault him for the letters being a day or two later than normal. Not when he had such a noble cause.

At least, that's what he told himself.

"Run along, Amy," Hugh urged, pulling her up. "Do allow Mr. Eastwood to teach you as you would not allow me."

Miss Paxton reluctantly stood, sending an annoyed glance to Hugh as she retrieved her racket from the grass nearby. William left his hat on his seat, draping his jacket and gloves over the top of it. He was glad to be rid of the black clothing, removing them every opportunity he could.

He was not mourning for his grandfather, but wearing the black jacket and gloves appeased Society enough to let them think he was in mourning. Still, he didn't really like the idea of wearing the clothes to honor such a man.

Setting any thought of his grandfather aside, he followed Miss Paxton to the clearing near the bracken and hedges.

Whispers followed him as he walked away, and he stole a quick glance back as Mr. Paxton scowled at Hugh, speaking under his breath.

Something was absolutely occurring, but William had no idea what it was.

"I'm sorry my brother pressed you into doing this, Mr. Eastwood," Miss Paxton said in a hushed tone over her shoulder. "I understand you are busy, so you needn't feel obligated to help me."

William's heart reached out to her. She didn't wish to impose —at least he knew that much about her now. But he *did* feel obligated to help her, just not at Battledore and Shuttlecock.

"I assure you, it is no trouble."

She made no response. The ribbon hanging down from her bodice rippled in the wind before catching on her hip.

He looked away. He shouldn't even be noticing such a thing.

When they reached the open area, Miss Paxton faced him. "So what do you suggest I do to improve my…my incompetence with this game?"

William studied her for a moment, wondering how long he should feign ignorance. Her family was far enough behind them so any conversation he might have with her would remain unheard. But he wouldn't wish to injure the girl by accusing her of lying—even though that was exactly what she was doing.

Perhaps he'd first give her the opportunity to confess herself.

"You have the correct grip on the racket," he began, eying her gloveless, elegant fingers encircling the handle with a light touch. "And your stance appears correct."

She remained silent, unmoving, apart from her eyes that focused over William's shoulder. After a subtle nod—no doubt in Hugh's direction—she looked to William.

"That is good to hear, at least," she said. "What do you suggest we do now?"

She was still taking Hugh's advice from across the garden. William drew a deep, calming breath. "I suppose we must see how you strike the shuttlecock."

"Very well. I'm ready when you are."

He hit the shuttlecock toward her, but she remained where she stood, reaching out in languid movements before it fell to the ground nearby. She scurried toward it, then gave a poor attempt to send the shuttlecock back.

"You see how terrible she is, Mr. Eastwood?" Hugh called out from behind as William bent to retrieve the shuttlecock.

Mr. Paxton frowned again at Hugh. Mrs. Paxton averted her gaze. And Miss Paxton's face shaded deep red—whether from embarrassment or frustration, William could not decipher.

Either way, he was finished. He respected people's privacy, for he knew what it was like to have none. But he could not go on like this any longer.

"All right, after observing you play, I have only one suggestion."

Her brow twitched. "And what is that?"

"You ought to stop losing on purpose."

He sent the shuttlecock toward her again. This time, her miss was not on purpose.

"Losing on purpose, sir? I have no idea as to what you are referring."

He raised a brow. "Do you not? Because only moments ago, I stood just there"—he pointed to the open view of the road—"where I was witness to the rather remarkable transformation that has taken place from the time you played so poorly at Birchwick, to you playing exceptionally well right here."

She reached for the shuttlecock, missing her first attempt to hit it back to him. "You must be mistaking me for another, sir. I haven't any idea what you're talking about."

Her voice no longer shook, and her chin was held high.

He hit the shuttlecock back, resulting in another miss. "I believe you do. And I believe your brother does, as well."

"You are imagining things."

"Am I?" Another hit, another miss. "Then how do you explain your sudden inability to strike the shuttlecock now, as opposed to when you were conquering in the game against your brother?"

She shrugged. "I had a stroke of luck, I suppose."

He shook his head in disbelief. He was getting nowhere with this tactic. Perhaps he ought to try out a different route.

"Very well, perhaps it *was* luck. Or perhaps you are failing to perform in the sport now—and at Birchwick, as well, I might add—because you are intimidated."

She tucked in her chin. "Intimidated? By what?"

"Me."

Her mouth parted, and a soft, incredulous laugh slipped through her lips. "I assure you, that is not the reason."

"Ah, so you admit that there is a reason then?"

Her grin disappeared. "No, I, well…"

William shouldn't have been so amused at the sight of her scrambling. But the answer was right there, the truth was within reach. All she needed to do was say it.

"I have already told you the reason, and that reason is pure and simple luck."

Blast. He'd been so close to the truth. He hit the shuttlecock toward her again, and it bounced to the ground and into the bracken behind her.

She bent over to retrieve it, and William quickly averted his gaze. "Very well, Miss Paxton. You can believe what you wish. But I still think you are intimidated by my presence, and that is why you cannot play as well as you typically do."

Her lips thinned. She did that sometimes when she spoke with Hugh.

William frowned. How did he know such a thing?

"I assure you. I am not intimidated by you." Her voice was firm, like when she'd scolded him for holding the chickens improperly.

"Then prove it, Miss Paxton."

CHAPTER TWELVE

illiam held his breath, awaiting Miss Paxton's reply. Would she snap at his bait? Prove to him that she had pride, that she could stand up to William and her brother?

Her eyes flitted beyond his shoulder but returned without a flinch. Was she ignoring Hugh's advice?

A slow smile spread across her lips. "Very well, Mr. Eastwood. I shall."

Pride twinkled in her eyes—not in that she thought she was above another, but that she was now no longer afraid to reveal the confidence she had in her abilities.

She *was* ignoring Hugh's advice, and William was completely enchanted with the change.

She tossed the shuttlecock up and down in her left hand. "Rather than playing as a team, perhaps we play as my brother and I have done since we were children? Whoever allows the shuttlecock to drop to the ground ten times forfeits the game. The player who wins the point serves."

"I think I can manage that."

"Are you ready?" She flashed a grin.

"Ready."

Without a moment's hesitation, she tossed the shuttlecock in the air, striking it with such force that it sailed past his racket before he even had the chance to swing.

"That's one point for me, I believe," she said.

He studied her, fighting off his look of astonishment as he hit the shuttlecock back for her next serve. "You aren't even going to allow me to hit it once, are you?"

She shrugged a single shoulder. "You asked me to play like this, did you not?"

She served again, but this time, William was ready, striking it with a flick of his racket. Miss Paxton lobbed it toward him, and they continued back and forth until he failed to hit it a fourth time.

"Two," she stated.

"Are you enjoying yourself, sister?" Hugh called from the table.

William didn't miss the warning in his tone.

Miss Paxton didn't even look at Hugh as she responded. "More than ever before, brother."

William had an inkling that perhaps Hugh encouraged Miss Paxton to perform poorly so as not to intimidate the gentlemen with whom she played. But William could not have been more impressed.

They continued their game, volleying often. Miss Paxton would strike the shuttlecock from one direction to the next, making William run back and forth across the garden. He did not possess one half of the control over his racket as she did.

He loosened his cravat and unbuttoned his waistcoat halfway. "Why do I feel as though you are making me run on purpose?"

She merely grinned, sending the shuttlecock toward him once again.

After another point toward Miss Paxton, William paused,

resting his hands on his hips as his chest rose and fell. He was out of breath and exhausted, yet still he smiled.

"You've made me break a sweat, Miss Paxton," he breathed, pulling out a handkerchief to swipe across his brow. "It's not even warm out."

Her breathing was nowhere near as ragged as his. "Perhaps you are merely intimidated by me."

Her teasing words struck him by surprise, and a bubble of laughter rose in his chest, escaping his mouth before he had the chance to stop it. How did she know just the thing to say to make him laugh?

And how did he not realize before now how good it felt, how light his heart was, when he *did* laugh?

After an abysmal dismantling of his pride by losing ten to three, William insisted they play again.

The next round was even worse, though the humor of the situation only rose. Together, the two of them laughed as they ran, hopped, and stretched to reach the shuttlecock each time it sailed above their heads.

William couldn't remember the last time he'd felt so invigorated. So happy. His heart was racing, his cheeks sore from his smiles.

At first, he chalked his joy up to not having played the sport in some time—he'd forgotten how much he enjoyed it.

But each time Miss Paxton's laughter rang out above the sound of the rustling leaves of the trees nearby and the soft, babbling brooklet, he knew she was the reason he enjoyed himself so fully.

And the thought sobered him instantly.

As Miss Paxton ran to retrieve the shuttlecock in a bed of flowers, his mind churned.

Charity didn't like Battledore and Shuttlecock. In fact, she didn't enjoy most games. When they would attend dinner parties or picnics—William always sneaking away without

Grandfather's consent—Charity would sit out during card games, outdoor games, or parlor games, desiring to speak instead.

William had followed suit the majority of the time, but when he did join in the games, he always enjoyed himself. It was nice at times to forget about life and have fun. Surely he could have such fun with Charity when she returned from London.

At any rate, he didn't need consistent laughter and exhilaration in his life. Not when he desired stability, comfort, and ease even more so. He was more of a serious person, anyway. Like Charity. The laughter he'd shared with Miss Paxton was clearly just a one time occurrence.

Something sailed toward him, pulling him from his unsettled thoughts, though not quickly enough for him to move.

As the shuttlecock hit him squarely on the brow, he pulled back, blinking at Miss Paxton, who stood away from him with a broad smile.

"The goal is to hit the shuttlecock with your racket, sir. Not your head."

He battled to push away his returning joy. Had this woman put him under some spell to make him happy with everything she said?

"I didn't know we had resorted to striking people during the game," he returned.

"I had to get your attention somehow."

"Is that your excuse?"

She shrugged her dainty shoulders once again.

He gave her a daring look then launched the shuttlecock directly toward her. She maneuvered out of the way just in time to return it, pelting him directly in the chest.

He gave a grunt, though the shuttlecock did anything but hurt him.

"You have to be quicker than that to avoid my strikes, sir."

He hit the shuttlecock back, this time pelting her just below the knees.

As they continued, they quickly lost count of who was winning or losing, though William hardly cared. Their laughter filled the air around them until he sent a final volley toward Miss Paxton, and he watched in horror as it struck her directly in her face.

"Oh!" She dropped her racket and covered her eyes with her hand.

William darted toward her, his jovial nature gone. "Miss Paxton, I'm terribly sorry. Are you all right?"

"I-I believe so."

She lowered her hand, squinting her eye so he could no longer see the blue in it. A small red mark had already formed at the corner of her long, dark lashes, but her blonde curls leaned forward, blocking the rest of the wound.

He winced, reaching forward to push back the curls, praying he hadn't broken the skin. The cork the shuttlecock was made out of was soft to a degree, but if he'd hit her hard enough…

No, thank goodness. The mark did not exceed half an inch, and no blood was visible. Still, his heart twisted. "Forgive me. I shouldn't have been playing so roughly."

Miss Paxton didn't respond. Was she upset with him? He wouldn't blame her.

He smoothed a thumb over the mark to feel for swelling, his eyes dropping to see if she looked angry. But when he caught her staring up at him, shoulders raised as if she didn't breathe, he stopped breathing, himself.

What was he doing, standing so close to this woman, veritably caressing her face? And what was he doing not moving away from her?

Every ounce of his logic screamed at him to turn, to look away, to do something other than study the curves of her face and the dark flecks of black in her otherwise blue eyes.

But he couldn't. He stared at the reflection of the trees in her wide eyes, sunshine glinting in their depths. Only, it wasn't sunshine. It was the light within Miss Paxton that made them radiate.

A light that infused his soul and lifted his spirits, that made his heart tremble in a way it should not have done.

In a way that had not once occurred when he was with Charity.

Finally, sense struck him like a bolt of lightning to a tall, vulnerable tree. He withdrew his hand from her smooth skin and took an abrupt step away.

With a swift look over his shoulder, he discovered the Paxtons and Hugh having moved to the far side of the garden, their backs turned so they would not have seen William's breach of proximity with their daughter and sister.

At least something was in his favor.

"You are—" He stopped, clearing his throat from the huskiness he hadn't expected. "You are sure you are well?"

"Yes, sir."

His heart tripped at her breathless tone. But it shouldn't have. He was not supposed to be having this sort of reaction to any woman but Charity.

He never should have agreed to play this silly sport.

"I suppose we had better end our playing." He buttoned his waistcoat and secured his cravat around his neck. "I wouldn't wish to injure you again."

"You hardly injured me, Mr. Eastwood."

He finished tying his cravat. "That red mark on your eye would beg to differ."

The corners of her lips curled. "I deserve it after thoroughly beating you."

He stared, conflicting emotions battling within him like multiple opposing armies—guilt, happiness, frustration. Even still, he couldn't stop his smile. "I suppose we are equal then."

He retrieved his racket and headed toward the table for the rest of his belongings. Before he had the chance to lift them from the seat at the now-empty table, Miss Paxton's words stopped him.

"Would you care for some refreshment?"

He hesitated. "Thank you, but I think I had better leave now. I've already stayed too late as it is. The Rutledges are expecting me for dinner tonight, and I still have my letters to post, as well as other matters of business."

Business item number one? Getting as far away from Miss Paxton as possible.

"Oh, I do apologize for keeping you so long as it is."

A fresh wave of regret rushed over him as Miss Paxton's cheeks flushed. She was clearly embarrassed by yet another rejection from him.

He shouldn't care, really. And yet...

"I suppose one refreshing drink won't hurt, though. I am exhausted, after all, from the exercise regime you have put me through."

His heart lifted as her eyes twinkled. "Lemonade or tea?"

"Lemonade, please."

That would be far quicker than tea.

Miss Paxton reached for the pitcher of lemonade, pouring a glass as William took a seat across from her. She extended the cup toward him, and though William was consciously careful as he retrieved it, his finger still brushed against hers. A pulse of energy shot up his arms, and he nearly dropped the glass in surprise, a splash or two falling onto his fingers.

"My apologies," Miss Paxton mumbled before sitting down across from him with a glass of her own.

Silence pursued. William studied the cool, yellow liquid in his glass.

A heaviness hung in the air between them, and he longed to

lift it as he would a heavy cloak from overheated shoulders. But what could he say?

Finally, he motioned to the rackets and shuttlecocks on the grass nearby. "May I ask how you became so proficient at the sport?"

She swallowed her sip of lemonade. "Practice, I suppose. Hugh and I would play regularly as children. He would often cheat, so I made it a goal of mine to play so well that even if he did try to swindle me, I would still win."

William would have laughed at the idea, had his next question not perched at the tip of his tongue, ready to dive forward into the open air between them.

Dare he ask it? After hearing what she'd just said, could he even help himself?

"So if Hugh knows you play so well, and you know you play so well, why did you say nothing when your brother claimed you play poorly?"

She pulled in her bottom lip, chewing it before responding. "I'm sorry, but I cannot say."

William's stomach hardened to stone. He knew instinctively that the rate of control between Hugh and Miss Paxton was nowhere near that of the power Grandfather had over his family.

But William had seen that same look of hesitance countless times—when he'd asked his parents why they didn't just move into the cottage or manor where they clearly wished to be instead of Birchwick. Or when he'd asked Father why William wasn't allowed to play with the other children. Or when he'd asked Mama why he would be staying home instead of attending Eton with the other boys.

Each time, the answer had been met with hesitation, then the typical, "I cannot say," was given in response.

But he knew the answer then, just as he knew now. It was

Grandfather's choice, and whatever Grandfather wished for... Grandfather received.

Just as it appeared with Hugh.

William's grip tightened on his glass. He couldn't bear this any longer. Not when he had the chance to improve Miss Paxton's life before it was ruined like his parents'.

After looking over his shoulder to ensure the Paxtons were still a good distance away, William leaned forward. "Miss Paxton, forgive me if I speak out of turn. In fact, I am most certain that I am. But I cannot hold my tongue any longer."

Warily, she eyed him, motioning for him to continue.

He drew a deep breath. "You do not have to do what your brother says."

She narrowed her eyes. "Whatever do you mean?"

He lowered his voice further. "I can see the control he has over you, Miss Paxton. I wish you to know that you have the power to stop his behavior, to rise above his repression. To make decisions of your own without seeking his advice, counsel, or permission."

At the end of his words, he'd expected her to cower in fear or perhaps shake her head in denial—like his parents did when he'd said the same to them. But when a surprised laugh escaped her lips, he pulled back.

"Why do you laugh? I speak the truth."

She shook her head, sobering at once. "I do apologize. I was not laughing at you, only the idea that Hugh could control me. I'm sorry, Mr. Eastwood, but you are quite mistaken about my brother."

William narrowed his eyes. Could she truly be speaking in earnest? She'd said the words with no hesitation—indeed, she'd laughed at his own. But then...

"If that is the truth, why do you do what he asks of you? Why do you look for his approval in everything?"

Her cheeks pinked a lovely shade, like the dahlias behind

her. "I'm afraid I cannot divulge that information, sir. I do seek his advice on matters regarding, well, that is not important." She looked away, the pink deepening. "But I can say with confidence that he is not controlling me. We have an agreement of sorts, that is all."

His mind raced over the past two weeks he'd known the Paxtons, seen them interacting with one another. Miss Paxton had never seemed as timid around Hugh as Mama and Father had been around Grandfather.

Miss Paxton had also stood up to her brother on multiple occasions—another sure sign of her confidence around him. So she really *was* only taking his advice? But there had to be something that she was not telling William, the whole truth behind her choice to follow her crazed brother.

He rubbed his jaw. "So I assume Hugh was the one to tell you to play poorly just now and at Birchwick?"

She ducked her head. "I'm afraid so. He believes I will make a poor impression on others if I play as well as I typically do at games, or if I speak of my pet hens."

Still reeling from his newfound knowledge, William shook his head, forgetting to curb his tongue. "Surely you've had experience with people liking you for you, hens and talents alike. Why the devil would you listen to such nonsense?"

Her voice was just a notch above a whisper, a touch of sorrow in her blue eyes. "People adore Hugh."

"And they do not adore you?"

His tone was soft, yet still, she winced. "I suppose I am a little too…too *myself* for some people."

He couldn't comprehend her words. Too *herself?* What did she mean, that she was too happy, too talented, too filled with light? "So you are willing to change yourself to be what your brother thinks you ought to be?"

"It cannot hurt to try."

She'd clearly made up her mind, and there was nothing he

could say to change it. Still, he longed to speak the truth to her, to share words of comfort. She ought not settle for any man who did not appreciate her for *her*. But he couldn't. Not when he was supposed to be saying such things to Charity.

Charity, whom Miss Paxton believed was only William's friend.

He needed to take his leave. "Well, I—"

"May I—"

William stopped as Miss Paxton started.

"Do go on," she said.

"No, please."

She hesitated. "I was going to ask you a question, since you asked me one."

His stomach tensed, like a hand had gripped his flesh between its nails. He knew what was coming. "Yes?"

CHAPTER THIRTEEN

"*W*ell, I merely wondered as to why there were chickens at the manor when the property was—is—uninhabitable."

William blinked, releasing a pent-up breath. Heavens, he was expecting a question about Grandfather, his childhood, even Charity. *This* he could respond to.

"I had purchased the hens a few months ago and they settled so nicely at the manor, I never moved them. Mr. Smith—who I've hired to care for the chickens—lives nearer to the manor than Birchwick, so it makes logical sense."

"And why hens of all creatures?"

"Well, I've always had the desire to have more animals to my name, perhaps even have charge over a small farm one day. Chickens seemed the logical first step."

"It would appear we both have a fondness for them then."

"Indeed, we do."

They shared a smile as she tipped her head to the side. "Although I still don't understand why you placed them firstly at the manor instead of Birchwick."

He swallowed, his throat dry, as if he'd had straight lemons instead of lemonade. "Well, we have no henhouse at the estate, and there was one ready-made at the manor, still in good shape."

"You couldn't have had one made closer to where you live?"

He slid a finger between his cravat and neck. This girl was as persistent as her brother. Perhaps if he gave her more of the truth—as she had with him—she'd fall back from her advance.

"Well, the truth of the matter is, my grandfather didn't like chickens. He despised them, actually, and did not want them on his property."

As usual, at the mention of Grandfather, William's palms grew sweaty, and his heart hardened.

"So he did not allow you to have them?"

William pursed his lips. "No, he did not. I merely kept them at the manor where I knew he'd never find them, as he hadn't been there since—"

The blood drained from his face at his near-slip-up. How had he been that close to sharing the tawdry details of his family's past?

Miss Paxton watched him with curious eyes. "Since?"

"Since he decided to focus his attention on Birchwick Hall instead." He cleared his throat, rushing on to avoid Miss Paxton's knowing gaze. "I have plans to move the hens, of course, to the estate. But for now, that task will have to wait until I find more time."

She nodded, clearly wishing to ask more, to seek clarification for his halted words, but to his great relief, she leaned back slightly in her chair. "Well, thank you for answering my question, sir. I've been rather concerned with the welfare of those hens since the day we met. I am pleased to hear they are in good hands. Hopefully hands that know how to hold them better than you do, of course."

Their gazes held, her eyes wrinkling at the corners as she delivered that teasing grin he so enjoyed.

His heart thumped against his chest, and he leaned forward to dispel the discomfort it caused him. As paper crinkled against his jacket pocket, the breath slipped from his lungs.

The letters. What was he doing, enjoying lemonade, chatting with this woman, when he had Charity and Mama with whom to correspond?

He cleared his throat and pushed back from the table. "Well, Miss Paxton, I fear I mustn't delay my departure any longer."

She stood, as well, pumping her head up and down, appearing rather flustered as she smoothed the bottom of her chignon. "Yes, I do apologize for keeping you. Do give my best to the Rutledges, and I wish you well with posting your letters of business."

His smile weakened. There it was again, letters of business. He really ought to tell her for whom one of these letters was written. Now was his chance to do something logical, to inform the woman of his attachment to another so they could both go their separate ways.

He parted his lips, his tongue latched to the roof of his mouth before he finally forced his words through.

"I thought you ought to know, I do not believe you should change yourself just to have another's approval. Especially when you are as charming and kind a woman as you are. People should be able to see your beauty on the inside as much as they can on the outside—for what is in your heart matters most."

That was not what he'd planned to say. Not even close.

Yet, as she peered up at him, warmth emanating from her eyes like the autumn sunshine, he could not find it inside himself to regret his words.

"Thank you, Mr. Eastwood," she said, smiling up at him.

His eyes lingered on hers for a moment longer before he retrieved his belongings, throwing his jacket over his arm and holding his gloves and hat in his hand.

With a tip of his head, he nodded. "Good day, Miss Paxton."

Then he left the garden and the glowing woman behind before his guilt had the chance to settle in too swiftly.

So much for keeping away from the cottage.

Amy leaned forward, peering around the edge of the tree-lined pathway she and her family walked along. Strumming her fingers impatiently against her skirts, she sighed.

There was still no sight of Mr. Eastwood. Why they'd chosen to walk instead of taking the carriage to Coniston Water was beyond her. Of course, the skies were clear, the sun was warm despite the biting air, and the walk was only twenty minutes from the cottage, but those were hardly good enough reasons now that her anxiousness filled every inch of her body.

"Do try to maintain some decorum, sister," Hugh said beside her with a chuckle. "I half-expect you to leap into his arms when you see him."

"Hugh!" Her eyes darted forward to ensure Mr. Eastwood was still nowhere in sight.

The very idea of leaping into the man's strong and capable arms sent her heart palpitating, but she couldn't very well have Mr. Eastwood hear her brother speak of such things.

Prepared to deliver a scathing retort, Amy faced Hugh, but Mama came to her defense before Amy could utter a word. "Leave her be, Hugh. If she is happy to see Mr. Eastwood, there is certainly nothing wrong with that."

Amy itched to bury her face in her warm, tan gloves. Was her anticipation of seeing the gentleman truly so noticeable?

When Papa spoke next, she knew that it was. "I must say, Amy, you will have to beat me to his arms first, as I am just as excited to see Mr. Eastwood as you are."

His comment earned him a few chuckles before the conversation shifted elsewhere, and Amy sent him a grateful look. Papa always knew just what to say to make her feel better.

Her peace was short-lived, however, as the pathway opened up and the gentleman appeared before them, standing at the edge of the lake beside three empty boats bobbing up and down in the water.

Swiftly, Amy smoothed her strands of hair that did not need to be smoothed and pinched her cheeks that were already pink from the nipping autumn wind.

She wanted to make a good impression, what with five long days having passed since they'd seen each other at the cottage. After playing Battledore and Shuttlecock, Mama had insisted on Mr. Eastwood setting a time to go boating before she'd allowed him to leave. He'd been very hesitant, though whether that was due to his busyness or because he didn't wish to spend more time with the Paxtons, Amy couldn't be sure.

Yet, now, as he turned to face them—his sleeves rolled up, hat and jacket nowhere to be seen—a genuine smile spread on his lips, and Amy's trepidations vanished.

He *was* pleased to see her.

"Good morning, Mr. Eastwood," Mama greeted first as they drew together. "How pleased we are for this day to have finally arrived."

"Indeed," Hugh agreed. "My sister has been practically beside herself with anticipation."

His words dampened her smile, and she turned to him with a warning, but Father was already clasping Hugh's shoulder in his hand in what appeared to be a friendly grasp, though his knuckles turned white. "Yes, son. We are all thrilled."

Mr. Eastwood's gaze lingered on them for a moment before motioning to the boats. "In that case, I suggest we do not delay."

He led the way forward. "Each boat will only hold a maximum of two people, so I'm afraid one of us gentlemen will have to row alone today. I will gladly offer to do so, so your family may keep together." He paused once they reached the boats, turning to face them. "Unless someone else wishes to go alone?"

Amy waited with baited breath, but when Hugh said nothing, she swallowed an exasperated sigh. She did not wait all of this time to go out on the lake with Mr. Eastwood to *not* go out on the lake with Mr. Eastwood.

With as subtle a movement as possible, Amy nudged Hugh with her pointed elbow. Fortunately, he understood her meaning, and even *more* fortunately, he was willing to follow through with it.

"Oh, I wouldn't mind going alone, of course," Hugh said at once. "But that would mean my sister will be with you —Roberts?"

Amy's eyes swung to Hugh's. Did he just call Mr. Eastwood what she thought he'd called him?

"It is Mr. Eastwood, you ninny," she hissed, her cheeks pooling with heat. To think of Mr. Eastwood now asking Amy who this Mr. Roberts was. Her brother was a fool.

Hugh's eyes locked straight ahead. "No, it is Mr. Roberts."

Amy's heart dropped as Hugh motioned past Mr. Eastwood's shoulders to where a gentleman stood, but she refused to believe him. Hugh was mistaken. It was not Mr. Roberts. It could not be Mr. Roberts.

And yet, there he was, sauntering toward their party with that same confidence Amy had once admired—that same confidence that she now could not bear.

What was he doing there? And how in heaven's name had he found them? She looked to Hugh for an explanation, but he appeared just as stunned with his friend's appearance as the rest of the Paxtons.

Amy's mind raced in search of an escape. She couldn't remain here any longer. She couldn't bear to be spoon-fed embarrassment again by this so-called gentleman. Would he now spread gossip about her name in Coniston as he'd done in Bath? Would Mr. Eastwood no longer speak with her if he learned of her humiliating behavior?

She backed away, intent on fleeing the situation before any conflict could begin, but her parents moved to stand at either side of her, silent sentinels keeping watch over their charge.

Their presence, their unspoken encouragement, finally gave Amy the courage for which she so desperately sought. She did not need to flee. She did not need to cower. She had moved beyond the infatuation she'd once held for this gentleman.

And now, she would not under any circumstances allow herself to be embarrassed again, especially in front of Mr. Eastwood, who, incidentally, just so happened to be standing by in a watchful silence as the exchange unfolded.

"Paxton!" Mr. Roberts greeted Hugh as he moved to greet him first. "I cannot express how relieved I am to have found you. I say, I've been on a dreadfully mad dash through all of Coniston just to do so. Tell me, why is the manor you said you'd be staying at in complete disarray?"

Amy's stomach twisted. The manor? Hugh had told Mr. Roberts of the manor?

"Oh, that is a long story, my friend," Hugh responded, clasping onto his shoulder. "One I shall tell you another time. But for now, you must come meet a new friend, and of course, speak with my family."

Amy straightened her back and raised her chin, forcing the confident poise to remain as he approached. His brown eyes she'd once thought warm and inviting settled on her, twisting her heart, but she refused to break eye contact.

"This is Mr. William Eastwood," Hugh said, pulling Mr. Roberts's attention away from Amy. "He owns the cottage where we are now staying. Mr. Eastwood, our good friend, Mr. Dominic Roberts."

Their good friend? Hugh must be out of his mind.

"Pleasure to meet you, Mr. Roberts," Mr. Eastwood said with a short bow.

Mr. Eastwood's eyes flicked between the gentleman and Amy, but she kept her eyes trained on Mr. Roberts, who barely responded to Mr. Eastwood before turning to face her.

"Miss Paxton." He said her name with an airy tone, as if he delighted in each syllable spoken. To think she had once fairly swooned over such a toothy grin. "How delighted I am to see you again. You look as lovely as when last we met."

Amy's confidence faltered, her blood boiling at the audacity he had to mention their last meeting in front of her family and this stranger. But then, he wasn't flashing a teasing grin, nor were his eyes twinkling. In fact, past his smile, he appeared rather contrite.

But she could not trust him.

She looked away, avoiding his gaze and Mr. Eastwood's alike.

"We are certainly surprised to see you here, sir," Mama said. Her lips pulled in a straight line.

Papa, on the other hand, did not even try, as disapproval creased his brow three times over.

Another boost of support buoyed her courage.

Mr. Roberts's smile faltered. He swallowed hard as he faced her parents. So he hadn't forgotten what he did to Amy then.

"Yes, I do apologize for not announcing my arrival."

Was that all for which he would apologize?

Hugh shook his head, seemingly the only one pleased with the man's sudden appearance. "Of course it is no trouble. We are thrilled to see you. Now tell us, what on earth are you doing here?"

Mr. Roberts sent another glance at Amy, but she remained as stony-faced as Papa. "I fear I have grown weary of Bath and its society, like all of you. I decided to accept your request to join you here."

The breath slipped from her lungs. No matter how she struggled, she could not haul it back. Hugh had invited Mr. Roberts to join them in Coniston? She should've known.

Hugh's wary eyes found Amy's, though he hurriedly looked away before revealing any more of his feelings.

Silence followed, and Mr. Roberts looked from person to person. "You do recall inviting me, do you not, Paxton? To stay with you during your time here?"

His words echoed jarringly against her chest. The same rigidity in her chest she'd felt that day in the gardens by the fountain crept back into her lungs.

How could Hugh have done such a thing? Her own brother, inviting this man who had rejected her, humiliated her, and spread gossip about her, to stay with them in Coniston? It was the worst sort of betrayal. One she could not readily forget.

Hugh lowered his voice. "Of course, my friend. But, I fear the cottage is too small to take on another person. I trust the Black Bull Inn will more than suffice your needs for the time being."

Mr. Roberts's face fell, though he nodded.

Amy pulled in her lips to keep from berating her brother's choices right then and there. How could he be so selfish?

"Of course that will be more than enough." Mr. Roberts gazed past Mama and Papa to eye the boats. "Well, it would appear that I've interrupted a family outing. Do excuse me. I will leave you now and return to the inn. Though I hope to speak with you all soon."

His eyes lingered on Amy as he took a step back. Just as she thought she might be free, Hugh stopped him. "Why do you not join us, Roberts? We were just discussing earlier how one of us would have had to row out alone. With you, we would be an even number." He paused, turning to Amy with an innocent expression. "In fact, you could even go out with my sister. I'm sure the two of you are anxious to speak with one another again."

Amy listened, horrified. What was Hugh thinking to suggest such a thing? Despite her scowl—and her parents' stern looks—Hugh merely continued to smile.

"Oh, I wouldn't wish to impose," Mr. Roberts said, a hopeful touch to his voice.

"It would not be an imposition at all, would it, Mr. Eastwood?" Hugh pressed.

Mr. Eastwood looked to the Paxtons, as if he sought for further clarification before answering. But as Mama, Papa, and Amy remained silent, he shook his head. "No, of course not."

"Excellent. Then I should be very happy to accompany you, Miss Paxton. If you wish it?"

Amy stared in stunned silence. How could she even answer such a question? Decline and embarrass the man, revealing to Mr. Eastwood her unkindness without his realizing why? Or accept Mr. Roberts's offer and spend the next whoever-knew-how-long boating with the gentleman who'd almost broken her heart?

She squared her shoulders. She knew just what she wished to do, and that was to confront Mr. Roberts about why he was *really* in Coniston. Then, after their time at the lake was finished, she would take Hugh and give him the verbal lashing he so thoroughly deserved.

"Yes, Mr. Roberts. You may accompany me."

CHAPTER FOURTEEN

This was just what William needed, for Miss Paxton to be occupied by someone other than himself. Now he would be free to enjoy his time on the lake without being distracted by her blonde strands of hair blowing across her pink lips or her eyes as deep and blue as Coniston Water peering over at him.

Of course he'd enjoyed his time laughing with her at Flit-field, but that was only because he hadn't laughed in so long. He wasn't disappointed in the slightest that she'd agreed to go with Mr. Roberts—whoever the devil that man was. In fact, William had more than expected it. After all, Miss Paxton was still doing whatever Hugh asked of her. And that was fine with William. More than fine.

But then, why did his heart struggle to beat, as if his chest had shriveled to half its normal size? And why did he regret now more than ever agreeing to Mrs. Paxton's insisting that he join them on the lake?

He held back as Mr. and Mrs. Paxton entered the first boat, followed shortly by Mr. Roberts and Miss Paxton in the next.

Miss Paxton disregarded the gentleman's helping hand and clambered in the boat herself.

As much as Hugh claimed to be friends with Mr. Roberts, the rest of the Paxtons appeared rather displeased with his arrival. Especially Miss Paxton.

Setting aside his thoughts—he had no reason to dwell on such things—he approached the final boat with Hugh.

"You wouldn't mind rowing out, would you, sir?" Hugh asked. "I'm not one for exerting myself when it comes to rowing. Or ever, really."

That came as no surprise. Hugh didn't appear to have done a lick of physical labor in his life. At any rate, William preferred rowing himself. That way they wouldn't end up banked in the mud at the opposite end of the lake or with the boat overturned due to some poor mishandling of the oars.

They set off across the lake in the direction of the others. After a few strides, William peered over his shoulder to ensure they were still on course, surprised to find they'd already caught up with Mr. Roberts and Miss Paxton.

As they passed by, William could better see the man's red face as he appeared to be concentrating very hard on keeping both oars steady, though they veered to the right once William moved ahead.

Miss Paxton hardly seemed to notice, her eyes focused on the water lapping at the boat's side. She'd removed her glove and was now threading her fingers through the lake, a small smile curving her lips.

He had rented a boat last year to spend some time on the water with Charity, but she had had a miserable time. She wasn't one for getting wet—as he'd discovered to his detriment when he'd attempted to playfully splash her. She hadn't spoken to him the rest of the evening until he'd contritely apologized, though he'd meant only to engage her in a bit of fun.

William didn't know how Miss Paxton would respond to such playful behavior, but based on how invigorated she'd appeared after being caught in the rain the day he'd been discovered in her room, he was certain he was fairly safe to assume the woman wouldn't hesitate to enjoy a good water fight now and again.

His brow pursed. Of course Charity would be upset with his splashing her if she didn't wish to be. And it was more than all right to not like water, or to *like* water. He needed to stop comparing the two women.

He chewed his cheek, keeping his gaze trained on the scenery around him. Early morning mist lingered atop the hills, cloaking the taller trees in a scant, white blanket. The bright green grass and gold and orange trees reflected perfectly in the still water at the edge of a lake, as if they peered over the side to view their beauty in Coniston's mirror.

As spectacular as the sight was, there was another view William wished to take in even more. One of a red-trimmed bonnet framing a pretty face. Of eyes that sparkled brighter than the stars when she smiled, and the faintest spattering of freckles across the bridge of her petite nose.

Squeezing his eyes shut, he gave a swift shake to his head. He sounded like an idiot. He was behaving like one, too.

Hugh sighed across from him, holding his head back and closing his eyes as the sun touched his face.

William stared. Perhaps he ought to speak with him. That would certainly provide a distraction worthy enough to keep him from staring at Miss Paxton.

"Will your friend be staying in Coniston long, do you think?"

Fool. Speaking of Mr. Roberts was a definite way to have the conversation steer toward Miss Paxton. Was his own tongue trying to betray him?

Hugh kept his eyes closed as he shrugged. "I haven't the

faintest. As I'm sure you noticed, his arrival came as a bit of a shock to all of us. Particularly my sister."

He cracked an eye open, but William refused to react, despite the inferno of questions burning inside him. Why would it come as a shock to Miss Paxton more than anyone? Had they some sort of attachment between them?

His eyes flitted to the boat now quite behind William's. As far as he could see, Mr. Roberts spoke while Miss Paxton still stared at the water. She hardly seemed attached to the man.

"I do apologize the manor was not ready for you and your family, especially now that Mr. Roberts will be forced to remain at the inn."

Hugh waved a flippant hand. "Roberts's idea of adventure is picnicking on his own grounds or taking a carriage ride with the top down." He sniffed a laugh. "Staying at the inn will be just the thing his spirit needs."

Finally, Hugh's eyes opened as he peered back at Mr. Roberts's boat. "As you can see, he doesn't boat very often, either."

Mr. Roberts and Miss Paxton were now circling toward the middle of the lake at a snail's pace. Hugh had known Mr. Roberts was rubbish at rowing, yet he still sent his sister with the man?

Frustration sparked in William's chest. Of course Hugh was not to be trusted, but William should've ensured Mr. Roberts could at least use the oars before allowing Miss Paxton out with him.

"Roberts and I have always been good friends," Hugh continued, still watching the other boat. "Though, Amy is closer to him now, I believe."

William's eyes snapped away from Miss Paxton, where he hadn't known they'd been.

A sly grin spread slowly across Hugh's face. "Do you wish for me to clarify my words?"

William's jaw tensed. "Surely that is none of my business."

If only to prove that he could stare at someone other than Miss Paxton, William turned to Mr. and Mrs. Paxton as they smiled at one another in their own boat.

At least those two seemed to be enjoying themselves.

Hugh stroked the side of his smooth jaw. "I see. You are one of *those* gentlemen. The ones who keep to themselves to avoid rumors and gossip."

William shrugged, moving the oars back and forth in rhythmic motion to keep the boat steady. Mr. Roberts was alternating between the oars, so the boat was only propelled forward by the water, which now moved and shimmered against the light of the sun in the growing wind.

"I suppose there is nothing wrong with wishing for one's privacy," Hugh continued. "So, I'm assuming you would then not take kindly to my asking after a certain Miss Charity Winslow?"

William's throat dried, as if all the water in Coniston could not wet it enough. He drew hardened eyes at Hugh. What was the man hinting toward? Did he claim to know more with Miss Cox as his confidant?

Either way, William would not stoop to such a level. "No. I would not take kindly to it."

Hugh laughed flippantly. "Oh, women and wives. Courtship and marriage. It is all rather complicated, is it not? This is why I shall never marry. There are far too many women to enjoy outside of the restrictions of marriage."

He winked, and William's stomach roiled.

"I take it by your silence that *you* will one day marry," Hugh stated.

"Yes, I will marry one day, and I do not see why any man would wish not to."

Especially with a woman as intelligent and level-headed as Charity. If—no, *when*—he married her, they would be at peace, they would have a life of ease. That was what he wanted more than anything. More than excitement and laughter, more than water fights and Battledore and Shuttlecock.

Besides, there was more to their relationship than a simple desire to marry. He *needed* to, if only to make up for what his grandfather did to Charity and her mother.

His eyes trailed to Miss Paxton, who stared at the Old Man rising over the autumn trees. Dark clouds hovered above the fell, as if trying to decide to make the journey toward Coniston or to move on to another village.

If only they'd draw closer to save him from this wretched conversation—this wretched day.

"May I make another assumption?" Hugh asked, drawing William's attention back to him.

William longed to stuff the flat end of the oar into Hugh's mouth to get him to stop talking, but the man forged on without a response from William.

"Am I right to assume, considering how well you get on with my sister, that you would not mind a wife who speaks her mind?"

William rolled his tongue along the back of his teeth. Hugh was either tempting him into an argument or testing his loyalty to Miss Paxton. Either way, he would not be giving this man any ammunition to use against his sister.

"No, I wouldn't mind such a wife. I don't believe there is anything wrong with a woman speaking her mind."

Hugh shook his head incredulously. "I'm afraid I'll never understand men like you. Mr. Roberts and I, of course, agree on the matter and have discussed this at length. Women ought to be amiable before vocal. Although, Mr. Roberts wishes to someday marry, and I do not."

William's temples pinched, a headache pulsing at the fore-front of his brow. So Mr. Roberts was of the same frame of mind, wishing for a subdued woman. Was this why Hugh was teaching Miss Paxton to behave such a way, so she might be prepared to marry Mr. Roberts?

Nausea curled within him, rising dangerously towards his throat. Mother had been pressured into becoming subdued and silent by Grandfather before Father had been allowed to marry her. She hadn't spoken her mind for so long, William wasn't sure she even *had* an opinion of her own.

How could he stand by idly and allow the same thing to happen to the kindhearted, joyful Miss Paxton?

Hugh continued. "Mr. Roberts and I, you see, we wish for peace. We wouldn't take to a woman telling us how to behave for the rest of our lives. What to wear, with whom to speak... with whom we are allowed to flirt."

He flashed a grin when he finally stopped, but William remained stoic. "I, too, wish for peace, sir. But such a life is possible even with a wife who is proud to be who she is, who is allowed—no, encouraged and supported—to be who she is. In fact, I believe one is even more likely to have peace in marriage, for when both partners are happy, they are more inclined to make each other happier, as well."

Hugh blew a breath, puffing out his cheeks. "That all sounds rather exhausting, does it not? Always working to ensure the happiness of your wife. It is far easier to find enjoyment when ladies are on their best behavior. Once they begin to show their true selves, it's far easier to leave and begin anew with another. Women are dispensable creatures, after all."

William stopped rowing, his soul hardening to stone. "And do your mother and sister know you feel such a way?"

Hugh chuckled. "Of course not. I would never say such words to them."

"And yet, though you may not speak such words aloud, your twisted ideology is certain to be reflected in the poor way in which you treat them."

Hugh's smile faltered for the first time since William could remember, but William could not stop now that he'd begun.

"Women are in no way lesser than their male counterparts. They are to be loved and treated with respect in the same way men ought to be. In an equal partnership, men and women alike both bring value. One can only spend so long in one's own company—or in the arms of various, fruitless women—before one realizes that bachelorhood, premier bachelorhood, does not, *cannot*, last forever."

Hugh's brow lowered, his lips thinning just as Miss Paxton's did when she was upset. "I must disagree with you, sir. But to avoid any residual ill feelings between the two of us, I suggest we change the topic."

"That perfectly suits me," William said, still seething.

He'd promised himself not to lose patience, not to be coaxed into arguing with this man who was fundamentally different than William in nearly every aspect.

Well, he'd certainly failed at that, hadn't he?

Amy looked over her shoulder at the dark clouds growing over the Old Man. Was the storm approaching the lake, or was it merely wishful thinking on her part?

With a heavy sigh, she faced Mr. Roberts. She'd attempted time and time again to confront the gentleman about his sudden arrival in Coniston, but he hadn't allowed her to get a word in since pushing off from the shore.

Not only had she been forced to listen to him recount all the happenings of Bath for the last twenty minutes, he was now resorting to asking her question after question, ranging from what she'd eaten for dinner the night before to if she still enjoyed walking.

The man was treading water vocally as poorly as he treaded water with the oars in this very boat. Had he ever rowed before? She would be very surprised if he had. They were nowhere near the others, having drifted with the water to the east side of the lake.

However, she was not too far away to miss Hugh's scowl, nor the way he shifted away from Mr. Eastwood. What on earth had happened between them? Hugh only ever looked that upset when he'd been scolded by Papa. Had Mr. Eastwood spoken harshly to him?

"You look happy here, Miss Paxton. As lovely as I can ever remember you being."

Amy cringed at yet another one of Mr. Roberts's forced compliments. How had she ever found this man charming?

"You do your hair differently, though, do you not?"

He was very clearly attempting to speak for longer so Amy might not have the opportunity to confront him about his motivations for being there, but she was quite finished with his words.

"I've done my hair in this way for more than six years, Mr. Roberts."

His smile faltered, and for a single moment, Amy's conscience was pricked. That is, until she recalled everything the man had done to *her*.

"Of course. I remember now. But that must be a new dress. I don't remember you ever wearing such a flattering color."

Amy was past the pleasantries. The question was at the tip of her tongue. Hugh would no doubt advise against her asking. But then, she'd been doing just fine getting along with Mr. Eastwood without her traitorous brother's advice.

All at once, everything—her brother's betrayal, her disappointment with how the boating was going, Mr. Roberts's appearance—weighed down on her shoulders. But she would not allow this man to ruin her life any more than he already had.

"And, Miss Paxton, I cannot say enough good things about—"

"What do you want, Mr. Roberts?"

He blinked. "Whatever do you mean?"

"Why are you here? Clearly there is some reason. After all, one does not typically travel across half the country simply to greet the woman he rejected months before."

Mr. Roberts stopped his rowing, though it was doing little good before. A cool draft of wind slid beneath Amy's spencer and round the back of her neck.

"I do apologize, Miss Paxton, truly. I thought to break the tension between us before I revealed to you the real reason behind my being here."

She scoffed. "It is amusing to me that you believe you can ease the tension between us, when that is impossible. This tension was made impenetrable after you told all of Bath what occurred between us."

He winced, shifting against the boat's wooden seat. To see his discomfort, to finally say the words she'd been longing to say for weeks, was nothing short of freeing. She was a bird sailing just above the lake, or the puff of clouds drifting across the blue skies. Nothing could stop her, not even her better judgment.

"How dare you?" she continued. "How dare you come here without any notice? How dare you speak to me as if the worst had not occurred between us, as if you cannot even remember it?"

He swallowed. "I will admit to my mistakes, Miss Paxton. I do not claim ignorance. I was in the wrong for a great many things—particularly when I...when I shared with a few of my closest friends what you had said to me."

The water started to churn below them, roughly lapping at

the boat's sides, but Amy hardly noticed. She had known all along what Mr. Roberts had done, but to hear the admission directly from his own mouth tore open the old wound that had not yet fully healed.

"How could you be so cruel? Even if you did not have any feelings for me of the romantic sort, I thought at the very least we were friends."

"We were friends. We *are* friends."

She gave a wary shake of her head, her voice softening. "Friends do not gossip about another's secret matter of the heart, sir."

His crestfallen face did little for the justice she wanted. "I know. I know, Miss Paxton. When they asked what had happened between us, I didn't know what else to say."

"And remaining silent never occurred to you?"

His shoulders slumped forward. "No, unfortunately it did not. Though that is precisely what I should have done. And for that, I am truly, truly sorry."

He was penitent, that much was clear. She really ought to forgive him, to allow her heart to heal, now that she no longer had feelings for him. But the wound was still too fresh.

"That is the real reason I am here," he continued. "To make amends for my abysmal behavior."

Amy shivered, a sudden chill enveloping her like a sodden blanket. The dark clouds over the fell had traveled swiftly and now hung over the lake like a foreboding canopy. The sun was no longer shining, but that was not the reasoning behind Amy's trepidation.

It was Mr. Roberts's intent gaze that pushed her over the edge.

She longed to tell him to stop, to keep his words to himself, but her tongue was bound.

He continued in a lower tone, his brown eyes focused solely on her. "When you expressed your feelings to me, I was shocked. So shocked, I could think of nothing to say but a hasty dismissal of my own feelings. But, as I've had time to think, I realized that all along, I do have feelings for you. And, well, now I long to rescind my previous cruelty and ask for your hand in marriage."

CHAPTER FIFTEEN

Thunder rumbled behind her, and Amy's face drained of all warmth. Mr. Roberts looked at her expectantly, but she could say nothing. How could she with such a proposal?

Gripping the sides of the boat, she attempted to find reasoning for his declaration. Was he truly in earnest? Did this mean that he loved her, wished to marry her? Her insides churned. This was not supposed to happen. Not with Mr. Roberts.

Weeks ago, her heart longed for nothing more than this man. But now...

"Miss Paxton, Mr. Roberts!"

Amy swiveled her head to Mr. Eastwood, who rowed swiftly toward them with Hugh. Mr. Eastwood's shoulders worked as he pumped the oars and shouted over his shoulder. "The storm is coming in quickly! We must get to shore before the water becomes dangerous!"

Amy realized only then how the water pelted the sides of their boats, splashing droplets atop her lap. The blue skies had been replaced by dark clouds, and the wind whistled in her ears. Her parents were already on their way toward the shore, and as

Mr. Eastwood turned his boat around, Mr. Roberts attempted to do the same.

"Have you any response, Miss Paxton?" The boat remained stationary as he pitifully skimmed the oars atop the water.

She glanced to where Mr. Eastwood stroked swiftly away from them. Now facing her, his eyes lingered on hers, but she broke their contact, afraid he might read her thoughts.

Save me from this man.

"I know my words will come as a surprise to you," Mr. Roberts said. "Especially after our last meeting. But I hope you will believe me when I say how thoroughly I regret what occurred between us."

A rough wave hit the side of the boat, splashing water inside to rest at the soles of her boots. "Perhaps we might defer this conversation until we have reached safety on land, sir."

"I cannot wait, Miss Paxton."

She closed her eyes, the swift, side-to-side movements of the boat churning her already upset stomach. Were the waves not so choppy, she'd jump from the blasted boat and swim to shore herself.

"I'm afraid you will *have* to wait, Mr. Roberts, or we will be having this conversation at the bottom of the lake."

Finally, after many grunts and huffs, Mr. Roberts managed to turn the boat around, but as he struggled against the waves, they lost more ground than they gained.

As she now faced the shoreline, she peered beyond his shoulder. Mr. Eastwood and Hugh were just reaching land, and Mama and Papa pointed out across the lake to where Amy perched like a veritable sitting duck with Mr. Roberts.

Curse this man and his words, and curse Hugh, too. Were it not for his encouragement, she never would have found herself in this predicament.

After a few more unsuccessful rows, Amy's worries

increased. "Perhaps I can help," she offered. At this rate, she was certain she could row better than this man.

"No, I am well. If you but agree to speak with me more on this matter, tomorrow perhaps, I'm certain that will give me the strength I need to make it back to shore."

His eyes were hopeful, but Amy could not stand to be pressured in such a way, nor could she bear the thought of this painful conversation continuing. If he *was* telling the truth and really did have feelings for her, she had to let him down gently, for she would hate to humiliate him in the same regard she had been.

"Sir, I apologize." She paused, another wave slamming against the side of the boat, wetting her feet and the side of her dress. "I once had feelings for you, but I must be honest and say that I do not any longer."

He stared at her, remaining stationary as shock pursed his brow. Could he truly be surprised after his treatment of her?

"How can that be?" he asked.

What could she say—because she never truly loved him? Because any chance she might have had to grow her feelings for him dissipated with his treatment of her? Because...because she might have feelings for another now?

A low rumble crawled across the sky, the boat tossing. Amy grasped onto the edge to steady herself, bracing her feet apart, no longer caring for decorum.

She could only spot Hugh and Mama on the shore. Had the others gone to secure the boats?

She leaned to the side, and relief flooded her limbs at the sight of Mr. Eastwood and Papa rowing toward them in a single boat.

They must have seen Mr. Roberts struggling against the water. Thank heavens. Not only was she to be freed from this conversation, but she would also be saved from a watery grave.

"Why do you smile?" Mr. Roberts asked, glancing over his

shoulder. He faced forward, his face red from exertion and now embarrassment. "They needn't come out here. I am perfectly capable of rowing back on my own."

As if to prove his words, he began vigorously working the oars against the water, but no matter how he tried, the boat did not budge. His technique was off, the rhythm of his rowing unbalanced—as was evident by Mr. Eastwood's fluid movements as he approached them at a quick pace.

Mr. Roberts spoke between grunts. "Before they arrive…will you please…tell me why…you no longer…have feelings for me?"

She shook her head. "No, sir. I cannot."

His eyes flitted over his shoulder. "Is it because…you have… attached yourself…to another?"

Her cheeks warmed, despite the cold wind nipping at her flesh. "No, it is not." She would not give him even a glimpse into her heart, afraid of what he might do with it. "And even if that was the reason, it certainly would not be any of your business."

Mr. Roberts frowned, finally falling silent. He no longer attempted to move the oars, waiting with his eyes directed at the water pooling in the bottom of the boat until their rescuers arrived.

"Are you well, Amy?" Father asked as they neared.

"Yes, Papa. We—"

"We were nearly to shore," Mr. Roberts interrupted, raising his chin and motioning to the paddles. "It's these blasted oars. I'm not used to such poor design. But I was maintaining just fine, I assure you. Perhaps if you tie the boats together and give us a little pull…"

Mr. Eastwood exchanged glances with Papa, who had not ceased sending disapproving stares toward Mr. Roberts.

"It will be far easier for Mr. Paxton and I to row to shore without having to drag a boat with two passengers behind us," Mr. Eastwood said.

"I heartily agree." Amy removed her sopping gloves and

shook the water free from the fabric, earning her an indiscernible look from Mr. Eastwood.

Mr. Roberts, however, was not quite ready to appear weak. "I merely needed a moment's reprieve. Now I am quite refreshed. If you two gentlemen will lead the way, I will be sure to bring Miss Paxton to land safely."

Worry gripped her, fearing they might actually go along with his asinine suggestion. Fortunately, Papa snorted and Mr. Eastwood gingerly spoke up.

"I'm certain Miss Paxton appreciates your valiant effort, sir, but it is time to admit to the facts. You haven't moved anywhere for nearly ten minutes. For Miss Paxton's safety—and all of ours—I suggest you take our advice immediately."

Mr. Roberts clamped his mouth shut, and Mr. Eastwood and Papa shared a visible look of relief.

"Are you ready, Mr. Paxton?" Mr. Eastwood asked.

Papa nodded.

When the front of the boats were brought together, Mr. Eastwood tossed a large, thick lead to Mr. Roberts, who missed the rope twice before managing to catch it.

"Tie it securely," Mr. Eastwood instructed.

Mr. Roberts fumbled with the knot, and Mr. Eastwood's nostrils flared as he eyed the boiling clouds above. Any moment now the rain would begin. Would the wind increase, making it even harder to row to shore?

Thank heavens Papa had come instead of Hugh. Her weedy brother would no doubt be worse at rowing than Mr. Roberts.

Finally, when the vessels were tied securely enough at the top of each boat to make the crossing, Amy made to stand, ready to join Father in the other boat, but he held up his hand to stop her. "You stay there, cricket. Mr. Roberts and Mr. Eastwood will swap places."

Mr. Eastwood, take her back to shore instead of Papa? Amy hesitated. "I can manage stepping into your boat, Father."

"No, I'll not risk you falling in. Mr. Eastwood is more than capable, I daresay. And Mr. Roberts, well, he will have to risk it." He gave the man a pointed look, as if willing him to misstep and plunge into the lake.

As Amy resituated herself on her seat, tucking in her legs to provide more room, Mr. Eastwood swiftly leapt into the adjoining boat. They rocked back and forth, and Mr. Eastwood hunkered down until they were steady.

Next, Mr. Roberts clambered forward, nearly falling twice before managing to step into Father's boat, though he tripped over the edge and landed with a grunt, barely catching himself before he could fall into the lake.

Papa glanced to Amy. "Pity," he mouthed out.

Amy's smile lasted only a moment as she returned her attention to Mr. Eastwood, who was now seated across from her, swiftly untying the weakened knots Mr. Roberts had made before tossing the leads back to Father.

"Keep her safe," Papa instructed.

Mr. Eastwood nodded. "I will, sir."

Papa gave Amy an encouraging nod then plunged the oars into the water, setting off toward the shore. Mr. Roberts folded his arms and stared at his lap.

As Mr. Eastwood launched their own boat into a turn, Amy centered herself on the bench, trying to breathe calmly. This was what she'd wanted all along—to row on Coniston Water with Mr. Eastwood. But Mr. Roberts's confession had certainly tainted any joy she might have felt. How was she to hide what had just occurred, now that she was with Mr. Eastwood?

A moment ticked by in silence, Amy struggling for something to say that didn't involve Mr. Roberts's words, or the argument that she assumed had occurred between Mr. Eastwood and Hugh.

"Thank you for coming to help us," she said softly, the rough waters no longer bothering her, now she knew she was in Mr.

Eastwood's safe hands. "We would have been treading water for hours had you not."

Mr. Eastwood glanced over his shoulder before facing her once more, rowing powerfully through the surging water. "It is no trouble, of course."

Their eyes met, his expression unreadable. The first drops of rain began to fall from the sky, one pelting her cheek.

"I'm sorry we didn't return before the rain set in." He motioned to her cheek with a flick of his chin.

"Oh, I don't mind a little water."

He stared at her, appearing to hesitate. "Am I safe to assume you do not mind getting embroiled in a fight with water now and again?"

She tipped her head to the side at his curious question. "Are you suggesting we start one, Mr. Eastwood?"

His lips curved. "No. I was merely curious."

She studied him for a moment, her eyes wandering over his forearms that flexed with each movement. That hard labor at the manor and with the Rutledges did a great many favors to his physique.

"Your assumption is correct, though, sir. I do enjoy a good battle, and water is often my weapon of choice."

Instead of smiling, his brow pursed, and he looked rather… disturbed. Should she not have admitted to such a thing?

"I'm sorry if you disapprove of such behavior."

"On the contrary, Miss Paxton. I heartily approve." He peered up at the sky, wincing as the rain pelted his face. "But might I request that you suppress any urge you might have to start a fight, as I fear we are both going to be very wet, indeed, from the storm instead."

Amy knew his comment was to make up for his look from earlier. But she couldn't very well press him on the issue. "I will restrain myself. But might I offer you the use of my bonnet to keep your head dry from the rain, sir?"

He smiled at her teasing. His cravat had been loosened since they'd started their expedition out on the water that morning. It hung low, opening his collar to reveal the angles of his neck each time he peered over his shoulder to gauge how close they were to land.

Her stare lingered a moment too long, for in the next moment, their eyes met, and the small twitch of Mr. Eastwood's lips revealed that he knew very well that she'd been admiring him.

With overheated cheeks, she drew her attention to the shoreline. Father and Mr. Roberts were just ahead of them, though they were too far away for any conversations to be overheard over the wind and rain. Both boats were making steady progress, now that capable men were at the helms.

"I assumed Hugh chose to stay ashore?" she asked.

"Yes, he did." Mr. Eastwood gripped the oars. Had his knuckles been that white before?

She bit her lip. She really should hold her tongue and not press for more information. But then, being blunt with the gentleman hadn't injured her thus far.

"You and my brother argued earlier."

He eyed her cautiously, though he did not deny her statement.

"May I ask what the argument was about?"

His jaw twitched. "Merely a difference in opinion."

Amy itched with curiosity, but his words held a finality to them that revealed how very little he wished to discuss the matter. With a nod, she relented. "I'm sorry you quarreled. Though I cannot say I am surprised, as I frequently disagree with my brother, as well."

She looked around her, the wind having somewhat calmed with the storm's arrival. Raindrops fell unceasingly from the low clouds, splashing into the lake, creating endless ripples with the soothing, rhythmic sound of water against water.

Despite the peace she felt, frustration still boiled within her at the thought of Hugh. "He's infuriating at times, but I suppose my lot in life is to forgive him and his many, many short-comings."

"And you do so every time?"

She shrugged. "What other choice do I have? After all, is that not what we are taught to do, to forgive others, so we may be forgiven ourselves?"

A furrowed crease slipped between Mr. Eastwood's brows.

"Do you not agree with me?"

"No, I do. I am merely impressed with your ability to do such a thing."

She gave a little laugh. "I assure you, it is not easy. And there are things that I have yet to forgive." Bringing Mr. Roberts to her, being one of them. "But I suppose all we can do is move forward each day."

Mr. Eastwood nodded, though his eyes wandered away as if he was deep in thought.

She studied him, wondering what he thought of before his eyes met hers. Her first instinct was to look swiftly away, embarrassed at having been caught staring again. But something within her made her hold his gaze.

The rain had seeped through the shoulders of her spencer, and the lap of her dress had completely soaked through. But despite the chills running up and down her spine, a warmth pervaded her limbs. He rowed the oars slower, moving back and forth in a deliberate manner.

As he leaned forward, the oars stopped, and his eyes flickered to her lips. Her breath caught in her throat as his own mouth parted. Was he...did he...

But the moment was gone in an instant. He pulled his eyes over his shoulder and began to paddle once again.

"Nearly there," he said, his voice gruff, the same way it sounded after he'd stroked her skin in the cottage gardens.

"Excellent," she said, though disappointment wedged firmly into her hopes.

Mr. Eastwood avoided her eyes the rest of the journey. She told herself it was because the gentleman did not wish to reveal his desires in front of her family. But a thread of doubt marred her dreams.

With a twisting stomach, Amy reached the shore shortly after Papa and Mr. Roberts. Her parents helped her out of the boat while Mr. Eastwood secured his vessel, and Mr. Roberts spoke in whispered tones to Hugh off to the side.

Would Mr. Roberts tell all of Coniston what had occurred between them, or would he keep it to himself now that the rejected party was himself? Either way, Hugh would be sure to *not* defend her.

"Are you well, my dear?" Mama wrapped her arms around Amy's sodden shoulders and led her toward the shelter of thick birch trees near the road.

"Yes, Mama."

Papa joined them with a crumpled brow. "Perhaps you two ought to remain here while I return to the cottage for our carriage. If I had any forethought, I would have insisted taking it in the first place."

"That is all right, my dear," Mama soothed. "We enjoyed the walk here. Did we not, Amy?"

Amy nodded, hiding how she'd really felt about not taking the carriage. "Of course, but there is no need for you to walk to the cottage on your own. We will arrive home faster if we join you."

"Oh, but the mud, Amy," Mama said.

"Why don't you come with me in my carriage?" Mr. Eastwood motioned to his carriage nearby. "I brought it in case of bad weather. It will be a tight squeeze with the six of us, but it certainly is better than catching a cold from all this rain."

"Oh, dear Mr. Eastwood," Mama said, resting a hand on his arm. "How can we ever thank you?"

"You can forgive me for choosing this day to go out boating."

They chuckled at Mr. Eastwood's joke. Amy tried to smile, but her spirits could not keep up with what her brain demanded.

As the carriage rolled toward them and Mr. Roberts's horse was tied to the back of it, the group gathered together. Hugh still frowned, and Mr. Roberts peered down at the mud on his boots. Mr. Eastwood hardly seemed to notice anyone else as he attempted to replace his gloves and jacket over his sodden hands and shirt. But as Papa helped Mama into the carriage, Mr. Eastwood gave up on dressing with an aggravated sigh, which finally proved to lift Amy's mood.

Amy followed Mama into the carriage, sitting beside her as Papa sat across from them, shuffling to the wall. Hugh followed, shifting to Papa's side with an unintelligible grumble.

Mr. Roberts was next, poking his head in the carriage with a look directly at Amy then to the empty seat beside her. Her heart sank. The carriage may be large enough for the six of them, but there would be an inordinate amount of bouncing into one another as they traveled along the inevitable muddy roads. She looked to Papa in a panic.

"Ah, Mr. Roberts," Papa said at once. "You'll be better off sitting beside Hugh. Mr. Eastwood is far larger than you and will not take kindly to having to squeeze into this side."

Mr. Roberts, though clearly disappointed, did not have the courage to say no to Papa. With a sigh, he settled down beside Hugh.

Amy sent a grateful look to Papa, who winked at her in response.

Her relief was short-lived, though, when Mr. Eastwood popped his head in next. His eyes skimmed the occupants of his carriage before landing on Amy. She hadn't had time before now to realize who would be sitting next to her, should Mr. Roberts not be. And though this was a far more agreeable option for *her*, Mr. Eastwood's grimace revealed his own feelings on being seated so closely beside her.

Swiftly, he sat down, shifting his body as close to the carriage wall as possible. Even still, their legs, shoulders, and elbows pressed closely together.

Amy tried to subdue her racing heart, the tips of her ears burning. Mr. Eastwood hardly appeared affected. In fact, he looked more perturbed than anything having to sit beside her.

As the carriage rolled forward, she dropped her eyes. Was he merely repulsed at the idea of sitting so closely to her? Did the thought of Miss Winslow lend to his aversion?

No, Mr. Eastwood himself had said they were just friends. And surely he did not believe Amy to have an attachment to Mr. Roberts, so he wouldn't be keeping away for that, either.

There was only one explanation to his sudden aversion of her. He must have seen her attraction to him and—unable to reciprocate her growing feelings—was now doing his best to discourage her from pursuing him.

Was she truly about to be rejected for a third time?

She closed her eyes, ignoring the burning sensation of her flesh where she made contact with Mr. Eastwood. She tried shifting subtly toward Mama, only then noticing part of her dress was under Mr. Eastwood's very firm, very wet thigh.

"My apologies," he murmured. He must have felt her attempt to gingerly tug it out.

He raised his leg a fraction, reaching down to pull the fabric out just as Amy did the same. Their bare hands brushed against each other, a shock of warmth and brightness shooting up her arm. She pulled back swiftly, his green eyes peering down at her. Her breathing halted, heart murmuring softer than a butterfly's wings as his gaze darted down to her lips once again.

This time, Amy could not deny the look of desire apparent in his focused eyes, nor in her own swirling chest.

Another bump in the road tossed them side to side, breaking their gaze, and Amy pulled back. Had anyone seen what had just occurred? Father leaned his head back against the carriage, closing his eyes, Hugh was scowling at his fingertips, and Mama was looking in the opposite direction. But Mr. Roberts stared across from her with narrowed eyes.

Instead of cowering from embarrassment, she raised her chin and turned away, vowing to never look in the man's direction again.

That would certainly be easy enough, for her mind was entirely too focused on how grateful she was for her spencer jacket, for if she had not worn the thicker fabric, she would have been sure to have felt every muscle working in Mr. Eastwood's arm through his thin, soaked shirt.

And that would have undone her completely.

CHAPTER SIXTEEN

*C*lack, clack, clack.

Amy groaned, rolling over in her bed and pressing her pillow over her head. For a moment, silence met her, and she breathed a sigh of relief.

Clack, clack.

In a swift movement, she sat upright, throwing her pillow at the foot of her bed and scowling fiercely at the window. That wretched gate. Would it never cease its—

Clack!

Her eyes narrowed. She would not receive a lick of rest tonight with that racket.

The gate had been left unlatched and now hit against the stone wall with annoying irregularity. If she was on the opposite side of the house, overlooking the lake, she no doubt would still be asleep.

Of course, the gate's discord was not the only reason she could not sleep that night, but that was beyond the point.

With a shake of her head, she tore off her covers and left her bed in search of her dressing gown, stomping around in the darkness, hoping to wake every member of her family though knowing she would not disturb a soul. *They* could sleep through anything.

Throwing her dressing gown round her shoulders, she clomped out of her room, passing by Hugh's chambers with particularly loud footsteps. After all, he was the reason for this terrible day, beginning with the disaster that was boating that morning and ending with the gate tapping on that wretched stone wall.

After her worthless brother had invited Mr. Roberts to stay for dinner—which kept Amy hidden away in her room from the moment they returned from boating—the two gentlemen had stayed awake drinking until eleven o'clock. She'd watched from her window as their shadows moved to the gate. After a wave of departure, highlighted only by the light of the moon, Mr. Roberts had opened the gate and failed to secure it behind him. Hugh returned indoors a moment later without latching it either.

She hadn't thought anything of it until a soft wind had picked up, and now it was all she could hear.

Clack, clack, clack, clack.

Terrible day, indeed.

After retrieving a lantern, she opened the door of the cottage, pausing on the threshold. She peered into the darkness with her raised lantern as the cold settled around her instantly. The rain had let up in the late afternoon, allowing clear skies the rest of the evening. Though the earth had yet to soak in all the moisture it had received, the moon shone forth in a bright light, outlining the trees in a glowing, silver paint and illuminating the pathway before her.

She stretched her lantern forth, clutching her dressing gown closer to ward off the cold as she tiptoed barefooted across the dewy ground. The gate must have sensed her approach and stopped its clacking at once, for the soft trickling of the brook was all that marred the silence of the evening.

Still, as she reached the wall, she flung the gate forward with a hard, satisfying swing. The wood rattled in protest, but Amy raised her chin and walked away with a gratifying swish of her skirts.

Now she would finally get some sleep.

Clack!

She swung around with wide eyes. The gate had escaped from its latch and once again tapped against the stone wall.

Was it broken? No doubt from Hugh and Mr. Roberts opening it. *Not* because of how hard she'd closed it just now.

She attempted to secure it once again, but the gate flapped open without hesitation. Pursing her lips, she shone the candlelight closer to the ground, settling on a large rock.

That would do nicely.

Placing her lantern securely on the stone wall, Amy bent down to retrieve the rock, cradling it between her arm and her side before turning to the gate, ready to stop its clacking once and for all. Finally. Her fingers were beginning to smart in the autumn temperatures.

"Miss Paxton?"

Amy gasped, cold air chilling her insides as she dropped the rock and jumped back in surprise. Her heart strummed against her chest. "Mr. Eastwood?"

The gentleman emerged from the shadows, hat, jacket, and gloves in hand as he stood in the gateway. His cravat was fully undone, hanging limply down either side of his neck, and his shirt hung open to his half-buttoned waistcoat. Candlelight flickered against his features, creating shadows across the top of his chest and at the base of his throat.

She pressed a hand against her heart to keep it from bursting right through her flesh. She couldn't remember the last time the man had appeared fully dressed before her—he hadn't even been wearing his jacket when she'd first seen him at the lake.

"Are you hurt?" he asked, peering down at her bare feet sticking out from her dressing gown.

Her dressing gown. Heavens above, what was happening right now? She tucked in her toes and nervously stroked her plaited hair draped over her shoulder. Thank heavens she'd forgone paper curls that evening, though her ringlets had all but died, and she was now left with stringy strands to frame her face. "No, the rock missed me only just."

"I apologize for startling you. I thought you heard my approach."

"No, I didn't." Her words faltered as their eyes met, and memories of their time that morning flooded her mind—their few moments in the boat, their ride in the carriage, his eyes on her lips...his apparent discomfort being near her.

She swallowed. "What are you doing out here so late at night?"

"My visit with the Rutledges ran late."

He shifted, though he didn't make to leave. Why did he linger? Did he wish to remain in her company, or was he doing so to be polite? And was he avoiding her earlier because he didn't like her, or because he *shouldn't* like her?

"Are you all right?"

Amy looked up, unaware that her brow was puckered. She blinked away her worry. "Yes, merely wondering if you were invited to have the pie that Mrs. Rutledge also promised me and my family. Although, I take it you earned the dessert by doing some act of service for them?"

His lips curved. "How did you know?"

"Because you are *always* helping someone in need."

"And do you disapprove of this?"

"Disapprove?" She forced her eyes away from the angle of his jaw, only enhanced by the lantern's light. "Quite the opposite, sir."

A moment ticked by in silence, her dressing gown now officially doing nothing in regards to warming her. Should she beg her leave now? She was fairly certain no passersby would find them, nor would her family see them out the window—what with their ridiculous ability to sleep through everything—but should they be caught speaking so late at night, and her in her dressing gown of all things...

"May I now ask what *you* are doing out here so late?"

Perhaps a moment longer in his company wouldn't hurt. She motioned to the gate. "Merely attempting to fix this before it's tapping drives me to lunacy."

He studied the latch. "It's broken again? How?"

Amy looked away. "I haven't the faintest idea."

He eyed her for a moment before placing his belongings atop the stone wall opposite the lantern. Hunkering down, he examined the latch more closely. "So, you were telling the truth earlier. You really can't sleep with irregular sounds occurring, can you?"

He peered up at her over his shoulder, a hint of a smile in his eyes.

He remembered? All those days ago, when she'd said she couldn't sleep with the dripping from the window in her room, he'd remembered?

With warmth swirling in her heart, she replied. "No, I'm afraid I cannot."

Returning his attention to the gate, he nodded. "The latch is a little off-centered, but I believe it will be an easy enough fix." He stood, brushing off his hands. "I'll be sure to send someone early tomorrow morning, if that will suffice."

"Send someone?" The question slipped from her tongue before she could stop it. She'd never known the man to send someone else to do his work.

He didn't meet her gaze. "Yes, I fear my day is excessively busy tomorrow, and I won't have time to fit this in also, with what I have planned. I hope that does not displease you or your family."

Amy clasped her hands together, trying to hold her tongue, but she couldn't bear it any longer. She needed to know. She *had* to know.

"As a matter of fact, it does displease me. Because I cannot help but think…" She drew in a deep breath. "If you do not wish to see me any longer, sir, or help us at the cottage, you needn't feel any obligation to do so. But I would appreciate a forthright response, if you would be so kind."

He blinked, taken aback at her blunt words, before a brief laugh escaped his lips. "You are not one for mincing words, are you, Miss Paxton?"

She shrugged helplessly. "I do try to be reserved at times, but I find life far easier to live when the truth is spoken first."

"And if the whole truth cannot be shared?"

His words shook her, as did the haunted look in his eyes. He peered toward the lantern, and only now did Amy notice the weary circles framing his eyes and the sunken attitude of his otherwise squared shoulders.

"Then I suppose partial truths will suffice," she responded.

He studied her, the soft trickling of the brook on the other side of the gate breaking up the silence. "Then I will tell you that I do wish to see you and to help at Flitfield. But I truly do have a great list of things to take care of tomorrow." He backed up a few paces, leaning against the stone wall where the gate hung open. Scrubbing his hands up and down his face, he sighed. "Though I apologize I cannot help your family myself."

As his shoulders sank further, Amy's heart constricted at having added to whatever burden weighed down upon him. "Do not apologize, sir, on our account. We are more than capable of living with a gate that does not latch properly."

He dropped his hands, and though he nodded, his weariness did not dissipate.

She winced, wishing to aid him in some way after all he'd done for her and her family. But what could she do? Offer a helping hand, a listening ear? She doubted that he'd want either.

Stepping toward the other side of the stone wall, she faced him as they stood in the open gateway. The light flickered behind Mr. Eastwood, silhouetting his sunken figure.

"You're tired."

He nodded, his head low.

"Perhaps you ought to return to Birchwick then." Keeping him at the cottage any longer would be purely selfish.

"I ought to. And you ought to return to bed."

"I ought to," she repeated.

Yet, both of them remained where they stood.

Amy studied him, knowing she ought to make the first move to leave, but there was something keeping the man here. What was it?

"Sir, do you wish to speak about something?"

Speak about something? Oh, yes. He very much wished to speak about a great many things. But he never had before. How could he start with Miss Paxton, the woman he was drawing danger-ously close to, the woman from whom he couldn't keep away?

He shouldn't even be out there with her in the dead of the night. Should someone happen upon them, should Charity discover their actions...

But, as Miss Paxton's soft eyes warmed his cold worries and spoke encouragement to his soul, his defenses fell. He would only speak for but a moment, then he would leave.

"It's Mr. Rutledge. He's...dying."

Saying the words aloud reinforced the fact he'd just been informed of that evening. He still hadn't processed the informa-tion, nor the grief in Mrs. Rutledge's eyes as she sat beside her husband in his bed, holding his hand. Mr. Rutledge could not hold hers in return.

Miss Paxton's breath puffed around her in a soft, white cloud, candlelight reflecting in her glistening eyes.

"I didn't know he was so very ill," she whispered.

William nodded. He'd said all he'd wished to say. He was a private person, and sharing his thoughts with this woman wouldn't do any good.

Yet he struggled to keep the words reined in as they continued to build up behind his restrictive tongue at an alarming rate. Where had this desire come from, to share his feelings with another? He'd not wanted to do such a thing since before Charity had taught him to do otherwise.

She'd spoken of her father's passing once when they were children, but she'd been so woeful afterward that she'd bottled it right back up, thereby teaching William to do the same with his own grief and troubles, if he wanted to avoid further pain. Thus far, it had worked just fine.

But perhaps...perhaps speaking with the friend he had in Miss Paxton would help. Perhaps if he merely shared a few words more, he'd finally be able to comprehend the grief now encompassing him.

"I thought the same," he began, his words slow and calculated, "that he had many years ahead of him, even with his weakness in his limbs." He shook his head, the words growing in force, spilling over the dam he'd built around his heart and rushing forward—shame, regret, and sorrow rolled into one. "I've been so preoccupied of late. I haven't made enough time for them to even notice the change in him." He rubbed his forefinger and thumb against his closed eyes. "He fell down the stairs a few days ago and hasn't left his bed since. The physician believes that he may never get up again. And I just can't imagine—"

His voice cracked, ending his words. He gritted his teeth. He shouldn't be revealing such emotion, such weakness, especially in front of Miss Paxton. But the truth of the matter was, he *was* weak. He was exhausted, weary, and worn down to the very earth. He needed to sleep, to rest from all he'd learned that evening. But he couldn't bear to be alone. Not right now.

He'd been alone for too long.

"I'm so sorry, Mr. Eastwood," Miss Paxton whispered. "I know how close you are to the both of them. I can't imagine the heartache you and Mrs. Rutledge must be experiencing."

He bit the inside of his cheek, blinking hard to push away the emotion rising within him, induced by her soft, compassionate tone.

The silence between them persisted, her empathy nearly tangible, and despite his best efforts, a tear escaped his eye and slipped down his cheek.

Hoping perhaps she hadn't seen the moisture in the darkness, William averted his gaze. But he stilled as Miss Paxton reached a tentative hand forward.

As her soft fingers finally made contact with his cheek, her gentle strokes removed any trace of moisture from his skin. He released a slow breath, unwittingly leaning into her touch. Instead of causing more grief and more pain, her caress drew out any remaining sorrow, all while immersing his person with reassurance and newfound strength.

He was soothed and comforted in a way he'd never known— all by a simple touch. When she pulled away, he opened his eyes, having no memory of closing them to begin with.

She peered up at him, and a vulnerability pulled his gaze to the floor. "I'm sorry," he whispered. "I didn't mean to..."

But she shook her head. "There is no need to apologize, not while showing grief for a loved one's ailment. It is natural. Healthy, even."

"You are right, of course." He cleared his throat. "I just didn't expect to..."

She nodded with understanding. "I'm sure you are tired. And you must allow yourself time to process your sorrow. He is very dear to you."

"He is. They both are. They…"

He paused. Miss Paxton looked up at him expectantly. Could he share with her what he wished to share? Speak about his past without losing control and turning into a blubbering mess?

Charity didn't like speaking of her feelings, or of the Rutledges. She'd never really befriended them as William had. She was too preoccupied with caring for her own mother since her father's passing…

He shook his head. He didn't really wish to speak of his past, did he? Yet, from somewhere deep inside, a desire rose up within him like a pillar of fire—a desire to tell Miss Paxton everything, in order to explain the depth of his relationship with the Rutledges.

But how could he, after keeping it inside for so long, swearing he'd never speak of it again? This had always been one of the main deciding factors in his choice to marry Charity. That, and how it would help both of their families heal wounds brought upon them long ago—wounds caused by Grandfather's pride and carelessness. With Charity as his wife, he wouldn't have to speak of his past to anyone.

Yet, right now, he *didn't* have to. Not once had Miss Paxton pressed him for information about his grandfather. She'd treated William with respect and civility, unlike countless people he'd grown up with—and that kindness was deserving of an explanation.

Now to see if his courage lasted.

Leaning against the stone wall with his hands behind him, he began. "I'm sure you've gathered enough from me and others to understand that I was raised in a very controlling household, dictated solely by my grandfather."

Miss Paxton nodded hesitantly. "I have, though I've done my

best not to listen to the rumors, sir. I know you value your privacy."

He nodded his gratitude for her words—words which were more proof that he could trust this woman with his family's sordid history.

"I appreciate the respect you've shown me. However, I should like to share more, if you care to hear?"

She nodded, a strand of hair falling from her plaited hair. "I should like that very much, Mr. Eastwood."

CHAPTER SEVENTEEN

*W*ith the cold air forgotten, William drew in a deep breath, expecting more resistance from his own tongue, but as soon as he began, the words did not stop. "Grandfather had a firm hold on both of my parents. He would say things—horrible things—to them, merely to break down their spirits so they would be more submissive. I watched this from a young age and knew straight from the beginning, I did not want such a life for myself.

"As I grew older, I attempted to rebel in every possible way— stealing boats, playing with the children he forbade me from seeing, walking instead of riding a horse, helping our tenants in any way I could imagine. Though, he still forced me to be privately tutored at home for years so he could have a closer watch over me."

Miss Paxton shook her head. "I can't imagine such a life."

"It was miserable, in the truest sense of the word. But somehow, Father encouraged Grandfather to allow me to go to Oxford. It was there I tasted true freedom, what life was like without living under the thumb of a ruthless despot."

"But you returned," Miss Paxton stated. "Forgive me, but I don't understand why you would."

His lip tugged up wryly. "I was naïve enough to believe I could convince my parents to change their ways, to stand up to Grandfather, so they could be happy, as I finally was. However, upon my return, I discovered things were far worse than when I left. Grandfather's health had deteriorated, and with it, he became all the more vindictive. All his properties, tenants, and friends had been neglected and forgotten, except for his precious Birchwick Hall."

William's lip twitched. How proud that man was of his estate, the immaculate gardens, the expanse of wealth emphasized in his fountains and statues, his hedge maze and grand trees. If William could demolish the entire estate, he would.

He shook his head and continued. "He no longer allowed my parents to leave Coniston. They couldn't attend any social gatherings, nor did he hold any at Birchwick. If he was not well enough to see anyone or do anything, no one could."

Miss Paxton's brow crumpled. "This is why you were so adamant I stand up to Hugh, because you thought he had the same hold over me as your grandfather had over your parents."

He nodded in silence, and she continued. "I can't imagine such a life. How could anyone be so cruel, so thoughtless?"

William hesitated for the first time. Was he really about to share the truth behind his grandfather's actions, why the estates were *really* mismanaged? Charity knew only because her mother told her, but the majority of those in town merely speculated the truth.

Yet he knew, deep down, he could trust Miss Paxton to keep it to herself. "My father told me that his own grandfather was just as controlling. They were taught from a very young age that a father's opinion surpassed all others and that women held lesser value. Grandfather had convinced Father that he needn't have any more children because one male heir was enough, though Mother always wished for more children. Despite Father doing most of what his own father said, he fortunately did not adopt the mindset that he was better than his wife."

Miss Paxton's lips twisted in disgust. "I cannot imagine living under such a mindset as your Grandfather's. The women in your family must have been as unhappy as the gentlemen."

William nodded somberly. "That was why I decided to never marry until Grandfather passed, so his cruelty would not be inflicted on any future wife I had. And as for my grandmother, I can only assume that she was just as unhappy as my mother. She died in childbirth, along with her second child. Though..." His lips thinned. "It was not my grandfather's."

Miss Paxton's brow pursed in confusion, then slowly, her lips parted. "Oh. Oh, I see." She looked away, the blush visible on her cheeks even in the darkness.

He regretted his words in an instant. "I'm sorry. I shouldn't speak of such matters. I—"

"No, I'm glad you did." She swallowed. "I was merely surprised, that is all."

"I was, too, when I first discovered the truth from Mrs...." He shook his head. That is one part of the story Miss Paxton did not need to know—how Charity's mother knew of his family's past more than he did. How her husband's death was caused by..."Much hearsay has been spread about me and my family, about my life. But this is the truth of the matter. This is why Grandfather left the manor and cottage in ruins. It was where he first discovered her betrayal. At first, he had leased the estates to gain more money to improve the state of Birchwick— his true love—but I believe the memory ate away at him, even to the day he died."

Miss Paxton blew out a breath, stroking the end of her plaited hair, tied off with a red ribbon. Were the strands as soft as they appeared?

"Was that his reasoning behind his neglect of his tenants, too? Including the Rutledges?" she asked.

William nodded. "After being wronged by his wife, Grandfather gave up on caring for anyone but himself. He forbade Father from helping, as well, but he could not stop me, though he threatened to strip me of my inheritance, along with countless other warnings."

He peered out to the side of him, candlelight reflecting off the brooklet like small crystals. He wasn't certain where his words were headed, but as they continued, he could not stop them. "Mr. and Mrs. Rutledge have been there for me since the beginning, in the darkest moments of my life. When I was twelve, I was determined to leave Birchwick and never return. Mrs. Rutledge found me late at night, wandering the streets of Coniston. She invited me in for a slice of pie, then both she and Mr. Rutledge encouraged me to return, for the sake of my parents—and for the sake of the tenants. I realized then where my duty lay, and I haven't looked back since. So I will continue to help my tenants, especially the Rutledges, until I can help them no longer."

"I'm certain they will forever be grateful for your help."

"I can only hope."

Their eyes met as his words finally ended, and an odd sensation occurred within him. He'd been afraid to share his feelings for so long—as if speaking aloud would make him relive the painful memories. But the opposite had occurred. Despite his grief over Mr. Rutledge's declining health, William almost felt...free.

But would this freedom have come if he'd spoken with anyone but Miss Paxton?

At the thought, a discomfort burgeoned in his chest. He told himself it was due to sharing almost everything he'd held inside for years. But deep down he knew, he knew the soreness was due to whatever was happening in his heart as Miss Paxton's eyes sparkled, staring up at him.

Charity's eyes had never shone in such a way.

He shifted his footing to dispel the thought, chuckling nervously as he rubbed a hand against his chest. "Look at me, chattering away as if the two of us weren't outside alone in the cold after midnight. I do apologize."

"That is all right." Her voice drifted around them in the otherwise sleeping earth. "I'm grateful you trusted me enough to speak of such things. I know it can't be easy."

William had been about to agree, to open up about how difficult it had been for him to share these things with anyone, but he bit his tongue. This woman must have a spell on him. There was no other explanation as to why he would wish to speak *so much*.

As the silence between them continued, he searched for a different topic, ignoring the fact that he really should be leaving for home. "I'm sorry our boating excursion ended so abruptly this morning. I'm certain you were all disappointed."

She shrugged. "My parents were. Though I was rather relieved to see it come to an end."

He'd already shared all the words he wished to say, and he now felt a great deal better. He really should leave. And yet…

"Why is that?" he asked.

"I suppose it did not turn out the way I had hoped it would."

Leave, William. Leave.

"You refer to Hugh's suggestion for you to boat with Mr. Roberts?" Blast his errant tongue.

She looked away. "You are too astute, sir."

His eyes traced the soft curve of her neck and the slight tip of her nose, and his heart reached out to her. "I wish you would not abide by his advice."

"And I wish you would tell me what the two of you argued over."

He smiled at her quip. "Perhaps I will, if you tell me exactly who Mr. Roberts is."

"He is Hugh's friend."

"And…" he prodded.

William didn't think Mr. Roberts was anyone special, at least not to Miss Paxton, as was evident by her clear discomfort around the gentleman. But he knew there was something more between them than she was letting on.

She fiddled with her plait again. How charming she looked in the candlelight, with her hair loose and hanging around her face, wearing her dressing gown.

His heart tripped. Thoughts of his past and Mr. Rutledge's ill health kept his mind from dwelling too much on her appearance. But now, with no distraction from her ethereal presence— her delicate, white dressing gown and blonde hair highlighted by the candlelight—he had nowhere else to look.

"I will answer your question," she began, "when you tell me who Miss Winslow is."

His heart dropped. This was the perfect time to be honest, to tell her his intention to marry his childhood friend. But then, what would that do to his relationship with Miss Paxton? Would they no longer be able to speak as comfortably as they did now? He'd certainly have to stop talking to her in such a compromising situation, but he wasn't ready to. Not yet. Besides, the chance of someone walking by and finding them together was highly unlikely.

"I already told you she is my friend."

She gave him a pointed look. "And?"

William shook his head, unable to provide more. The silence between them was as thick as the darkness beyond the brook.

"If you will not say more," she began, "I will admit that I am not engaged."

He couldn't explain the odd rush of relief flooding his limbs, nor the airiness to his heart.

"Nor am I," he said.

He attributed his response to the lightheadedness he felt. Logic certainly couldn't have dictated his words, though true as they may be.

"Well, then," she said, her voice barely above a whisper, "I suppose we know a little more about one another then."

"Indeed."

She pushed away from the wall she had leaned against and disappointment struck. Was she making ready to leave?

"Tell me," he began, desperate to keep her there, to maintain her company for a little while longer, though he had no idea where his words were headed, "will you always do what Hugh asks of you?"

"No, not always."

He pushed away from the wall, as well, taking a step toward her. "What about other gentlemen? Will you do what they ask of you?"

She raised her chin. "I suppose it would depend on what gentleman it was."

Their eyes locked. William had taken leave of his senses, but he hardly cared. He was much too focused on the perfect features of her face. On her soft hair he needed to touch. On her full lips he needed to taste. "Suppose *I* was the gentleman."

She swallowed, taking a step back. "I-I suppose it would then depend on what it was that you were asking me to do."

He raised the side of his lip, though he didn't say a word. If he did, he might not have the courage to continue.

He reached around her, bringing the gate from where it tapped softly against the stone wall in the slight breeze. Gently, he brought it forward, bumping against Miss Paxton so she had to take slow steps toward him until the gate was latched securely in its place.

She stared down at it, no doubt wondering how it stayed. He wasn't about to tell her it wasn't a permanent fix, that one push would send the broken gate swinging back against the stone. He wanted her close to him. He *needed* her close to him.

And close they were, their bodies a mere breath apart. He looked down at her, studied every inch of her face before settling on her lips.

"You never answered me, Mr. Eastwood, what it is you're asking of me."

"I think you know, Miss Paxton."

She wet her lips, and suddenly, all sense threatened to flee as those pink lips glistened in the candlelight.

He reached up his hand, hesitating, hovering just above her cheekbone. If he did this, if *they* did this, everything would change—his life, his future, their relationship. Was he prepared for that? Was she?

"My question now," he breathed, smoothing back her hair with the slightest brush of his fingertips, "is if you will be asking Hugh for permission, or if you will choose for yourself what it is you want."

"I will not be asking Hugh his permission for anything."

His eyes flicked between hers. "Then what will it be, Miss Paxton?"

"I choose to…"

Her eyelids fluttered to a close, and William's breathing refused to function any longer. Finally, he allowed his fingertips the touch they so desperately craved. Her skin was cool and soft, even softer than he'd imagined. He slid his fingers along her cheekbone before cradling her face in his palm.

She leaned into his hand with a prolonged sigh, though she said nothing still. What did she fear? Merely the fact that they were outside alone—or was there something else keeping her from agreeing to their kiss?

Slowly, he trailed his free hand down her opposite arm until his fingers found hers. He brought them up, resting them against his chest. She stiffened when she touched his bare skin just below his throat, then her touch softened.

She most certainly could feel his heart thumping, but somehow, he didn't mind. He longed to let her know the effect she had on him, if only to encourage her to finally give him permission.

"Miss Paxton," he whispered, leaning close enough for their noses to touch, "what is your decision?"

He waited with baited breath. He needed her consent to continue, to finally allow himself to kiss her. Then he knew he would not be taking advantage of her. Then he would know that she wished to kiss him in return.

Then he could justify his actions.

"I..." She raised her chin, her breath on his lips. "I want—"

She broke off in a gasp, slipping from his grasp as the gate clicked open and gave way. Swiftly, he reached forward, wrapping his arms around her before she could fall.

"Are you all right?" he asked.

She looked back then forward to face him, steadying her feet on the ground. "Yes," she breathed.

They paused, their arms around each other, faces inches apart.

But the moment had passed, and logic resumed.

Abruptly, he released her, ensuring she was steady before taking a step away. "Forgive me. I have taken leave of my senses."

It was after midnight. They were alone in her garden. And he was going to marry Charity.

Wasn't he?

He shook his head at his own thoughts. "The gate will be fixed in the morning. Goodnight, Miss Paxton."

He retrieved his belongings swiftly then crossed over the small foot bridge. Only then did he register the confusion on her brow and the worry in her eyes. He stopped, turning back to face her as she walked to the house with the lantern aloft.

"Miss Paxton?"

She turned around, her brow raised. "Yes?"

His mind raced. Should he apologize again? Explain his behavior? With a shake of his head, he scrambled for the words. "Will you be at the festival tomorrow, by the fields near Birchwick?"

She studied him for a moment then gave a single nod. "I believe so."

"Excellent. Then I will see you there."

The small curve of those blasted, tempting lips was more than worth the effort it took for him to turn back around.

With a nod of his head, he left once again, not stopping until he was hidden completely in the shadows of the trees.

Holding his breath, he turned around in time to see the lantern disappearing into the cottage and the door closing behind Miss Paxton.

Once alone, he dropped to his knees beside the brooklet and flung splash after splash of icy water across his face. He blew out a pent-up breath.

How could he have allowed such a thing to occur when he fully intended on marrying another?

Unless, of course, Charity returned from London with news that she'd found another.

As a flash of hope illuminated his sunken chest, confusion crippled his mind. If he did not wish to marry Charity...did he want to marry someone else entirely?

He leaned back with a silent groan, raking his nails through his hair. No. No, he could not entertain such thoughts. He'd planned his entire life to marry Charity, to live a life of ease, and to perform his duty to fix what Grandfather had done to the Winslows. One night of fleeting desire could not change that. Not only that, their marriage would not only benefit *them*, but their entire families. For perhaps the past could then finally be forgotten—the part of his past he'd not had the courage to share with Miss Paxton.

Light flickered in the corner of his eye, drawing his attention to the top window of the cottage. A slender silhouette appeared in front of the light as Miss Paxton stared up at the bright moon in the sky.

His heart twisted as he tried to wring out any remaining feelings for the woman—but it was of no use. Those feelings had surfaced that evening from a deep-rooted connection he'd had with Miss Paxton. A connection he could not explain nor deny.

But then, what did that mean for the connection he thought he'd shared with Charity? The connection that had begun to feel more and more like a burdensome duty than a blessing?

CHAPTER EIGHTEEN

*A*my's eyes trailed after the large, black-spotted pig as it walked round its makeshift enclosure. Mr. Smith, the owner, rattled off various facts about the animal and his superb pedigree while those gathered around the enclosure listened with interest, asking questions and expressing their appreciation for such a fine animal.

Amy, however, propped her chin on her fist and leaned against the tall fence, doing her best to listen to the farmer, though her attention constantly shifted over her shoulder, where Mr. Eastwood stood speaking with a group of gentlemen.

He wore his hat and jacket today, a far cry different than how he'd appeared before her last evening.

Last evening. She still couldn't believe he'd shared so much about his past with her, nor his feelings concerning the Rutledges. And the kiss that almost was... She sighed, shaking her head. His departure had been disappointing to say the least. But she'd merely chalked it up to his respect for her.

After all, no man should be kissing a lady after dark alone in her garden, no matter how she desired it.

Mr. Eastwood's laughter brought her back to the present,

and she unknowingly smiled just as his eyes caught hers. She faced forward, her cheeks stinging. Again.

That had to be the hundredth time he'd captured her staring. This time—*this time*—she'd keep her eyes on the pig.

"Fascinating, isn't it, cricket?" Papa asked beside her, motioning to the animal. "Who knew there could be so much to learn about pigs?"

"Indeed, Father. I hadn't any notion."

Nor did she understand *why* they needed to learn so much about them. Perhaps Papa had a certain fondness for pigs as she had for chickens? Or perhaps he simply liked to learn about his food before eating it?

"Might we go explore the booths next?" she asked.

Mama, who stood on Father's opposite side, leaned forward to reply, though her eyes remained on the livestock. "Yes, my dear, in just a moment."

Amy stifled a sigh. She'd been to many a rural fair before, and this one was no different, even though they'd not arrived until later. She enjoyed lumbering about the open fields, looking at the animals and exploring the booths and carts filled with food, earthenware, and tools as much as the next person. But her parents always took an unduly length of time at each location. At this rate, they wouldn't be round the entire fair until next Friday.

She tapped her fingers anxiously against the fence, wondering if Mr. Eastwood might come speak with her. He'd been speaking there for nearly a quarter of an hour. And she knew he'd seen her.

Perhaps she ought to look one last time, just to see if he was still there or if he'd moved elsewhere. Slowly, she peered over her shoulder with as much indifference as she could muster.

But Mr. Eastwood no longer stood with the group of gentlemen. Instead, he was headed in her direction with a confident stride that made her heart tremble. She swung her body round to face away from him again, the blood rushing from her head.

"Are you well, Amy?" Papa peered down at her as she clung to the top of the fence.

"Yes," she said in a high-pitched tone.

She plastered on a smile to be more convincing, though he still watched her with a curious eye.

The pig, look at the pig.

What was the matter with her? She'd spoken with the gentleman countless times before. Heavens, she'd nearly kissed him! So why, now, was she ready to swoon at the thought of his approach?

Yet, as he spoke her name from behind—his deep voice like smooth cream pouring over warm pudding—she knew why.

"Good evening, Miss Paxton."

Pulling on her best surprised expression, Amy turned to face the gentleman. "Oh, Mr. Eastwood. Good evening."

His eyes twinkled as if to convey his knowledge about her feigned surprise, though he remained silent on the matter, allowing her to maintain her dignity.

"Lovely to see you again, Mr. Eastwood," Mama said as she and Papa turned to greet him, as well. "Coniston certainly knows how to put on a lively fair."

He gave her a nod of gratitude.

"I take it you've seen Mr. Smith's lovely pig before?" Father asked, turning back to the animal.

Mr. Eastwood came to stand beside Amy, his sleeve brushing against her arm as he clasped his hands behind his back. "Indeed, I have. He's quite proud of the creature, as he is with all of his animals."

"Has he brought more?" Father asked.

"Indeed. The majority of the animals here belong to him."

"And what of your hens, Mr. Eastwood?" Mama asked. "Did you bring them?"

"Of course. I could not pass on the opportunity to boast of their beauty to the entire town. They are just beyond there." He motioned to the opposite side of the field where more animals were situated in even more makeshift enclosures. "I'm certain they would not mind a little reunion of their own, Miss Paxton, if you'd care to see them in return?"

Her chest swelled. She sent a quick glance to her parents, who nodded their approval at once.

Amy had told her parents about declining Mr. Roberts in the boat, but she hadn't the courage to speak to them of yet another one of her poor decisions—lingering out of doors alone with the very gentleman before them. If they would have known, surely they would have been less apt to allow their daughter to walk away with him.

With a slightly guilt-ridden conscience, she faced Mr. Eastwood. "I would be most delighted, thank you."

"We will join you there in a moment," Papa said, then he and Mama faced the pig once more.

Mr. Eastwood offered his arm to her, and she wrapped her hand around his forearm, careful not to grasp too tightly, though she longed to feel for herself the muscles she'd observed working time and time again.

"Are you having a pleasant evening?" he asked, keeping his gaze trained forward.

"I am. And you?"

"Yes, thank you."

The air between them was as stilted as their conversation. Amy could think of nothing to say, her mind dwelling entirely on last night and the way he'd stared at her parted lips.

She blinked away the image and drew in a deep breath.

"I hope you don't mind my pulling you away from the pig," he said next. "I couldn't help but notice the look of boredom on your face."

She cringed. "My parents have an unfounded fascination

with the animal, I'm afraid. I will never be able to thank you enough for saving me from suffering through what was sure to be another half an hour of their admiration."

He chuckled, and the tension between them lessened. "Surely pigs are not so very dull."

"It is not their dullness that bothers me, but their stench."

"Ah, yes. I must agree with you there. But am I right to assume you'd rather stare at a pig than walk through another field of cows?"

He motioned to the left of them where two large, Highland cows stood, tied to a small stake buried in the ground. They bellowed as the two walked by, and Amy flinched, instinctively grasping Mr. Eastwood's jacket tighter.

He laughed, resting his hand atop hers. "Worry not. We'll steer clear of them from this point forward."

The comforting pressure of his hand on hers, the warmth percolating through both of their gloves, soothed her worries, and the rest of her discomfort melted away.

Her confidence and security grew with her arm laced through his, and as her comfort improved, her eyes found more pleasure in the sights around her.

The evening sun still glowed brightly, casting a golden light across the green fields. The orange and yellow trees at the edge of the grass caught the light, as if lit by a warm, gleaming fire.

Despite the long day they'd already had, the country folk still stood by their carts and booths, determined to stay until the last minute to sell the rest of their bright red apples and sharp-smelling cheese, of their handmade leather satchels and clay pots and plates.

As she and Mr. Eastwood meandered through the center of the fair, children ran past with their pastries and small baskets of strawberries, their mothers skittering after them with flustered cheeks and wide eyes. A lasting game of croquet in a nearby open area sent a large crack through the air each time a ball was struck, and a small group of young people gathered nearby to dance to a lively tune played on the violin by a man with a long, white beard.

The air breathed of life and joy, of laughter and music and friends.

Then she noticed the stares.

At first, she thought she'd imagined them, the lingering eyes of old and young women alike, the clear absence of smiles as they did so. Even Miss Booth and her mother, who had been so kind at the picnic, sent penetrating stares in their direction, looking away without a response to Amy's greeting smile.

Mr. Eastwood hardly seemed to notice, pointing out various craftsmanship that his own tenants had created or the smooth, brown eggs his very own hens had laid.

Amy did her best to listen and respond, but when they finally reached his chickens, standing outside a thrown-up henhouse, whispers from nearby reached her ears.

"Mr. Eastwood, walking with her?" came the first. "I can't believe it."

"I didn't even know they knew each other well enough to walk in such a way together," came the next.

"Do you think she knows about *her*?"

"Oh, she must. The whole town knows."

A coldness rushed down Amy's spine. No, she would not focus on this issue again. Mr. Eastwood had denied a relationship with Miss Winslow *twice* now. He'd said the town loved to speculate about him and his family. This was just another thing for people to pry and gossip over, surely.

"Are they not as lovely as you remember?" he asked beside her, bringing her attention to the present.

"What? Oh, no, of course they are."

"Then why do you appear so…disturbed?"

She removed her frown. "Merely because I was fearing that *you* were the one to carry them here."

He chuckled, the sound instantly warming the coolness within her soul. "Worry not. A woman once told me how to hold the hens, and since then, they've been more than happy."

"Ah, she must have been a very wise woman," she teased. "How fortunate you are to have met her."

"Indeed, I am fortunate."

His tone had changed, all mischief gone, replaced with such sincerity Amy wasn't sure what to respond with other than another blush.

"Miss Paxton—"

"Amy, there you are."

Amy blinked, coming out of the perfect bubble Mr. Eastwood had formed around them to face one of the last men she wished to see that evening.

"Hugh," she said dully.

She'd managed to avoid her brother and Mr. Roberts since boating the day before, though they'd both been at the fair the entire day with Miss Cox, sampling all the ale and cheese they could find.

Amy was still not ready to speak with Hugh since his betrayal, nor was she ready to have him interrupt her time with Mr. Eastwood.

"I must speak with you for a moment, sister," Hugh said, directing his body away from Mr. Eastwood without a word of greeting.

Mr. Eastwood stared down at him with a tight-lipped expression. Was he considering the argument he'd had with Hugh the day before?

"It can wait, Hugh," she stated firmly. "As you can see, I'm speaking with Mr. Eastwood."

Hugh's eyes didn't flicker from hers, his smile void of any happiness. "I'm well aware. But I fear this cannot wait."

Amy's determination faltered. His eyes truly did speak of an urgency he did not often show—unless, of course, he was anxious to meet with a woman. So what could he have to say to Amy?

With a regretful sigh, she nodded. "Mr. Eastwood, would you mind so very much excusing me for a moment?"

Mr. Eastwood's jaw tightened, though he nodded all the same. "Of course, Miss Paxton. I'll wait here for you."

He gave what could only be read as a warning glance to Hugh then turned to face his chickens.

Amy begrudgingly followed her brother away from Mr. Eastwood and past a few carts before stopping in a quiet area near the border of the trees. Their footsteps barely had time to stop before Amy's patience fled from her grasp.

"What is the meaning of this, Hugh?" she hissed, making sure to keep her voice checked. "If pulling me away from Mr. Eastwood is some poor attempt to make my decisions for me, you must be mad, indeed. After what you did to me with Mr. Roberts, I will never heed your advice again!"

"Do calm yourself, Amy."

He raised his hands in the air as if to calm a rabid dog on the streets—which only proved to infuriate her all the more.

"I will not calm myself! How could you, Hugh? How could you bring him here after what he did to me, after the rumors he spread, after—"

"I didn't!" He shook his head, his eyes wide. "I swear to you, I didn't."

Her mouth dropped at his obvious lie. "How can you lie so effortlessly? Mr. Roberts himself said you'd invited him!"

"No, no, that was before. I admit, many months ago when you had first shown an interest in Mr. Roberts, I told him to join us in the Lake District. But that was the one and only time I ever mentioned it to him. He must have taken that verbal invitation and used it as an excuse to join us here."

Amy narrowed her eyes, mistrust swirling inside her.

"I speak the truth, Amy. You heard him say yourself that he

was looking for the manor instead of the cottage. Had I invited him later, he would've known exactly where to find us."

As his words spoke sense to her frustrations, Amy sighed. She hated the way Hugh could talk himself out of any situation —even if he was speaking the truth. "Very well, I believe you in that regard. But don't think we can go back to the way things were. I'm not going to follow your advice any longer. I cannot trust you."

He shrugged, looking very apathetic to her releasing him from her services. "Whatever you desire. Though, you may wish to reconsider when I earn your trust back by telling you the real reason Mr. Roberts has come to Coniston."

Amy's brow twitched. "He has already told me."

"That his feelings for you matched your own two months past? Surely you know that is not the whole truth, Amy."

The breath slowly seeped from her lungs. Mr. Roberts had lied to her? Her throat dried. "Then what *is* the whole truth?"

Hugh must have sensed her hesitancy, for instead of bounding forth with his information, he had the decency to pause for a moment.

"I will be the first to admit that I would not mind having Roberts for a brother-in-law. He and I were friends, if you recall, before any of this occurred between the two of you."

She looked away. She should not be the one to feel any semblance of guilt right now.

"Last night, Mr. Roberts had enough drinks to tell me the truth behind his sudden appearance. Apparently, his parents are finished with his inability to commit to marriage. They've refused him finances to gamble, purchase clothes, everything, until he finds himself a wife."

Amy's mind scrambled to make sense of the information. "So he came all the way to Coniston to attempt to marry me? Why not one of the thousands of women in Bath?"

"He tried to do so for a month, but one evening, he drunkenly told half of Bath his reasoning to marry."

"The man cannot hold his liquor, can he?"

"No, indeed. He's worse at drinking than he is at rowing."

Despite herself, Amy shared a smile with Hugh before he continued.

"Now the women he'd been pursuing will not even entertain the idea of being with him, for they all believe in the notion of marrying for love." Hugh scoffed. "After many failed attempts, Mr. Roberts hoped to come here before news of his true intentions reached you."

Amy shook her head in disbelief. Thank heavens she hadn't accepted the man's deceitful, desperate words enough to even consider being with him.

"I tried to tell you all of this earlier today, but since you've been avoiding me—"

"For good reason," she interrupted.

"Yes, for good reason. But now you see I am not in the wrong. Perhaps you and our parents will have a better opinion of me now."

Amy's heart reached out to him, despite her best efforts to remain apathetic. She didn't know if he truly worried over having people respect him or not, but it wouldn't hurt to give him a little encouragement. "Yes, perhaps we will."

He leaned toward her. "So, now that I've made amends with you, am I allowed to help you make your decisions again? Because I really think you ought to allow Mr. Roberts's pursual of you."

Amy's lips parted, her brow furrowing. "You can't be serious."

He did not have his usual teasing grin on his lips. "I am. Perfectly."

This time, it was her turn to scoff. "Hugh John Paxton, you have gone insane."

She made to walk past him, but he stopped her with an outstretched hand. "Come now, Amy, just listen for a moment. Mr. Roberts may not be perfect, but he's a good man inside. He was honest about his true intentions, was he not?"

"Oh, yes. Very honest, indeed. Only a few glasses of ale had to pull it out of him."

Hugh shrugged. "What does that matter if he is wealthy, Amy, with a good family name and a better reputation than your brother's? He also admitted that he does have a fondness for you."

"A fondness?" She pulled back. Weeks ago, she might've been flattered. But now, having his *fondness* was hardly appealing. "How flattering."

"You nearly loved him before. What is to stop you from doing so again?"

What was to stop her? One very great reason—and that specific reason was whom she needed to get back to this very moment.

With a shake of her head, she moved past Hugh, speaking over her shoulder. "You only want me to marry him because he's your friend. It's purely selfish motives with you, Hugh. As always."

"If you believe you are to marry Mr. Eastwood, I would rethink that logic, sister."

CHAPTER NINETEEN

*A*my's steps faltered. She turned around to face Hugh, anger flushing through her as she wondered if he was making threats or predictions. "Why is that?"

He stepped toward her. "I admit, I pushed you and Mr. Roberts to be on the boat together because I had thought perhaps this would encourage Mr. Eastwood to share his feelings for you out of sheer jealousy. But after spending more time with Mr. Eastwood, all I can say is that you would be better off with Mr. Roberts than that supposed gentleman."

"You only say that because of your argument with him. What did he do, stand up to you? Share his disapproval for your inappropriate behavior?" She leaned forward. "Express his disappointment in you like Mother and Father always have to do?"

His eyes hardened, and Amy regretted the words in an instant. As upset as she was, there was no reason for her to pick at Hugh's own wounds.

"Forgive me," she muttered. "Mr. Eastwood is a fine gentleman, and you know how I've grown to care for him. I do not appreciate..." She trailed off as he shook his head. "What is it?"

"Would a fine gentleman pursue a woman while he is already engaged to another?"

This again? When would the rumors stop? And when would her heart cease its dropping whenever she heard mention of it?

"He is not engaged. I've heard it from his own mouth." And she would trust him, like he'd trusted her with stories of his past.

"Don't be ridiculous, Amy. Why do you think the man is not yet married?"

She knew why. He'd told her himself he'd chosen not to marry until his grandfather passed. But she wasn't about to let Hugh know such a thing. She raised her chin. "Perhaps because he has not found the right woman."

Hugh barked out a mirthless laugh. "Oh, I assure you, he's found the perfect woman for him in Miss Charity Winslow. She's strong, as he clearly wishes his wife to be. She has been supporting her mother since Mr. Winslow passed. And she knows Mr. Eastwood better than any other woman in town."

She winced. Was there some truth to his words? Had Mr. Eastwood pulled away before he could kiss her because his conscience had spoken to him?

No. She refused to believe Hugh's words. They were friends. Mr. Eastwood and Miss Winslow were only friends.

"You are merely listening to Miss Cox and her gossip again, that is all," she said, if only to reassure herself.

"I've heard the same story from multiple sources. And I tell you now only to save you from future embarrassment. If you pursue Mr. Eastwood, you will be hurt, Amy. If you agree to marry Mr. Roberts, you will be contentedly settled for the rest of your life."

She closed her eyes, tears brimming at the edge, but she refused to release them. "No. No, I will not listen to this. I will not marry a man who does not love me."

"But you'll agree to marry a man who loves another?"

She gritted her teeth, trying to push aside the negative words infiltrating her mind. "Don't speak to me, Hugh. Don't ever speak to me again!"

She spun on her heel, rounding the corner of an empty, forsaken booth and barreling straight into Mr. Eastwood's chest. She pulled back, his hands around her upper arms to steady her in an instant.

"Miss Paxton?" Concern creased his brow as his eyes lingered on her tears. "What happened? Are you well?"

"Yes, I assure you."

"Ah, Mr. Eastwood. Here you are again."

Amy spun around as Hugh approached them, a pointed look in his eyes. Would he confront Mr. Eastwood about Miss Winslow? Or…or would he tell Mr. Eastwood about Amy's failed attempt to marry Mr. Roberts?

Her insides broiled. She wanted to believe Hugh would respect her enough to keep his words to himself, but there was no way she could.

"Are you the cause of your sister's distress, sir?" Mr. Eastwood said, taking a step forward to stand equally beside Amy.

Hugh barked a bitter laugh. "I wouldn't say *I* was, Mr. Eastwood."

"Hugh, stop," Amy pleaded.

He wouldn't look at her.

"Forgive me, but I find that difficult to believe." Mr. Eastwood took another step toward him. "Especially when you continuously give her poor advice on how to behave. What gives you the right to do such a thing?"

A wicked smile spread across Hugh's lips. "Oh, so my sister has not told you why she's chosen me to make her decisions for her?"

Amy's breathing grew heavy. This could not be happening. She could not allow this conversation to continue.

Mr. Eastwood's eyes flicked to Amy's. "It matters not what

her reasonings are. What matters is that I have had enough of seeing the way you treat her."

"Oh, the way *I* treat her?" Hugh shook his head. "And what of yourself, sir?"

Mr. Eastwood's fists clenched. "I've treated your sister with nothing but respect from the start."

"Respect? Funny way to show it."

Amy shook her head. She was the one who needed to tell Mr. Eastwood about everything—about Mr. Roberts, about the rumors—everything.

And she would do it now, before anything further happened.

"What do you mean by that, sir?" Mr. Eastwood asked.

"I mean, how can you show respect when you are—"

"Hugh!" Amy said through clenched teeth. Never had she spoken so harshly, never had she been so angry. With a look of warning, she held up her hand. "Stop, now."

Finally, he did, his chest rising and falling. She turned to Mr. Eastwood. "Please, come with me."

Mr. Eastwood hesitated, still staring at Hugh, but when she pressed an entreating hand against his arm, he finally relented.

They walked away, and Amy looked over her shoulder to ensure Hugh stayed put. He was already walking in the opposite direction with a shake of his head.

Amy could not yet breathe a sigh of relief, for she expected the next conversation to be even more difficult than the last.

They remained silent as Amy led the way past more people and booths and food until they reached the field opposite the fair, where two large draft horses stood near the fence.

"May I speak candidly with you, Mr. Eastwood?" she asked as they paused near the horses.

"Of course." His brow pursed warily.

She turned to face the Clydesdales, focusing on their dark brown coats and white, feathered feet as the horses grazed lazily in the grass.

"I don't really know where to begin," she said in a sort of daze, "but I do wish to explain to you a few things, things that I believe will help you to understand my behavior—as well as the argument I've just had with my brother."

Mr. Eastwood stared down at her. Though he remained silent, she could see the intrigue in his eyes.

"You see, I never would have asked Hugh to make my decisions for me—or rather, to advise me on certain decisions I made—were it not for my utter incompetence around gentlemen."

Mr. Eastwood gave a soft laugh. "Forgive me, but I find such an incompetence from you hard to believe."

Though flattered by his words, she shook her head. "No, it is true. I am inept. Truly. You see..." She looked to the horses again. "A few months ago, before we came to Coniston, I found myself quite enraptured by Mr. Roberts. I told him, without any prompting or any notion of his feelings, that I wished to marry him."

William blinked hard to keep his eyes from widening. Miss Paxton had said such a thing? And to Mr. Roberts? He *knew* there had to be something between them. So...she'd liked him enough to share such words with him? A knot the size of Cumbria tied in his stomach.

Miss Paxton continued. "Mr. Roberts was rightfully taken aback. He swiftly expressed his lack of feelings for me, and that was that. I decided to enlist Hugh's help to stop my poor decision-making before I could humiliate myself any further."

"I see."

And he *could* see. He knew how Miss Paxton disliked to be embarrassed. He also knew her aptitude for being rather blunt. Most gentlemen would be frightened of such forward behavior, though William himself would not —*was* not.

Still, confusion muddled his mind.

He pressed a hand to his brow. "Forgive me, I cannot understand why making one slightly poor decision would lead you to seeking your brother's help, of all people."

Her cheeks shaded pink. "Well, it was not just the one time. It happened before with a distant cousin of ours a year ago. And...and I've been known to lose friendships due to men and women alike being put off by my forthright behavior."

Understanding dawned. But still. "Why Hugh?"

She shrugged. "It is as I said before. Most people seem to like him. Present company excluded."

They shared a wry smile before she released a sigh.

"Of course, the poorest of decisions I've ever made was asking him to decide my life for me."

William nodded, his mind wandering from question after question before finally settling on one. "Do you know why Mr. Roberts has come to visit here?" William had to know if it was Hugh's invitation that brought him here or something else.

Miss Paxton's shoulders fell. "That is what I was just discussing with Hugh. You see, on the boat, Mr. Roberts expressed his devotion to me, that he was wrong before about his lack of feelings, then ended with a proposal."

William swallowed the anger rising within him. There was no reason to be upset with the man who had clearly not won Miss Paxton's hand. But still, the thought of his unkindness shifting to a proposal was beyond him.

"However," she continued, "Hugh has informed me that Mr. Roberts only wishes to marry me to get back his restricted finances—as no other woman in Bath would."

William shook his head in disbelief. "So he feigned feelings for you simply to receive money?"

"Yes. And this was after fleeing Bath to escape the rumors

he'd so graciously left in my stead." She laughed derisively. "What a gentleman, is he not?"

He pulled up a lip in disgust. He couldn't understand Mr. Roberts as much as he couldn't understand Hugh. How could any gentleman refuse Miss Paxton, then spread rumors about a woman so good and kind as she?

"So there you have it," she finally finished. "The pitiful tale of Miss Amy Paxton. Too unlikeable and too desperate to have any gentleman appreciate her enough for herself."

She'd spoken the words with a smile, but William had not missed the sorrow in her tone. His heart reached out to her, unsure of what to say. He'd been hesitant to see her today after last evening, after what might have occurred.

But when her eyes continually stole toward him, he'd been unable to keep himself from her any longer. He'd done quite a lot of soul-searching the night before, and though he hadn't come to any real conclusions, he did know one thing—he needed to be honest about his relationship with Charity.

Perhaps then he'd be rewarded with more clarity. Or so he'd hoped. But then Hugh had interrupted, and Miss Paxton's confession had come. Now was not the right time. Not when she was already beaten down by her confrontation with her miserable brother.

"I'm sorry you've been injured so many times," he began. "But please, don't call yourself desperate."

She peered up at him, clearly hanging on to his every word.

His voice softened. "There is nothing wrong with wishing for love, or wanting to be loved in return. That is what the world thrives on, after all."

His eyes dropped to her hand resting on the fence. "But there are people in this world who do care for you, who accept you for who you are—blunt words, talented in Battledore and Shuttlecock, love of hens and all."

Her lips curled, tears brimming in her eyes, and his heart

swirled, light and airy, as if caught in a draft of wind. He needed to stop, to be honest with her.

But wasn't he being honest with her right now?

He reached forward, resting his hand atop hers. "All you must do is learn to accept yourself, to be happy with yourself. Because you, Miss Paxton, shine brighter than any person I know."

Her brow raised, and a tear slid down her cheek. She laughed embarrassedly, hurriedly wiping it away.

"You certainly have a way with words, Mr. Eastwood. Thank you."

Their eyes met, and his heart twisted with feelings he did not wish to understand. He wished to revel in the joy he felt in making her smile, in the happiness he experienced whenever he was near this woman.

But his conscience prevented him. "Miss Paxton—"

"Mr. Eastwood—" She began at the same time. "Oh, go on."

"No, you, please."

"All right. There was something else Hugh and I argued over. Regarding you."

He swallowed with a nod. "Yes?"

"About the rumors surrounding your name…with Miss Winslow."

The breath slipped from his lungs.

"I told Hugh I would not listen to the rumors, but today, there were stares as you and I walked together. Stares and whispers. I do not wish to pry, nor press you into speaking of something you don't wish to speak of, but I cannot help but wonder…"

William wet his lips, nodding his head up and down in a quick motion. He needed to be honest. But how could he tell the truth now that his feelings for her filled his heart so full, he could no longer deny them?

He would tell her now. He would tell her that he had

planned his whole life to marry Charity Winslow, but now that he'd met Amy Paxton…

"William?"

No. No, it couldn't be. And yet, he knew that voice.

Charity.

CHAPTER TWENTY

*A*my swiveled her head around as Mr. Eastwood did the same.

Three strangers stood before them. One, a young woman with dark curls shining in the evening sunlight. The other two, an older man and woman, stood on either side of the young lady.

The gentleman looked far too similar to William to be a coincidence.

Amy's throat tightened. She knew exactly who these people were, and the sudden shift in Mr. Eastwood's mood confirmed it.

"Mother, Father?" He swiped his hand swiftly from Amy's as he swallowed. "Charity."

The words were a blow to Amy's confidence. He'd called her Charity.

This time, she could not find the strength to deny the imposing thought. Now the stares and the whispers, the rumors and the talk, all made perfect sense. He and Miss Winslow were more than friends.

Amy stood in a stupor as he moved forward, greeting his

parents as the three sets of eyes examined her as if she were one of the farm animals on display.

Amy had done nothing wrong. But then, why did she feel guilty, as if her childish hands had been caught pulling flowers from her mother's rose garden?

"What on earth are you doing here?" Mr. Eastwood asked as he kissed his mother's cheek and nodded toward his father with a strained smile. "I wasn't expecting any of you for months."

"We thought to surprise you." The woman Amy knew must be Mrs. Eastwood sent another lasting glance toward her. "It was Charity's idea."

Charity. The young woman's dark eyes finally pulled away from Amy and focused on Mr. Eastwood.

"William." Her tone was as smooth as silk. "How pleased I am to have returned to you at last."

She stood on the tips of her toes and placed a lingering kiss to William's cheek.

Amy's heart stuttered to a halt. That was no kiss of friend-ship, nor was that look she was giving him now.

Despite all Mr. Eastwood had said, despite all Amy had believed, there was something more between the two of them, just as she'd feared. Just as Hugh had warned her.

And there she was, standing like the gullible simpleton that she was.

Longing to escape, she took a furtive step to the side, but her movement, slight as it was, drew the attention back to her.

"Well, son," Mr. Eastwood's father said, "we are anxious to speak with you, but for now, perhaps you might introduce us to this young lady."

"Yes, yes, of course."

Mr. Eastwood turned toward Amy. She didn't know what to feel as their eyes met. Anger bubbled within her first, followed swiftly by sheer, utter humiliation. Why? Why would he lie in such a way?

In that split second their eyes met, a whole conversation seemed to occur.

"How could you?"

"I'm sorry."

"I thought you said..."

"I can't explain it. Not right now."

"William?" his mother prodded.

He tore his eyes away. "This is Miss Amy Paxton. Miss Paxton, my parents, Mr. and Mrs. Eastwood. And my...and this is Miss Charity Winslow."

Miss Winslow's eyes snapped to Mr. Eastwood's at his clear hesitance, though her rehearsed smile did not falter. "Pleasure to meet you, Miss Paxton. I assume you are visiting our wonderful Coniston?"

"Yes." Amy's voice croaked like the frogs Hugh had once hidden in her room when she was a child. She cleared her throat with a blush. "Yes, I am staying at the cottage with my family for the autumn."

"The cottage?" Mr. Eastwood's father sent a sharp gaze to his son.

"Yes, Father. I wrote to you about the situation."

"No, I'm afraid you didn't, son."

Silence thickened the tension already enveloping the group. Had his father truly not known? Were they upset about it, enough to evict the Paxtons? Or did Mr. Eastwood have enough control that they'd be safe at Flitfield?

"Well," Mrs. Eastwood piped in, "I do hope you enjoy the rest of your stay, Miss Paxton. I look forward to getting to know you and your family a little better."

Amy could only nod her appreciation.

Silence cloaked the group once again, and finally, Amy's senses returned.

She inched away from the group. "It was lovely to meet you all, but if you'll excuse me, my mother and father will be wondering where I am."

They murmured their goodbyes, Mr. Eastwood's eyes lingering the longest on her, but Amy refused to meet his gaze. She couldn't let him see the tears sliding down her cheeks.

Amy had told her parents what happened only after they'd promised to never relay the information to Hugh. He would surely hear of it soon enough, but for right now, she could not bear his waving the proverbial flag of victory, drawing attention to yet another one of her follies.

She and her parents had left the fair early together—without Hugh and Mr. Roberts—and Amy had shared with them her argument with her brother first before recounting her heartache over Mr. Eastwood and the woman he'd assured her twice was merely his friend.

Father had listened in silence, neither stewing nor threatening Mr. Eastwood. Mama, however, had wrapped her arms around Amy, just like the last two times she'd been rejected.

Of course, this time was different. This time, Mr. Eastwood had not outright rejected her. He only lied to her from the beginning, hiding his relationship with Miss Winslow.

And this time, Amy's heart had not merely been wounded by embarrassment. It had been broken. Because she was not merely infatuated with Mr. Eastwood.

She was in love with him.

She'd realized this truth as the coming days began to blur together into one, continuous, never-ending monotony. Without the knowledge that she would get to see Mr. Eastwood —hear his encouragement, feel his support—that he would instead be spending his days with Miss Winslow, Amy had hardly managed to pull herself out of bed.

Hugh had to know something had occurred, especially since

she was fairly certain the entire town knew of Miss Winslow's return, so she'd kept away from everyone, eating her meals in her room and refusing to leave for anything. Hugh had come to her a few times, but she'd refused to answer, even after his soft apologies were whispered between the crack of the door and wall.

After four days, however, Mama came to her room, entreating Amy to leave the house.

"It's a beautiful day," she said, drawing back the curtains so the sunshine spilled forward in speckled rays across the dusty room. "I think your soul is in need of a little sunshine."

Amy grumbled an indecipherable answer, throwing the covers over her head, but Mama tossed them right back.

"Come along. I must make a call and would appreciate the company."

"I cannot stomach a call today."

"Not even with Mrs. Rutledge?"

Heavens, especially Mrs. Rutledge. There would be no way to avoid thinking of Mr. Eastwood in the woman's home, where there were sure to be constant reminders and conversations centered around the gentleman.

"Amy, she will surely be disappointed if you do not join me. I know she's felt remorse over not yet having us over for the pie, even after all she has been through."

Amy finally rolled out of bed, her conscience pricked. She would be selfish, indeed, if she refused to call upon a woman going through so much.

After dressing, Amy and her mother walked the short distance to town. A few stray clouds drifted over the sun, sending alternating waves of cool and warmth across their shoulders until they reached the Rutledges.

As they sat and visited with the woman whose cheery spirits had remained almost unaltered, despite her husband's waning health, Amy found her mood slowly shifting. For days, she'd been wallowing over the loss of a love she'd known for only weeks. Mrs. Rutledge had to have been married for nearly forty years. Despite the grief she must have felt acutely, the woman could still get out of bed that morning and smile for visitors.

Surely Amy could do the same.

"It is difficult," Mrs. Rutledge whispered as she set her half-eaten piece of pie to the side. Her voice was low to not disturb her sleeping husband. "To watch his suffering our entire lives, and to have it end this way, it is nothing short of heartbreaking. But how grateful I am to have had the time I did with him. And how grateful I am for my own health, so I could take care of him. We truly are blessed."

By the end of their visit, Amy left the small home utterly chastened. She had been behaving ridiculously, moping about her room for days. It was time to make a change.

"What a remarkable woman," Mama commented as they moved down the road.

Amy could only nod. No wonder Mr. Eastwood had been drawn to the couple. They were the best sorts of people.

A cold draft blew up the street, greeting Amy with a tickle across her neck. Dense clouds had gathered in the sky while they'd visited Mrs. Rutledge, and thick raindrops just now began to slip down from above. In a matter of moments, the steady trickling turned into a full-on storm, as if water flowed forth from a pump in the sky.

Amy was used to the sudden rainstorms they often received in the Lake District, what with how frequently they occurred. But the cold rain would be unbearable if they left it for too long.

"We really ought to stop putting our faith in the weather and take our carriage next time we leave the cottage," Mama said. She motioned down the street. "The bakery. Let us warm up with a cup of tea and see if we cannot wait for this rain to settle.

Amy smiled, following Mama at once. "Perhaps we may bring back a few buns for Father."

Mama gave her a warm smile. "Wonderful idea."

Amy thought so, too, until she walked into the bakery and noticed who occupied the far corner of the otherwise empty room. Mr. Eastwood sat next to Miss Winslow at a small table, and across from them were his parents and a woman with graying temples.

Amy swiveled around, her back facing the others. "Mama, we must leave at once."

Mama pursed her brow before settling her eyes on Mr. East-wood. "Yes, let us go."

They only managed a single step, however, before Mrs. Eastwood spoke from behind them. "Miss Paxton? Is that you?"

Blast. Amy couldn't leave now without being considered the most uncivil lady in all of Coniston. With a deflated sigh, she slowly turned to face the others.

Mr. Eastwood stood with his father as Amy and Mama approached, glancing between Amy and Miss Winslow before settling on his teacup still resting on the table.

"How lovely to see you again, Miss Paxton," Mrs. Eastwood said, her words hinting of all politeness, though her smile seemed anything but genuine. "This must be your mother."

Had Mr. Eastwood told his loved ones about the time he'd spent with Amy? Or did they all suspect that Amy was in love with Mr. Eastwood? Setting her questions aside, she introduced Mama to the Eastwoods and Miss Winslow, stopping on the woman with graying temples.

"This is Mrs. Winslow," Mrs. Eastwood added. "Miss Winslow's mother."

Mrs. Winslow's eyes had narrowed even more than her daughter's. "Pleasure," she said stiffly.

"I assume you've decided to take shelter from the rain, too?" Mrs. Eastwood said next.

Amy felt eyes watching her, and she glanced in time to see

Mr. Eastwood pull swiftly away. Miss Winslow looked between them, and Amy's ears burned.

"Indeed, we have," Mama replied. "Though only for a moment to purchase a few items. We wouldn't wish to interrupt you further, though. Please, excuse us."

Amy had never been more grateful for a compassionate mother than in that moment. Being soaked through was far better than staying there a second longer.

They turned to approach the front counter, but a young woman with a dark blue apron came up right beside them before they could move an inch.

"Care for some tea?"

"No, thank you. Just a few Chelsea buns to take along with us."

"In this weather?" The young woman eyed the rain still dotting the window with loud plinks against the glass. "That can hardly be wise, ma'am. I insist you allow me to bring you a cup of tea" She motioned to the Eastwoods and Winslows. "Then you can join your friends here."

Amy gritted her teeth. Could the girl not feel the tension between the families?

"Oh, we wouldn't wish to intrude," Mama said with a glance to the others.

Silence followed, and the young server eyed the Eastwoods and Winslows expectantly.

Finally, the elder Mr. Eastwood nodded. "It wouldn't be an intrusion at all. In fact, I insist you join us."

Before Mother or Amy could protest again, he'd enlisted his son to aid in drawing another table to theirs.

"Mrs. Paxton," the father said, motioning to the chair beside his own wife.

The movements happened so swiftly, Amy remained standing in a daze. How did they manage to be maneuvered into such an uncomfortable situation?

"Miss Paxton?"

She blinked, only then noticing Mr. Eastwood standing by the only empty seat remaining—the seat next to his.

As all eyes fell on Amy, she moved slowly forward, sitting at the very far side of her seat to avoid any accidental touch of the gentleman.

An awkward silence gripped the group. If the tea was delivered faster, they could leave in a shorter amount of time. Amy peered over her shoulder to the empty front counter. Of course *now* the girl was nowhere to be seen.

"I trust you're enjoying your stay in the cottage," Mrs. Eastwood said, finally breaking the stillness.

Amy glanced to the elder Mr. Eastwood. At the mention of Flitfield last time, he'd visibly stiffened. Now, however, he seemed quite at ease. Had he and his son discussed the occurrence? Did he trust in Mr. Eastwood's ability to improve and profit honorably from their estates?

She longed to glance to Mr. Eastwood, but seated so closely beside him, surely the others would notice.

"We are, indeed," Mama replied. "It is a pleasant change from our estate just outside of Bath. There's certainly a different pace here. One we quite enjoy."

"And when will you be returning to Bath?" Mrs. Winslow asked.

"We are scheduled to leave in just another month."

Mrs. Eastwood's smile faltered. "How lovely that we shall get to know you a little better then."

Mama and Amy exchanged glances. They'd both heard the woman's disappointment over their staying longer.

"I hope you enjoy the remainder of your visit." Miss Winslow leaned forward with a polite glance at Amy.

Amy nodded her gratitude, leaning back in her seat to hide from the woman's calculating gaze.

Mr. Eastwood didn't move.

Finally, the tea was brought forth for Amy and Mama, and Amy did her best not to chug the scalding liquid to escape faster. It mattered not how quickly she drank it anyway. Mama would never drink in an unladylike fashion.

The conversation focused on the beauty of Coniston for a moment before Miss Winslow turned to Mr. Eastwood. "Oh, William, won't it be lovely to enjoy the scenery again together? I have very much missed our daily rides across the countryside."

"Indeed," Mr. Eastwood mumbled.

Amy sipped her tea.

"Oh, but we must wait until there is no chance at being caught in a storm," Miss Winslow continued. "You know I cannot abide getting wet. I'm sure you recall the time we rode as children and were drenched through?"

"Yes, I remember."

Amy lowered her gaze. Was that why William had stared at her on the boat when she'd admitted to not minding a little rain or lake water? He'd been comparing her to his perfect Miss Winslow who was too ladylike to enjoy such a thing?

Miss Winslow then proceeded to face the others, detailing a very lengthy story that Amy was certain could have been told in one sentence.

Amy knew she was unwelcome with these two families. Unwelcome and unwanted. Mr. Eastwood must have felt her discomfort, too, but he did nothing to quell her unease, simply remaining silent, not looking in her direction once.

If he hadn't visited her in four days to explain his lies, she didn't know why she'd expect him to comfort her now.

Amy recalled her determination to remain more positive, to remain unaffected by what had happened—or rather, had not happened—between her and Mr. Eastwood.

But as story after story was told by Miss Winslow about her time with Mr. Eastwood—riding horses and reading books— Amy could hardly bear it. Nor could she bear the fact that Mr.

Eastwood did not say a single word to her as she sat beside him, though he had more than one opportunity to do so.

This was just another sign that he was attached to Miss Winslow, as well as the fact that Mrs. Eastwood and Mrs. Winslow could not seem to keep their disconcerting gazes off of Amy. They suspected something between Amy and Mr. Eastwood, of course. And they were judging her for it.

But Amy had not known Mr. Eastwood was engaged.

Her insides curled like a fallen leaf in the heat of the sun. She may not have known he was engaged, but she *had* suspected something. And she'd still gone ahead and fallen in love with him anyway.

She was no better than he was for lying.

As the tea sloshed, discomfited in her stomach, Amy peered out the window. The rain had settled, and a break in the clouds allowed the sun to blare forth, twinkling the droplets on the glass like round stars.

When conversation lulled—or rather, when Miss Winslow finally ceased her stories—Amy caught her mother's attention and motioned to the window.

"Mama, the rain has let up for a moment. Perhaps we ought to take our leave before it begins again."

Mama nodded her understanding at once, stepping away from the table. "Fine idea, my dear." She faced the others. "Thank you all so much for allowing us to join you."

A murmur of farewell followed.

"It was lovely to get to know you a little better, Miss Paxton," Miss Winslow said, though Amy had hardly said a word. "It's a shame you'll be leaving us in only a month's time. There are so many gentlemen here who would have loved to have made your acquaintance, I'm sure. Perhaps before you leave, my William and I will be able to introduce you to them."

Amy's cheeks burned. *Her* William.

Embarrassment flushed freely throughout her—which had

no doubt been Miss Winslow's intention. Amy could not blame her. If William *was* Charity's, she had every right to stake her claim.

Still, Amy raised her chin all the same. "As you said, our visit will not be long enough to necessitate such introductions. But I thank you for the offer, all the same."

With a nod and her small parcel of Chelsea buns in hand for Papa, Amy left the bakery with Mama, sending only a fleeting glance back at the others. Miss Winslow was the only one watching her, and though the woman smiled, she slid her arm through Mr. Eastwood's with a pointed look at Amy.

Without another glance at Mr. Eastwood, Amy left the shop.

"Oh, my dear," Mama said at once, wrapping her arm around Amy's shoulders. "I'm so sorry."

Amy shook her head. "You needn't apologize. I blame my own stupidity for allowing myself to fall for the gentleman in the first place."

"It is not as if you knew he was soon to be engaged."

Amy swallowed, turning away from Mama. That was one thing she'd omitted from her parents when she'd recounted all that had occurred between her and Mr. Eastwood. She couldn't bear her parents yet again thinking she was a simpleton by not seeing the signs that Mr. Eastwood was, indeed, attached to Miss Winslow—despite his frequent denials.

They continued down the road, the sun having swiftly been shadowed by the dark clouds once again. As the first raindrop hit against their bonnets, they increased their speed, moving past the shops to reach the small, terraced houses.

The wind increased, blowing an errant drop against her face. Amy reached for her handkerchief to wipe the moisture from her brow, only then realizing she did not have her reticule.

"Oh, no," she breathed, her pace slowing as she closed her eyes.

"What is it?" Mama asked.

"I've left my reticule at the bakery."

"I'll return for it," Mama decided at once.

Relief flooded Amy's limbs, but as another drop fell from the sky, she hesitated. She could not ask her mother to do such a thing if it meant Mama would be in the rain for even longer.

She sighed with lowered shoulders. "No, I will do so."

"Are you sure?"

"Yes. I'll slip in and out of the shop. They are most likely gone anyway. You carry on, and I will catch up with you directly."

Amy left her hesitant mother, scurrying through the streets, though dread filled her to face the families again.

Perhaps they'd be gone. Or perhaps they would ignore her as much as she wished to ignore them?

She continued rifling through different scenarios until she looked ahead and saw the very man she wished to avoid walking toward her, and her heart stumbled.

CHAPTER TWENTY-ONE

*A*my slowed her steps, ready to turn back around to avoid another awkward confrontation with Mr. Eastwood, but as she realized his family was nowhere in sight, and that he clutched her reticule in his hand, she paused.

There was no logical reason for her to run away now. Especially when his eyes locked onto hers until he stopped a few paces away from her.

He nodded his head in a simple greeting.

"I was just returning for that." She motioned to her reticule he still grasped in his hand.

"Oh, yes." He extended it toward her, and she was careful not to touch him as she retrieved it. "I noticed you dropped it only a moment after you left."

Amy nodded, eying the rain speckling his black jacket. "Well, I must thank you for saving me from making the entire journey back."

She took a step away at the same time he moved forward. "Did you enjoy the tea at the bakery?" he asked.

What was his purpose in drawing out this unpleasant, stilted conversation? Did he not worry that Miss Winslow would discover him and call him out for his behavior? Or did he think he could get away with lying to both women?

"I did."

He nodded. "I'm sorry I didn't have the opportunity to speak with you more."

Frustration sparked inside her. She tried to hold her tongue, to remain pleasant as he was, but then, why should she?

"You did not have the opportunity?" she asked, tipping her head to the side. "Or you did not wish to speak to me in front of Miss Winslow?"

Mr. Eastwood's cheeks turned a shade Amy had never seen before. "Miss Paxton, forgive me. There is no excuse for my behavior toward you. I wished to come to the cottage to explain, but my time has not been my own. And I tried so often to tell you the truth before this."

His clear discomfort fanned the flame of her confidence. "The truth? The truth about what exactly? That you are, in fact, engaged?"

"I am *not* engaged to her."

She blew out an incredulous laugh. "How can you say such a thing?"

He drew closer to her, his brow furrowed. "Because it is the truth. We are not officially engaged. We never have been. However…" He swallowed, wincing. "We have discussed at length about…about marriage."

Hearing the admission, knowing it was the truth, was the final dagger to her heart. The breath rushed from her lungs, her anger dissipating as hurt rushed to fill the hole his dishonesty had caused.

"I don't understand why you didn't tell me when I gave you opportunity after opportunity to be honest with me."

"I tried," he rushed on, a pained expression on his brow. "I did. When you first asked me about Miss Winslow, I did not tell you because I wished to keep my business to myself. As the weeks passed by and we spent more time together, I knew I could trust you enough to tell you, but I did not wish for our friendship to change."

She shook her head, attempting to swallow the information he'd given. "Did you not consider that our friendship *would* change upon the arrival of Miss Winslow?"

He lowered his head. "I thought you would be gone from Coniston long before she returned."

The words struck Amy to her very core. Of course. He was simply having fun with Amy. She was just a friend to help pass the time before Miss Winslow returned. He cared not for Amy, only for his own well-being.

"So you were using my presence as a balm to ease your missing Miss Winslow?"

His brow furrowed. "No, that is not what our friendship is at all, Miss Paxton."

With a shake of her head, she backed away, unwilling to listen any longer. "Well, you may have your wish now, Mr. Eastwood. I'll remain at the cottage until we depart Coniston so you will never have to see me again. Good day, sir."

She left him there, standing in the rain, as dejected as a child who'd lost himself and his missing dog in the woods.

It wasn't too far from the truth. Mr. Eastwood had lost his pet in Amy. She only hoped Miss Winslow knew what she was getting into by marrying someone so dishonest.

Miss Winslow. Her footsteps slowed until she stopped altogether. Turning on her heel, she found Mr. Eastwood still in the same spot as before.

She hesitated only a moment. She really should not be discussing such private matters, especially in the middle of the village, but honestly, what did she have to lose now?

"I can understand how you could be dishonest with me, sir," she said, slowly stepping toward him. "After all, you have known me for a mere month. Miss Winslow, on the other hand...I assume she knows nothing about the fact that we nearly kissed."

Mr. Eastwood flinched, but his eyes remained on hers. "No, she does not."

"How could you keep that from her? How could you be so dishonest with the woman you love?"

"I don't lo—" He stopped abruptly, turning to face the opposite side of the street. His jaw twitched. "There is no excuse for my behavior, for my treatment of either one of you."

Amy narrowed her eyes, her heart pattering against her chest for reasons she could not understand. "You do not love her?"

He moved toward her, lowering his voice. "I didn't say such a thing."

But she'd heard him nearly say it. And Miss Winslow had to love him, didn't she? What with how possessive she'd been and the way she stared at him with sparkling eyes.

Mr. Eastwood gave a heavy sigh. "It is complicated between the two of us. Our pasts are intertwined in an inexplicable sort of way."

"So you marry her due to a connection between your families?"

She really had no right to be asking such questions. But then, he had forfeited the right to privacy by lying to her, had he not?

"No, there are other reasons."

Amy waited, but he kept silent. Clearly, he was unwilling to divulge any more information. And Amy was finished waiting. She needn't hear what he had to say anyway. No matter what it was, it wouldn't change what had occurred between them—or the fact that Mr. Eastwood would marry Miss Winslow.

"Miss Paxton—"

"Excuse me, Mr. Eastwood. I must return to Mama before the storm worsens."

She turned away, but he ran in front of her, blocking her

path with a raised hand. "No, surely you must understand. My life has been dictated by Grandfather from the beginning. When I was a young man, I made the choice to marry Miss Winslow because Grandfather did not approve of her. But since then, I've been made to realize certain facts about our families. I must marry Charity because I owe it to the Winslows."

Amy shook her head. "This is none of my business, Mr. Eastwood."

She wasn't going to listen to this. Nothing he said would ease her broken heart. She walked past him with a raised chin.

"Please, Miss Paxton," he called after her. The pleading in his voice made her feet stop of their own accord. Slowly she turned to face him.

Sorrow flooded his green eyes, and the helpless expression on his face reminded her again of that little boy lost in the woods. "My grandfather is the reason Miss Winslow's father is dead."

"What?" she breathed.

Mr. Eastwood took a step closer to her, lowering his voice. "When my grandfather discovered his wife with another man... that man was Mr. Abraham Winslow, Miss Winslow's grandfather."

The breath rushed from her lungs, though confusion still lingered before Mr. Eastwood continued.

"Miss Winslow and I were not alive for any of this, though my father and hers were both nearing ten years old and remembered the rumors around their two families. Grandfather did not discover the truth about his wife until years later when he found letters at the manor written from Mr. Abraham Winslow. Naturally, he challenged him to a duel. Mr. Abraham Winslow failed to appear on the date settled and was labeled a coward."

William winced as he continued. "As years passed, Miss Winslow's father grew, and at age seven and twenty, when Miss Winslow was merely six years of age, he, along with his father—

who had died from disease of the lungs years earlier—were publicly called cowards by my grandfather. Mr. Winslow would not stand for the humiliation, nor to have all of Society know about his father's abandonment of the duel. He then challenged my grandfather to a duel. Given their significant age difference, Grandfather should have refused. But he accepted, and Mr. Winslow was killed."

Amy's mind swirled as she attempted to piece together the information, Mr. Eastwood rushing forward.

"The duel was kept quiet, and only our two families—and the Rutledges—know the full truth of what occurred. Miss Winslow and I had no notion until her mother informed us. My grandfather forbade me to have any contact with the Winslows. But knowing what I did, that Grandfather was the reason their family struggles to make ends meet every day, I could not keep away."

He paused, searching Amy's expression. "Do you see, Miss Paxton? My relationship with Miss Winslow is not simple. I am required to do this, to fix what Grandfather destroyed years ago. To help her family in any way I can. I could not share with you all of this before, no matter how I wished to."

Amy shook her head, her breathing calm. "I understand. I understand your desire to keep such a history quiet between your two families. But that still does not explain to me why you could not have said you were going to marry Miss Winslow."

Amy would not feel remorse for her honest question, not even with Mr. Eastwood's crestfallen face.

"Because I was afraid. I was afraid you would no longer speak with me. I was afraid to lose the light you'd brought into my life."

Her chest constricted. What was he saying?

"Amy," he breathed, her Christian name on his lips making her legs tremble. "My feelings for you…"

She squeezed her eyes closed, shaking her head firmly.

She couldn't. She couldn't listen to him say it, no matter how badly she wished to hear it. She couldn't hear him express any feelings he might have for her. Not when his reasons for being with Miss Winslow were so valiant, and so very convoluted.

And Amy would not hurt Miss Winslow like Amy had just been hurt herself.

"Amy?"

"No." She backed away, shaking her head. "No, Mr. Eastwood. Go back to your family. To Miss Winslow. And I will go back to mine." Emotion swelled in her throat. "Hugh was right. I never should have pursued you."

~

The last of the rain dissipated as William returned to the bakery. Shortly after, the clouds dispersed, warming Coniston and its inhabitants with bright sunshine.

But William could not feel any warmth. After sharing the full truth with Miss Paxton, he longed to believe that she'd left him alone in the road because she disapproved of his past and his family so very greatly.

But he knew she'd left because she'd disapproved of *him* so greatly.

He followed his family and the Winslows down the road for another hour, browsing through shop windows and purchasing a few goods before they made to leave.

"William, would you mind if we walked instead of taking the carriage?" Charity asked as the others filed in. "I have a sudden desire to stretch my legs a little longer."

He swallowed. Charity never chose to walk over ride. She despised walking more than she despised getting caught in the rain. Surely she and his family had seen him holding Amy's hand, as well as the looks shared between them. No one had mentioned a word about it. But would that end with this walk?

"Oh, but the streets will be so very muddy, Charity," Mrs. Winslow said, concerned as ever for her daughter's well-being.

"That is true," William agreed.

"I'm certain William will see she returns clean and in one piece," Mother said. "Will you not, son?"

William nodded. "Of course."

The carriage pulled away, and William moved toward the outskirts of town, only to be halted a brief moment as Charity threaded her hand through his arm.

When Miss Paxton had done the very same, it had taken a great deal of focus to keep moving one step in front of the other. With Charity, there was not even a stirring of his heart.

Did he expect there to be one, after he'd declared—to Miss Paxton, no less—that he did not love Charity?

In truth, he knew all along that he did not, though he'd regretted his words the moment they'd left his mouth. He knew Miss Paxton would never tell a soul, but admitting to not loving the woman he'd planned to marry was not ideal.

"What are you thinking of so deeply, William?"

He blinked. "Nothing of importance. I'm glad you suggested to walk. It is proving to be a fine day after all."

Charity squeezed his arm. His heart didn't respond. "I must admit, I had an ulterior motive in asking you. You do recall how I dislike walking?"

"Of course." Amy enjoyed walking, like he did.

"It is just that, well, we've not had much time with only the two of us since my return, and I would very much like to discuss our future."

He'd always admired her boldness. She had been the only woman he knew who did not dance around with words—until he met Miss Paxton. Now Miss Paxton's boldness impressed him, and Charity's, well, frankly, it frightened him.

Would she be discussing how their future was affected by his obvious attachment to Miss Paxton?

He tugged at his cravat with his free hand. "Very well."

"The Paxtons seem like a fine family."

Those weren't the words he'd expected. He answered carefully. "Yes, I believe they are."

"And Miss Paxton is as lovely a woman as I have ever seen."

William swallowed, unable to respond. Why was it so blasted hot in the middle of autumn? Where was the cool rain from before? The rain that had slid down the edge of Miss Paxton's straw bonnet and speckled the blue of her gown.

Charity kept her gaze focused forward. "Did you have much time to get to know her?"

He struggled to draw a deep breath, his vision beginning to blur. "I suppose I did. I was required to mend the cottage often, so naturally I grew to know her and her family."

Would Charity accept his skirted response?

She stopped walking, turning to face him directly. Her dark eyes peered into his. For years, they had been friends, for years they'd spoken daily and gotten to know one another better than anyone. He knew she suspected something more was going on. Would she press it? Would she make him say the truth—that he had deep, undeniable feelings for Miss Paxton? Or did she wish to avoid hearing the words aloud as much as he did?

A lifetime passed before she finally spoke again, her voice as soft as the brooklet they stood beside. "We were both aware of our agreement, were we not? If I returned from London without having given away my heart to another, we would make our final arrangements for our marriage."

William's brow twitched. That was not all of their agreement, if he recalled. Didn't he have a say in it, as well?

"I have returned unengaged, and I still wish to marry." She gave a pregnant pause. "Do you?"

William stiffened. He'd expected the question for days now, and he'd torn himself to pieces like a scrap paper, trying to decide his answer. Of course, this was an easier question than, "Have you fallen in love with Miss Paxton?"

So did he still wish to marry? Of course he did. But did he still wish to marry *Charity*? He…did not know. Surely he could not give up their relationship, the years of planning, the stability he always had with her, the healing it would do for both of their families—not to mention the very real duty he had to the Winslows. After what Grandfather had done to them, William had to make it right. Didn't he?

After all, Charity expected this marriage. As did his parents. They'd waited for it for as long as he had.

But then, had his feelings not changed? Did his heart not face a different direction now? He glanced up the road, realizing only then how near they stood to the cottage—so near he could see the thatched roof peeking through the golden leaves of the trees.

So near he could see Miss Paxton's room.

He pulled away, forcing his eyes on Charity. He could not forget his responsibility to his family, to the Winslows, or to Charity simply because his soul longed for something other than what logic and duty required.

Miss Paxton may have brought peace and joy, excitement and laughter to his life. But Charity would bring a life of ease. She would never speak of her troubles or listen to his, just like now. She may not smile or laugh or carry chickens or run from Highland cows. But that was not all a marriage was, was it?

Besides, how well could he really know Miss Paxton after only a few weeks? He'd known Charity his whole life.

He drew a deep breath. "Yes, Charity. We will marry."

She blew out a slow breath, the faintest whisper of a smile on her lips. "Wonderful. We must get straight to planning then. I intend for the banns to be read this very week, if possible."

He nodded, unable to speak, his throat as dry as the brittle leaves crunched and broken beneath his boots.

She stood on the tips of her toes, placing a kiss to his cheek. This time, his heart picked up, but only because he saw a hint of Miss Paxton pulling away from her window in the cottage.

But he must have imagined it, for in the next instant, the vision was gone.

It was better this way. He had made his decision. He would be happy with Charity. He knew that he would.

But then, why could he not stop himself from gazing up at Miss Paxton's window again, hoping, praying for a glimpse of the one woman who *had* managed to set his heart aflame?

Amy swiped the tears away from her eyes, smoothed her gown, straightened her hair, and left her room.

She was finished with the games, with the heartache, and the loneliness. And she was going to do something about it.

With determined steps, she marched down the stairs, gentlemen's voices growing louder as she approached the sitting room.

Without hesitation, she entered the room, abruptly stopping in the center.

"Amy?" Mama said, tipping her head to the side. "What is it?"

Amy didn't look at her mother. Or her father or brother.

Instead, she looked directly at Mr. Roberts. "Sir, I wish to speak with you for a moment. In private."

CHAPTER TWENTY-TWO

A few days later, with Birchwick Hall's ledger, a quill, and an extra bottle of ink in hand, William made his way back to the drawing room. Charity and their mothers were busy with preparations for the wedding, and though he had very little opinion about what food they ate, what he wore, or which guests were invited, the women insisted he be present.

"William?"

He paused, turning as his father left the library William had just passed. "Father. Good morning. What are you keeping busy with today?"

"Merely reading for a moment." He removed his spectacles and held them in the same hand which grasped his closed book. "And you?" He motioned to William's own full hands. "Moving your station of work, I take it?"

William sniffed. "It would appear so. The ladies require my presence for their wedding plans, but I thought I might as well do something productive whilst I wait for them to summon me."

Father's smile didn't reach his hazel eyes. "I'm proud of you, son, for marrying Miss Winslow. For performing your duty and mending the bridge broken between our families. It is a good thing you are doing, a choice with which your mother and I are very pleased."

William dropped his gaze. Duty. That was precisely what this wedding was. The more time that passed, the more he realized it, as the desire all but fled him to fix what his grandfather ruined.

"Are you looking forward to the wedding?" Father asked next.

"Doesn't every groom?"

William could never answer directly when asked about the wedding. It was always one slight falsehood after the next.

"Are you so very happy, Mr. Eastwood?"

"I have no reason not to be."

"You must be so pleased this is coming about so quickly."

"Yes, very quickly, indeed."

"Is Miss Winslow beside herself with joy?"

"Yes, enough joy for the both of us, it would seem."

Even to his own parents he needed to twist his answer to avoid any further guilt. For as much as he wanted to be the same as before—to feel the same as before—his heart was not in his decision.

But he had made his choice. And now he would live with it for the rest of his life.

"William?"

William blinked. "Sorry, yes?"

Father gave him an odd look before repeating the words William had not heard. "I was merely expressing my appreciation for what you've done with the estates while we've been away. I know I was hesitant at first, especially allowing people to lease the cottage, but now I see how it will benefit us. You are a wise man. Far wiser than my own father."

William looked away. They never spoke of Grandfather. They didn't need to start now. "I had hoped to make a great many more changes before you arrived. But, perhaps we can work on them together, now you are here."

William had never done much with Father, the two having very little in common. William usually spent his time with Mr. Rutledge instead. But it certainly wouldn't hurt attempting to gain a better relationship now Grandfather was gone.

Father peered down at his book and spectacles. "Oh, no. I haven't the intellect for that, I'm afraid. I've a mind much more suited to reading."

He gave a departing nod then moved down the hallway.

William watched after him, his nerves sparking with frustration. How often had Grandfather said those exact words, destroying Father's confidence and making him feel as tall as a blade of grass. How could Grandfather's influence still be constricting Father?

But then, wasn't marrying Charity constricting William?

He shook his head, though the truth had already penetrated.

Before, he would have married Charity because he wanted to. Now, he was following through with their marriage because of his duty.

He was no better than his father.

With a heart as shriveled as the curling petals of a dying rose, William entered the drawing room.

Mother greeted him with a happy smile from across the room, while Charity and Mrs. Winslow nodded their salutations before returning their attention to the papers scattered before them.

Mother motioned him forward. "Finally, you have returned. Come. Give us your opinion on which food will be best served at the gathering after the wedding."

William deposited his belongings on the table and stifled a sigh, taking a few steps toward them to put in some effort. "I always enjoy a strawberry tart."

"A strawberry tart?" Mrs. Winslow said. "Heavens, no.

Imagine the stains that might occur. No, let us choose something a little safer."

"That is a valid point, Mama, but if William wishes for a strawberry tart at his own wedding, he should have the right to have it," Charity defended.

William backed away from the women. There was no place for him there. "No, no. It's all right. You may choose to serve whatever you'd like."

Charity's eyes followed him as he retreated across the room. Ever since her return, she'd taken to staring at William for long, unexplained moments, as if trying to decipher his very thoughts. Typically, William would leave her sight to avoid the discomfort her stares caused.

This time, however, he hardly noticed, settling down on his chair behind the small desk. With a sigh, he opened his ledger, grateful for the distraction that came with running three estates. He'd have enough to distract him for the rest of his life, if he wished for it. But over time, he wouldn't need the distraction. Over time, he'd forget Amy and be happy with Charity.

And at some point, he and Charity would find more in common.

He paused, his quill lingering in the open bottle of ink.

"Charity," he called across the room without another thought, "would you like to play Battledore and Shuttlecock with me?"

She pulled back, and the mothers exchanged odd glances. "What, right this moment?"

He shrugged. "It could be an enjoyable use of our time."

"You know I dislike the sport."

"I do, but perhaps if I pressed you to play, you'd be more inclined?"

"No, that would make me more *disinclined*."

Mrs. Winslow laughed. "It would appear that our Mr. Eastwood has forgotten how stubborn my daughter is. She is strong in mind. That is just what a gentleman needs to keep him in line."

She smiled proudly at her daughter, who peered down at the papers once more, avoiding further eye contact. "Perhaps another time, my dear. There is much to be decided upon before we are to wed."

William chewed the inside of his cheek. Over the last few days, Charity had immersed herself in her—*their*—wedding plans, becoming rather manic about the whole ordeal.

He couldn't decide if that was because she actually enjoyed the planning, or because she was keeping busy to prevent her mind from dwelling on other things—like the fact her betrothed was in love with someone else.

He cringed. She couldn't suspect his feelings for Miss Paxton now. Not after he'd still agreed to wed. He was no doubt being overly anxious about the whole thing.

"Mr. Eastwood. Mr. Hugh Paxton to see you, sir."

William started, looking to the door in surprise as the butler stood to the side to allow Hugh Paxton—Hugh Paxton, of all people—into the drawing room.

What the devil was he doing here? Especially alone and with that smirk on his lips?

After bows and curtsies, Hugh straightened. "Good morning."

William hesitated, wishing to ask outright what the man was doing there. But with the surprised looks on each of the women's faces, he knew he needed to make the introductions first.

As the women resumed their seats by the far window—though still close enough to hear the conversation—William placed a strained smile on his lips. "So, Mr. Paxton, to what do we owe the pleasure?"

Hugh strode about the room like he was master of Birchwick, eying the pictures on the wall and the gilded mirror behind the marble hearth as he spoke. "I do apologize for my lack of notice. I was merely riding by and recalled that I have been entirely remiss in congratulating you and your lovely bride-to-be. I thought to remedy my oversight with a short visit. I understand the two of you are to be married very soon?"

Charity responded before William had the chance. "We are, sir. And we are very much looking forward to it."

"Oh, indeed, we are," Mother piped in, looking at the list she created with Charity and Mrs. Winslow. "My husband and I could not be happier with the decision our son has made to marry Miss Winslow. The pride we feel..." She trailed off with a happy shake of her head.

Hugh's gaze shifted to William, whose stomach tossed back and forth like the choppy waves of Coniston Water.

Hugh paused near a shelf and ran his fingers along the spines of a few books. William watched him with a heavy gaze. Did Hugh's family know he was there? Was Miss Paxton aware of his presence?

"How is your family?" he asked with nonchalance. Charity's eyes were on him in an instant, but he didn't meet her stare. He didn't need to. He was merely asking after the state of his tenants.

Hugh pulled a book from a shelf and flipped through the worn pages. "Oh, we are well, of course. Looking forward to our return to Bath. Even more so now that my sister has a wedding to plan."

Shock cut through William. His breathing shallowed, and his mind blurred. Surely he'd misheard Hugh's words. Surely, he was mistaken.

"Pardon?" he managed.

Finally, Hugh looked up. The look in his eyes was far too innocent, as was the innocuous smile playing about his lips. "Oh, haven't you heard? Amy is to be married. To Mr. Roberts."

William's heart dropped, his chest concaving. All words fled him, his thoughts spinning so swiftly, he thought he might fall over.

Miss Paxton was to marry Mr. Roberts? It wasn't true. How could it be? After all she'd said of him, how could this be happening?

"Well that is delightful, isn't it?" came Charity's voice from somewhere across the room.

William leaned his knuckles against the desk to ground himself. Surely Miss Paxton had not made the decision herself to marry the man. Surely she'd been talked into it by no one else but Hugh.

His fists curled.

"When will they be wed?" Charity asked.

Her voice sounded distant as fiery blood rushed through his ears. He was only vaguely aware of her watchful gaze on William.

"The moment we return to Bath, the banns will be read," Hugh explained. "I must say, I'm quite looking forward to having Mr. Roberts as part of our family. He is a good friend, after all. And always so kind and respectful to Amy." He stared at William. "Most importantly, he's honest."

William's legs tensed. He drew in a deep breath, ready to accuse Hugh of his treachery, but Hugh replaced the book in the shelf with a sigh.

"Well, I do apologize for such a swift visit, but I shan't intrude any longer. Thank you for allowing me to share with you my good news and felicitations on your own. Good day to you all."

The ladies stood and curtsied as Hugh departed, but William could not even suffer a bow.

His insides tied in knots, pulsing heat flooding through every vein. He could not bear the idea of Miss Paxton marrying such a man—especially because he *knew* she was convinced to do such a thing by her brother.

"William, are you well?" Mother asked across the room, apparently having seen his reddened face.

He blinked, unable to look their way. "Yes. I..." He couldn't take this any longer. Abruptly, he pushed away from the desk and strode directly from the room. "I will return in just a moment."

"William?" Charity called as soon as he left, but he did not stop.

He hardly cared if they suspected anything at this moment. He had only one thing on his mind, and he would not stop until he confronted Hugh about his duplicity.

He stormed down the corridors as the front door clicked open and closed. Picking up his pace, William ran past his bewildered butler and left the house just as Hugh was reaching for the reins of his horse.

"Hugh!" William shouted, taking the steps two at a time.

Hugh turned, his brow raised before a smile tugged his lips. "Mr. Eastwood. Didn't have enough of my visit, eh?"

"Hardly," William growled. "Tell me what happened."

"I don't know what you mean, sir."

Losing all control, William grasped onto the lapels of Hugh's jacket and raised him toward him. The groom who'd delivered Hugh's horse eyed the two gentlemen before scurrying back to the stables.

"Tell me what happened between your sister and Mr. Roberts."

Hugh sputtered. "Unhand me at once, sir."

William seethed, speaking through clenched teeth. "If I discover that you played any part in her agreeing to marry that cad, you will answer to me."

Fear flickered in Hugh's eyes, but he hid it with a raise of his chin. "Should you not be more concerned over your own betrothed instead of Mr. Roberts's?"

William shook his head, disgust rising within him. He

released Hugh, pushing him away as the man stumbled a few feet back and bumped against his horse. The steed skittered back and tossed his head in protest.

Hugh straightened his collar with a swift tug, but William was already walking toward the stables.

In a matter of moments, he rode out on his own horse, sailing across the countryside at full-speed until he reached the cottage, intent on barging in through the front door and demanding answers from Miss Paxton.

But she was not inside.

He slowed his horse to a canter, eying her as she stood near the brooklet on the outside of the gate, picking apart a burnt orange leaf and tossing the pieces one by one into the water. Her expression was solemn, the edges of her lips pulled down, her eyes missing the signature light he'd grown so accustomed to seeing.

His taut chest deflated. The woman had clearly been coerced into doing something she did not want to do—again. There was no reason for William to be upset with *her*.

He dismounted, walking toward her as she looked up to discover him.

"Mr. Eastwood?" She immediately brushed the rest of the torn leaf from her hands and faced him. "It is a pleasure to see you."

Her words were formal. Too formal. Too...not like Miss Paxton.

But this was not the time for pleasantries. He would be blunt, just like she was.

"You are marrying Mr. Roberts?"

CHAPTER TWENTY-THREE

*A*my's heartbeat thudded in her ears. Mr. Eastwood's words were not spoken in anger, though he did not look particularly happy either.

"Why?" he asked when she remained silent.

She'd already answered the same question from Mother, Father, Hugh, and Mr. Roberts.

She'd been expecting to do the very same for Mr. Eastwood. Mr. Eastwood, who knew of her disdain—*past* disdain—for Mr. Roberts's actions.

Each response had differed, depending on with whom she had spoken.

"Mama, I have very little choice on the matter of whom I marry now. With three rejections and three spent Seasons, I've run out of options."

"Father, you know I will not allow him to treat me with anything other than respect."

"Hugh, you said yourself. I liked him once. I can do so again."

"Mr. Roberts, you and I are both desperate. You, for money, myself, to marry."

And her answer for Mr. Eastwood?

"Because I wish to," she stated.

Each of the answers held a partial truth, but no one knew the entire truth.

Amy had been using her fear of becoming a burden on her parents as the main reason to find a husband. But, in actuality, she knew her parents would never regret a single day they spent with their daughter.

The truth was, Amy *wished* to marry. She longed for companionship, for a spouse to care for her for the rest of her days. She longed for children, for a house of her own, and for love.

Since she'd lost that love with William, she knew she would never find it again. So her next best option was to settle for mere companionship instead with Mr. Roberts—for he was the only gentleman to have ever expressed any desire to marry her.

"Because you wish to?" Mr. Eastwood repeated, shaking his head at her response, just as she'd expected him to. "That is not true, and you and I both know it. I've heard from your own mouth that you did not wish to marry that man—that you could not *stand* him."

He tied his horse to a low tree branch then progressed toward her, lowering his voice. "You do not love him. And you must know that he does not love you."

Amy pulled back, her pride wounded. Of course that was the truth, but was it necessary to fling such harsh realities at her?

"That hardly matters. You of all people should know, marriage does not require love. Does it?"

She stared at him pointedly, and he looked away. "That is beyond the point."

"Then what is the point, sir?"

"The point is that you should not marry him because… because you clearly do not wish to."

"That is where you are wrong. I do wish to marry him. This was my decision, and I will—"

"Was it?"

She blinked. "What do you mean?"

"Was it your decision?"

"Of course it was. Who do you think…" She trailed off, understanding finally dawning. "You believe Hugh made this decision for me?"

"There is no other logical explanation. I cannot allow you to marry him. I forbid it!"

A derisive laugh escaped her lips. "Who are you to say such things? You forbid it? You cannot *allow* it? I thought you were different from your grandfather, sir?"

Mr. Eastwood flinched, and he took a step back in silence.

The words were cruel, but Amy couldn't help it. Who was he to try to make her decisions for her?

"The *logical* explanation," she continued, "is that I chose him for myself, Mr. Eastwood."

Finally, he found his voice again. "I am not trying to control you, Miss Paxton. I simply…" He tossed out his arms to the side of him. "I cannot understand how *that* is logical. The man wishes to marry you to receive his fortune!"

"If you recall, *I* was the one who told you that very fact." She took a step toward him. "But Mr. Roberts told me his side willingly before I agreed to wed him. *He* was honest with me."

He winced, pulling his eyes from hers. "Is that true?"

"Yes. It is."

It *was* true. When Amy had pulled Mr. Roberts away from her family to speak, she'd told him she would reconsider his offer of marriage if he merely promised one thing—to help Amy be happy.

"Of course, Miss Paxton," Mr. Roberts had agreed instantly. "I will strive to do so each day of my life. Only…" He had paused, his brow crumpling. "To make that so, I must be honest with you about something first."

Apparently, Hugh had not told Mr. Roberts that Amy was

aware of his real reasoning behind his proposal and then proceeded to share the truth with Amy.

"I do admire you, though, Miss Paxton," he'd said. "And I will strive to make you happy."

And Amy believed him. He'd always been more honorable than Hugh. Or at least, so she hoped. At any rate, the fact that he'd shared the truth with her had solidified her desire—not to mention he was her only option. Mr. Fisher and Mr. Payne had long been forgotten, and she did not know them as well as she knew Mr. Roberts.

She may not be in love with him, but at least he was honest. And at least she would no longer be alone.

Mr. Eastwood ran his fingers through his hair, holding his hat in his opposite hand, bringing her attention back to the present. "I just…I cannot understand it. I cannot understand how you can shift so swiftly from despising the gentleman to marrying him."

Angered at his continuous disapproval, Amy took a step forward. "And I cannot understand how you can shift so swiftly from merely being *friends* with Miss Winslow to now being engaged."

He swallowed, his nostrils flaring.

"Yes, that is right, sir. I have heard that your engagement has been made official. Miss Winslow must be relieved to know you will actually tell other women that you are, in fact, spoken for. Or is your plan to remain quiet about that fact long after you're married?"

His brow furrowed. She knew she was being heartless, her words borne from her pain, but in her anger, the man deserved this treatment.

"Yes, Miss Winslow and I are engaged. Now that it is official, I will not hesitate to share the news. But I will not feel sorrow for something I did not do—which was lie about our relationship."

Amy scoffed, turning away. "This again?"

"Yes, this again." He ran up to her, grasping her arm with a firm grip. "I have already admitted I was wrong in not informing you that I was intending to marry Charity. I have already expressed my sorrow, my regret. My utter shame." His eyes, dark and stormy like the sea-green ocean, bore into hers. "But I will not say that I did so to be cruel, underhanded, or deceitful. Miss Winslow and I agreed to pursue marriage if she returned unattached to another—and if *I* remained unattached, as well."

As he maintained his hold of her arm, Amy stared up at him, trying to make sense of his words. That was what Miss Winslow had been doing in London—looking for other men? So Mr. Eastwood had been allowed to pursue other women, as well?

All this time, Amy had thought Mr. Eastwood was willfully being dishonest with the woman.

Her breathing shallowed, and she peered up at him in silence.

As their eyes locked, Mr. Eastwood blinked, his grip on her arm softening until he released her altogether. "Forgive me, I should not have spoken to you in such a way. I cannot bear the thought of you marrying such a man."

"Why?" she breathed. "Why does it bother you so?"

He shook his head, backing away. "I don't know. It shouldn't. It doesn't."

But Amy had seen the answer in his eyes. She had seen it when he'd nearly kissed her, when he'd held her hand at the fair. When he'd brushed her hair back in the garden at the cottage.

A few days before, she'd stopped him from saying how he truly felt. But now, was there nothing she could say to have him share his feelings?

Her heart flapped like a bird anxious to escape its cage. She had to try. Advancing upon him, she blurted out, "Do you wish to know the real reason I am to marry Mr. Roberts?"

He slowed, hanging his head, though he did not say a word.

"It is to ease the bleeding of my heart."

His shoulders tensed, and he turned halfway toward her.

Her voice broke. "It is because I have thought myself in love with three men in the last year. But now I know…I was only ever in love with one."

Tears pricked her eyes as the truth filled her heart. The sheer joy he'd brought into her life, the way he encouraged her to be who she was. The way her heart swirled was unlike anything she'd ever felt with anyone.

Yes, she was engaged to Mr. Roberts.

Yes, Mr. Eastwood was engaged to Miss Winslow.

But surely…surely love would…

Worry wrung out her hope like a wet rag. Mr. Eastwood had yet to look at her, his head hanging low. She was perched on a precarious limb, offering herself up with the risk of being rejected once again.

"Mr. Eastwood," she said, taking a few steps toward him. Her nerves threatened to swallow the question she longed to ask, but she drew a deep breath and pushed forward. "You told me that you and Miss Winslow would marry if you both remained unattached. She clearly has. But have you become attached to another?"

He closed his eyes, his shoulders falling before finally, he looked at her. Sorrow twisted his features. "Amy," he whispered, "I wish I could tell you. I wish I could express my…" He trailed off with a sigh. "But my parents, Miss Winslow, our families. They've been expecting this since…I am sorry, but I-I can't."

He turned swiftly away, but not before Amy caught the tears shining in his eyes.

As she wiped away her own, she drew in a deep breath, watching Mr. Eastwood fleeing on his horse until he disappeared down the tree-covered road.

She would not cry any longer about his decision. At least,

not right now. She'd seen his turmoil. She knew of his pull to do his duty, to help his parents and Miss Winslow.

Had her heart not been broken, she would have understood him even better.

Because things *were* better this way. They'd already made their promises to Miss Winslow and Mr. Roberts. And at least now that Amy would be wed, she would no longer make stupid decisions—like declaring her feelings to yet another gentleman.

Yes, they had all chosen their own lives.

And now it was time to live them.

"So you've finally made it official with Miss Winslow. You have my sincerest well wishes, son."

William nodded at Mr. Rutledge's comment. Dark brown walls and a crackling fire provided a comfortable atmosphere to the elderly man's small room, despite the somberness William felt at Mr. Rutledge's weakened tone. He had not improved in weeks, but still he clung to life, lying in his bed, unable to lift hardly a finger.

Mrs. Rutledge cooked dinner in the room just below them, pots and pans clanging through the paper-thin walls.

"It certainly has been a number of years, has it not?" William responded. He tried to smile. After all, such a thing should be easy for a gentleman who would be wedded in a fortnight.

Instead of a smile, however, he must have grimaced instead, for Mr. Rutledge's weak expression further faltered. "Is something bothering you?"

"Not at all." To prove his words, William raised a flippant shoulder from where he sat on the chair beside Mr. Rutledge's bed.

William had visited Mr. Rutledge once a day since discovering more about his poor health, but William still had not grown used to seeing his father-like figure in such a state. He wouldn't speak of anything that might upset the ailing man further.

But Mr. Rutledge narrowed his eyes. "Come now. Tell me what is wrong. I haven't the energy to fight you on this, but you know I will."

William sniffed a laugh. The Rutledges always knew how to coerce the truth from him—a talent he both loved and despised. "It is nothing really. I just have a lot on my mind as of right now."

Mr. Rutledge stared, waiting a moment before continuing. "Are you looking forward to the wedding?"

"Very much so." Why did his words always turn out so flat? He pushed a more upbeat tone. "Why would I not be?"

"Only because you look as excited as Mrs. Rutledge does each time she must clean up after dinner."

William gave a half-smile, turning to eye the single window pouring afternoon light and a soft breeze into the otherwise stale room. "Surely a wedding will be more exciting than washing dinnerware."

"I am not sure about a wedding, but a marriage, most certainly. At least, that is for what one hopes."

William looked away from Mr. Rutledge's pointed stare. William had not always wanted an exciting marriage. He had been perfectly content with the notion of a simple life with Charity until Miss Paxton rode into town with her blue eyes, and contagious smile, and—

No. He'd promised himself he'd no longer think about her. He'd broken her heart—and his in the process. He could not go back now.

"Do you believe you and Miss Winslow will be happy together?"

William searched his mind for a reply that would not give away the truth. "Yes, we will be quite content."

There was no reason for them not to be content, so long as Charity did not prevent him from visiting the Rutledges as she'd tried to do that morning.

"Must you really go out when there is a wedding to be planned?" she'd asked gingerly.

"Charity, Mr. Rutledge is ill. He will very likely not live to even see our wedding."

She'd lowered her eyes. "Very well. And…is that the only call you will be making today? Or need you see other tenants?"

William knew she'd been referring to the Paxtons, especially after his mad dash from Birchwick. With a clenched stomach, he had shaken his head. "No, only the Rutledges."

"Content?" Mr. Rutledge repeated, bringing William's mind back to the present. "There is that familiar word, one you use so often in regard to your life. Tell me, son. Have you ever been more than content? Happy, perhaps?"

William pushed away the image of playing Battledore and Shuttlecock, of eyes that sparkled joy so radiantly that it was impossible for him not to feel the same happiness. "Occasionally."

Mr. Rutledge stared. "Mrs. Rutledge says you were the happiest she'd ever seen you a few weeks ago. Something tells me that had to do with a woman. A woman who is not your betrothed."

William's cheeks warmed, and he stared down at his hands as he leaned forward on the creaking, wooden chair, resting his elbows on his knees. "I haven't any idea to whom you are referring."

"Come now, William. When have we ever minced words with one another? You know I speak of Miss Paxton, the lovely girl living in the cottage. Now tell me, have you feelings for her more than Miss Winslow?"

He should've expected such a question. The Rutledges were

not exactly couth. Funny how he was drawn to a certain sort of people.

"I should not have feelings for her."

"But you do."

William rubbed the back of his neck, slowly nodding. "I do. But it doesn't matter how I feel. I've a duty to Miss Winslow and her family. My parents expect it. Society expects it. I expect it. Or rather, I did."

Mr. Rutledge hmphed, drawing William's surprised gaze toward him. "Since when have you ever done what Society expects of you, or what your family tells you to do? If I recall, you always did the very opposite."

William certainly couldn't refute that. "That is true in every instance but when I am striving to make amends for the faults of my grandfather."

Mr. Rutledge peered into his eyes, unflinching. "You are doing an honorable thing by mending the bridge between your two families, as well as by making up for your grandfather's neglect of his homes and tenants. But there is a difference between sacrificing your time and hard work for the sake of those in need…and sacrificing the rest of your life by marrying someone you do not love, merely for the sake of healing a wound not caused by yourself." He narrowed his eyes, his voice gaining strength. "It is not too late to have what your heart desires, Will."

William's shoulders lowered, the truth of Mr. Rutledge's words weighing heavily upon him. "You are right, of course. I agreed to marry Charity out of duty, but now I see the folly of my actions. But it *is* too late now. If I end the engagement between us, I would ruin her reputation. I cannot do that to her."

Mr. Rutledge sighed, the edges of his lips turned down. His voice fell back to the weakened state from before. "Does she know you have feelings for Miss Paxton?"

"No, but I do not doubt that she suspects it."

Mr. Rutledge pressed his lips together, staring at the fire. The logs settled farther in the hearth, and the flames snapped in the silence.

"What is it?" William asked.

As Mr. Rutledge responded, his eyes remained on the fire, his voice hardly above a whisper. "The best decision I ever made was marrying Mrs. Rutledge. We have been happy together, despite my ailments and struggles. Though, I know it would not have been that way had I not been honest from the start." His eyes found William's with a pointed stare. "Had I not been honest with her about the level of care I would need as I grew older and as my ailments increased, she might have grown to resent me. But because of my honesty, the both of us were able to live with the facts."

He paused, reaching his fingers toward William with a grimace. William leaned the rest of the way, taking his friend's warm, wrinkled hand in his own as Mr. Rutledge continued. "You must do the same with Miss Winslow. She deserves to know the truth."

William winced. "Even if I hurt her?"

"The truth will always come out, Will. Better to hurt her now than in years to come."

His words slurred, and his eyes fluttered to a close—evidence of his exhaustion. William cursed his own selfishness in discussing such a difficult matter in Mr. Rutledge's weakened state.

"Rest now, sir," he whispered. "We may speak later."

The faintest hint of a squeeze came from Mr. Rutledge's fingers—clearly all he could manage. "You've overcome much in your life, William. You will overcome this, too."

CHAPTER TWENTY-FOUR

*T*hree days later, Mr. Rutledge drew his last pained breath.

Having had no children of their own, William was the only one there to comfort Mrs. Rutledge, though he knew little of what he could do besides be present for her.

The day of the funeral was simple—just as Mr. Rutledge would have wished for it to be. The procession lasted only a few moments as they rode toward the churchyard, then the closest thing William had to a loving mentor was laid in the ground, encased in a pine coffin—paid for by William.

The sun was shining, giving him no way to hide his tears. But he did not care who was witness to his emotion. Mr. Rutledge meant the world to him, and he would never deny it.

Afterward, a small gathering was held at the Rutledge home with two of their closest friends—and Miss Paxton and her parents.

William had seen the Paxtons lining the street as they walked by in the procession. Tears had brimmed in Miss Paxton's eyes as she looked at William, and he'd almost broken down right there from her compassion.

Charity had not come to the procession or afterward.

"I cannot bear the heartbreak," she'd said with brows raised. "Besides, Mother does not like me to attend such morbid things."

Never mind that she'd made the effort to attend Grandfather's funeral from afar. She'd merely never understood William's attachment to the Rutledges and did not feel the need to attend this one.

After the funeral, he stood near the small hearth in Mrs. Rutledge's minute sitting room. He watched from the corner of his eye as Miss Paxton and Mrs. Rutledge embraced, sharing soft words with each other before Mr. and Mrs. Paxton spoke next.

Miss Paxton moved on, fixing her eyes on William, slowly approaching him.

"Mr. Eastwood," she said with a soft nod. "Allow me to express my condolences, sir."

He gave a hint of a smile. "Thank you for coming. I know Mrs. Rutledge appreciates your presence here and during the procession, as do I."

Their eyes met, the words that had passed between them the last time they'd seen one another flashing through his mind.

"I wouldn't have missed it," she whispered. "I know how much this family means to you."

Her voice cracked, and with it, William's heart. Her compassion, her generosity, was unmatched. How had he allowed this woman to slip straight through his fingers?

"When do you leave Coniston?" he asked.

"Tomorrow."

He blinked. Mr. Paxton had written to him, alerting him of their intent to vacate Flitfield Cottage. But in spending the last week with the Rutledges and preparing for Mr. Rutledge's funeral, William had lost count of the days.

So the Paxtons would be leaving Coniston tomorrow. And he would never see Miss Paxton again.

Miss Paxton opened her mouth, appearing to hesitate before shaking her head. "I truly am sorry for your loss." She made to walk away, her eyes brimming with tears. But she turned back toward him, reaching up to place a soft kiss to his cheek.

Though it passed as swiftly as a single raindrop falling from the sky, he closed his eyes, breathing in the sweet scent of her hair as she pulled away.

"Goodbye, Mr. Eastwood."

And then she was gone, taking William's heart along with her.

He had tried to deny the facts, to convince himself that he did not truly love Miss Paxton.

But each day that passed without seeing her, each moment that occurred in her presence, he became more and more aware of the fact that he did love her. He loved her more than life itself.

And coming to this realization, he would finally honor Mr. Rutledge's last request.

He would speak with Charity.

Instead of returning to Birchwick that afternoon, William made a late call to Charity's home.

"Are you to join us for dinner, Mr. Eastwood?" Mrs. Winslow offered after he was shown into the drawing room where she and her daughter gathered.

"Thank you, but no. I do apologize for intruding at such an untimely hour, but I was hoping to speak with your daughter." He glanced to Charity. "Alone."

Mrs. Winslow left them with an uneasy glance, leaving them behind with the door open.

William waited for her footsteps to retreat down the corridor before facing Charity.

"How was the funeral?" she asked, her brow creased.

"It was…difficult." He hesitated. Typically, they didn't speak of such things. Life was already too challenging. But then, what if *he* wished to talk? "Mrs. Rutledge was upset, but she did her best to put on a smile for her guests. And seeing Mr. Rutledge laid to rest…"

Charity's eyes flicked over his shoulder, evidence of her disinterest, and his words trailed off. So she didn't wish to speak of the funeral after all.

"How was your day?" he asked.

She instantly brightened. "Very constructive, I must say. We've finalized the food, and I've only just posted a letter to my aunt in London, the one whom we were staying with before. She will be so pleased to hear of our engagement. She was the one who helped me to convince Mama to have us return early from our stay there."

He nodded absentmindedly—just as she'd done moments ago with his own words. Did they truly have such little care over what the other had to say?

"So are you to tell me why you've requested a private audience with me?" She stared up at him, her eyes lingering on his lips.

It was time. He paced a few steps in front of where she sat on the settee. "Yes, I have been thinking a great deal about us lately. About our relationship and the wedding. And I…" He swallowed. "I must now be honest with you. I fear—"

"You've fallen in love with her, haven't you?"

Their eyes met, and at once, William knew whom she was referring to. For a single, fleeting moment, his desire to cower from her direct question nearly won out. But he planted his feet to the floral rug beneath his boots and spoke softly. "Yes. I love her."

She pulled in her lips, eyes glistening. Her voice cracked as she spoke. "I feared as much after seeing the two of you holding hands at the fair and after observing the looks she gave you at the bakery. I'd merely hoped her love was one-sided."

William's heart bowed in pain, like a feeble tree branch in a fierce wind. "I'm sorry, Charity. Truly, I am. I did not mean to fall in love with her."

Her eyes swung back to meet his, and she swiftly blinked away her tears as her gaze hardened. "That makes all of this better then, doesn't it? The fact that you *did not mean to*." She stood abruptly, anger laced throughout her words. "I waited for you my whole life. I waited for your grandfather to die, for you to take charge of the estates, for you to grow older and be more secure in yourself." She shook her head, her voice lowering. "I've wasted my entire life on you, William Eastwood."

He winced. "Charity, I—"

"I told Mother this would happen. I knew if I left Coniston you would find someone to replace me."

He shook his head, reaching forward to rest a hand on her arm, but she pulled swiftly away. Her anger was warranted, but that did not mean he still didn't wish to ease her pain. "It is not like that, Charity. I did not find her to take your place. You've been my closest friend for years. I could not ever replace the help you've provided me for so long."

She dropped her gaze, and her shoulders fell forward. "That is just the problem though. You see me as only your friend."

William longed to refute her words, to ensure her she was wrong, but he was finished with being a coward.

"I only wish..." Her voice filled with emotion, and she paused to clear her throat. "I only wish that you would have told me before we became engaged. Before I alerted my family. Before I even returned from London. My reputation, William. I'll be ruined. I'll—"

"I still intend to marry you."

She stiffened. "What?"

"We made an agreement. I intend to follow through with it."

"Oh."

He gathered all the courage he could muster. "I am not blind to how I would ruin your reputation if I broke off the engagement, and I could not do that to you. Believe it or not, I care for you, Charity."

"Just not as much as you care for Miss Paxton?"

He could not hurt her further by agreeing with her words. Instead, he reached forward, taking her hand in his. This time, she allowed him to. "I promise to care for you and to respect you as my wife for as long as I live."

"But can you love me?"

She stared up at him expectantly, but William tensed. He'd heard of marriages that began with a friendship eventually ending in love, but how could he promise that when his heart belonged to another?

"I'm sorry, Charity. I can promise no such thing."

Tears once more sprung to her eyes, but she looked away with a raised chin. "If you cannot promise me that, I will not marry you. You are free to pursue Miss Paxton." She walked to the door, her black curls barely moving at her slow pace.

William stifled the rising hope in his heart. His mind swirled as he tried to comprehend all that had occurred. He was no longer engaged. He was no longer beholden to Charity. A weight lifted from his shoulders, and he felt as if he could breathe for the first time in weeks.

Then the guilt settled in.

"I...I will not pursue her," he said just as Charity reached the door. "Miss Paxton is engaged to another and will be leaving Coniston tomorrow."

She paused with her hand on the frame, turning back to look at him, a haunted look in her eyes that pierced his soul. "It is none of my concern how you intend to live out the rest of your days, William. But if she loves you as much as you love her, you'd be a fool not to fight for her." She turned away, her voice lowering even further. "And if you *truly* love her, you would not risk breaking her heart as you just did mine."

"I'm sorry," he breathed. "For everything."

She did not look back at him. "I know."

And then she was gone.

William stared at the empty doorway, unable to process his conflicting emotions. After a moment, he wandered through the house and out the door, stepping into the golden, evening light and taking the reins of his horse from the groom.

He paused before mounting, focusing on Charity's words that had struck him to his core.

She'd told him to go after Miss Paxton, to not break the heart of the woman he loved. But surely he did not deserve happiness with Miss Paxton when he was the cause of Charity's grief. He would only be hurting his friend if he sought Miss Paxton so swiftly. But if he waited a day or two, Miss Paxton would be gone—with her betrothed.

His heart pumped faster, and his breathing shallowed. He knew Miss Paxton did not love Mr. Roberts. She loved William. But would she accept William even after how dishonest he'd been before? Would she end her own engagement just to be with him?

He had never meant to hurt Charity. And he would regret that for the rest of his life. But he loved Miss Paxton more than anything. He wanted to *be* with her more than anything. And if he did not act now, he would regret *that* for the rest of his life.

In a single movement, William leapt onto his horse and urged him forward. He was finished waiting to do the right thing. He was finished waiting to be honest. That was exactly what had caused his problems in the first place.

He would go to Amy. He would be truthful. And he would

plead for her forgiveness, for the chance to prove his love for the rest of his days.

Now he could only pray that she accepted his offer.

～

Amy stifled a yawn as she sat with her family and Mr. Roberts in the sitting room of the cottage. She knew she ought to retire, but knowing this was her last night in the house she'd so grown to love, she couldn't break away.

She eyed the chipped paint, the fading wallpaper, and the small hearth, wondering how she'd ever *not* found them charming—wondering how she was going to leave all of this behind.

"We are a quiet party this evening, are we not?" Mama said, eying the silent room. "Or are we preparing for the long journey ahead of us tomorrow?"

Tomorrow. They would be leaving tomorrow. That was two weeks earlier than they had planned. But this was for the best. She'd be home faster. She'd be away from Mr. Eastwood quicker. And she would marry Mr. Roberts sooner.

Instead of relief flooding through her, Amy's stomach merely tightened, causing the food she'd just eaten to roil about inside her.

Hugh rolled his head back until he leaned it against the sofa. "I'm merely trying to digest the food given us. Cook certainly fed us enough to last the whole of our journey."

"Indeed. She is marvelous." Mr. Roberts pumped his head up and down. "Although, the cook at Pagemore Place is just as talented. You will be sure to enjoy her cooking, as well, Miss Paxton."

Amy stared for a moment, a split-second of confusion pursing her brow, then she realized...Mr. Roberts was speaking of when Amy would move in with him at his family's estate.

The food in her stomach rose. Of course she'd had the thought before—having to move from Roseley House to Pagemore, having to be with the man romantically. She'd always had a sour taste in her mouth, like she'd eaten an unripe apple.

But this time was different. This time, the image in her mind's eye made her head spin. She would be eating at his table, surrounded by his family. Then she would retire with a man she did not love.

Heat burgeoned within her, swirling from her limbs and stifling her breath. Fire swept across her cheeks and brow. How could she follow through with the notion?

No. She needed to relax. She'd been through all of this before—the panic, the second-guessing. All she needed was some fresh air and some time alone to think.

She stood abruptly from her seat.

"Are you well, Amy?" Mama asked, concern pursing her brow.

"Yes, of course. I'm just going to stretch my legs for a moment before I retire."

"Would you care for some company?" Papa asked.

"Oh, I was going to offer the same," Mr. Roberts piped in, scooting forward on his seat, though he moved a little too eagerly, as if he was merely copying Papa.

Papa sent him a look of annoyance. He'd been silent for days, ever since she'd agreed to marry Mr. Roberts. Papa was protective of her, and she couldn't quite get herself to convince him to be otherwise.

She would not have minded walking with just him, but to do so without Mr. Roberts now would be impossible.

"Thank you both for the offer, but I'll just take a turn around the garden before the sun sets. I won't be long."

"Are you certain you don't wish to take your betrothed with you, Amy?" Hugh asked, quirking a brow.

Hugh had been insufferable ever since Amy's engagement.

He'd expressed his sorrow for her being hurt by Mr. Eastwood, but he couldn't hide his satisfaction over her attachment to his friend.

Thank heavens she was no longer taking his advice.

"Yes, Hugh. I am certain," she said, and with a pointed look in his direction, she left the room and the cottage behind.

She didn't want to offend her...her betrothed, but heavens, she needed a break.

The moment she stepped outside, the tension in her shoulders eased. It wouldn't always be like this, feeling awkward and tense around Mr. Roberts, would it? Surely things would be far more comfortable when they returned to Bath. Surely.

However, she was not naïve enough to expect a great joy to overcome her at her marriage, nor any love to blossom between her and her husband. How could she, when her heart was already spoken for?

Her eyes fell on the gate—still broken, just like her spirits. Mr. Eastwood had forgotten to send someone to fix it, but knowing how busy he was with the Rutledges—and Miss Winslow—she had pushed aside the thought of asking him to fix it again.

Now, part of her regretted not requesting it of him, for she could have seen him at least one more time.

She closed her eyes, turning her back to the gate as she wandered around the side of the house. She paused beside the cottage where a view of Coniston Water opened up before her, and she drew in a deep, soothing breath. The lake sparkled in the evening light, shimmering colors of blinding white and yellow with shades of dark blue and black.

The early October air was cool, invigorating her limbs as it blew her curls about her temples.

She would miss the peaceful atmosphere of this place. She would miss the quaint cottage and the many walks she could take in solitude. And she would miss Mr. Eastwood.

Her shoulders fell forward. There he was again, where he always was—lurking in every corner of her mind, in every piece of her heart.

The thought struck her like a blast of cold wind. Mr. Eastwood would *never* leave her...even when she married Mr. Roberts. And how was that fair to him? How was that being an honest and faithful wife?

Her heart twisted. A rhythmic pulse beat against her brow, and she raised a hand to settle it. She'd made a mistake. A grave error. This had to be the worst decision she had ever made. When would she learn?

She could not, in good conscience, marry the man. Not when she couldn't be faithful to him. Not when she couldn't even bear the mere thought of being with him, mentally or physically.

She would be miserable without Mr. Eastwood. She would be lonely without a companion to love for the rest of her life. But she would be both if she agreed to a loveless marriage.

Footsteps approached, and her heart skipped a beat. She blew out a steady, silent sigh. Mr. Roberts. She would talk to him. She would be honest with him now.

"Mr. Roberts. I..."

Her words trailed away when she turned to see the gentleman approaching.

But it was not Mr. Roberts.

"Mr. Eastwood?"

CHAPTER TWENTY-FIVE

*A*my's heart flew about like a shuttlecock sailing through the air. How she wished she could go back to that day, playing the sport with him, the only care in the world being that if she played too well, the man might be *too* impressed.

He stopped a few paces before her, his eyes flitting from here to there. "Miss Paxton," he greeted with a short bow. He removed his hat and clasped it behind his back. "I trust you are well?"

"I am, thank you. And yourself?"

He gave a quick nod then fell silent. Amy studied him, waiting for an explanation as to why he found his way to the cottage alone that evening.

"Were you just now leaving Mrs. Rutledge's?" she asked.

"No."

Amy paused, waiting for him to continue.

"I came to…to bid farewell to your family."

Her family. Not her. "They are in the sitting room. You may go through if you wish." She nodded her head in dismissal then walked away.

"Will you not join me?"

She paused, turning back to face him. After only just escaping Mr. Roberts, whom she would now be breaking things off with? "No, I'd rather walk."

His eyes pulled to the front of the house.

"Do not feel as if you must stay out here on my account," she said, turning to face the lake once more. "I'm quite content being alone."

Unless, of course, she was referring to the rest of her life. In that case, she apparently required a husband who had spread rumors about her and only wished to wed her to receive his fortune again.

What a fool she'd been.

She fully expected Mr. Eastwood to move indoors. After all, he was engaged and should not be seen outside alone with another female. So when his footsteps neared her, she reminded him of the fact.

"Where is Miss Winslow?"

He stopped at her side. "At her house."

She bit her lip. "Does she know you're here?"

"No."

She took a few steps forward, resting a hand on the edge of the cottage, desperate to create more space between them. "Then you had better leave."

"Is that what you want?"

Amy fixed her eyes on the shimmering lake, the small waves kissing the edge of the land as it lapped the grassy shoreline. No, she never wanted him to leave. Which was exactly why he needed to.

"I think it is best if you do. Your betrothed would not approve of you being here." And for good reason.

Mr. Eastwood was silent for a moment. "She is no longer my betrothed."

Shock rattled Amy's heart. Slowly, she turned to face him, a solemn expression on his brow. "What?"

He took a step toward her. Pulling his hat in front of him, he curled his fingers round the bridge of it. "Miss Winslow and I are no longer engaged."

Amy searched his eyes. "How? How did this happen?"

"She broke off the engagement after I told her the truth."

"The truth about what exactly?" Hope tried to break forth from the cage she'd held it in ever since Miss Winslow had returned, but she wouldn't allow it to come forth.

His eyes bore into hers. "That I do not love her. That I...love someone else."

Her legs shook. She took a step back, pressing her hand against the stone of the cottage. Was he saying...Could she dare to hope that he...

"Miss Paxton," he whispered, taking a step toward her, "I do not profess to...I cannot..." He released an aggravated sigh as he struggled for words, tugging at his cravat. "I wanted to say that I wish you every happiness with your upcoming marriage to Mr. Roberts."

He ended with another sigh, scrubbing a hand over his face.

Amy frowned. After ending his engagement with Miss Winslow and hinting at his love for Amy, *that* is what he wanted to tell her?

She pressed her lips together, pride and frustration pushing the words from her mouth before she could stop them. "Thank you. I'm sure we will be very happy together."

Now why in heaven's name did she have to say that? She wasn't even going to marry the man! And they certainly would not have been happy together.

Mr. Eastwood ceased his fidgeting, his expression falling. "I hope you will be. Goodbye, Miss Paxton."

He turned on his heel, walking away from the cottage with swift footing. Amy bit her tongue to keep herself from calling after him, no matter how her heart longed to connect with his.

She'd put herself out there too many times. If Mr. Eastwood was unwilling to fight for her, then...

Then what was he doing stopping? Her breathing constricted, her heart leaping to her throat.

In a single moment, Mr. Eastwood turned, his gaze fixed on her. "No. No, actually, that is not true."

She shook her head in confusion. "What do you—"

"I do not wish for you and Mr. Roberts to be happy together." He strode toward her, one deliberate step at a time. "I don't wish you to be happy with any man. Unless that man is me."

Her breathing shuddered, but she would not allow any further misunderstanding. "What are you saying, Mr. Eastwood?"

He stopped only a step away from her. "Tell me that I am selfish. Tell me that I am desperate or hopeless or a fool. But never—*never*—tell me that I am the man who gave you up for another."

Tears sprung to her eyes, and she bit her lip to keep her chin from quivering. Was this truly happening?

His expression softened, his eyes caressing her face. "I will always hold a fondness for Miss Winslow as my friend." He leaned forward, taking Amy's gloved hand in his. "But you, my darling Amy. You are and always will be my first—my only —love."

A smile spread across her lips, her chest swelling so greatly, she feared it might burst. How she'd longed for this moment, to hear him say such words. And now it was here, she could hardly believe it was true.

Mr. Eastwood reached forward, brushing aside a curl that had blown across her brow. "If you choose to honor your agreement with Mr. Roberts, I will respect your decision. But, please, have it be *your* decision. Not mine, nor Mr. Roberts's. Certainly not your brother's. Yours."

Amy's heart soared higher than the birds coasting above

Coniston Water. This, this was what she had wanted, for the choice to be hers. To not be influenced by Hugh, or by her fear and worry over being alone. She wanted to make her choice out of love, out of the deepest desires of her heart.

Looking up at him, a tear escaped her eye. "You, William. My choice is you."

He released a sigh. His own glassy eyes focused on hers before shifting to her lips.

Her heart flipped with desire, and she leaned toward him.

But…she couldn't. Not yet.

"William, wait…"

He pulled back at once, concern in his eyes. "I'm sorry. We don't have to…"

She shook her head. "No, I must first speak with Mr. Roberts. It would not be right to—"

"Eastwood! What the devil do you think you are doing?"

William dropped his hand from Miss Paxton's—from Amy's arm, turning to face Mr. Roberts as he approached.

"That is my betrothed!" Mr. Roberts shouted, coming upon them as rage popped his eyes into wide circles.

More footsteps pattered behind the man, and they were soon joined by the entire Paxton family. Hugh eyed the distance between William and Amy, his lips in a firm line. Mr. and Mrs. Paxton, however…William couldn't be sure, but he was fairly certain the look they exchanged with each other was filled with wide, hopeful eyes.

"Have you no explanation for your behavior?" Mr. Roberts shouted, his face red.

William squared his shoulders. "None whatsoever."

Mr. Roberts's face scrunched together. "Then I require you to meet me, sir."

William grimaced. He had to have known such a thing would occur after nearly kissing another man's intended. But how could he agree to a duel when his grandfather's dueling had been the very thing to have started this entire mess in the first place?

Then again, how could he honorably decline?

Mr. Paxton stepped forward. "Just a moment, surely there is another way this may be solved."

"Yes, Mr. Roberts, be reasonable," Mrs. Paxton added.

Hugh remained silent, his eyes hungrily taking in the ordeal. He looked very much like he could pop back with a piece of pie and watch the entire thing unfold before his eyes.

"I'll be reasonable when I receive justice!" Mr. Roberts belted out, his voice jarring against the calming sound of Coniston behind them.

Amy stepped forward. "Mr. Roberts, do calm yourself. A duel is hardly necessary."

"Hardly necessary?" he shouted. "You were in the arms of another man! Do you still expect us to wed after this?"

"No, of course I don't."

William could have cheered with pride over her confident stance. Mr. Paxton's lips twitched. Mrs. Paxton covered her mouth with her hand. Even Hugh blinked in stunned silence.

Mr. Roberts, however, merely crumpled his face into a greater frown. "I can only imagine what all of Bath will say when they hear about your shameful behavior, Miss Paxton."

William's fists clenched. Before he could defend the woman he loved, however, Amy's lips thinned.

She walked toward Mr. Roberts, pointing her finger at his chest. "How dare you threaten me! How dare you even consider such a thing after the rumors you've already spread! Mr. Eastwood and I have not even so much as kissed, as I wished to end our engagement first—out of respect for you. Well, sir, consider this the formal end of our relationship. I wish you luck in finding another woman who will agree to marry you for you to regain your fortune."

He blinked, sputtering. "I-I will not stand for this. I will hold you to our engagement, or—"

"Or you will what?" Mr. Paxton demanded. He moved forward, standing to his full height.

Mr. Roberts cowered at once, taking a step back. "Very well, the engagement is void. But I still demand justice from Mr. Eastwood."

Hugh cleared his throat, inching toward Mr. Roberts with a hand on his shoulder. "Roberts, perhaps you ought to rethink this. After all, you're more rubbish at swords and pistols than you are at rowing a boat."

Mr. Roberts's angry eyes swung to Hugh's. A moment later, however, his shoulders fell.

"And," Hugh said, his voice lowering so William could only just make out his words, "your parents won't allow you a single pence back if they discover you've been dueling."

A silent, tense moment passed as all eyes watched Mr. Roberts. Finally, he released an aggravated sigh. "I never should have entangled myself with such a family. You are all a waste of my time."

With a spiteful look at Amy, he turned on his heel and headed straight for the road.

"You'll get back to Bath far quicker if you ride your horse instead of walk, Mr. Roberts," Mrs. Paxton called out, her eyes twinkling.

Mr. Roberts hesitated then turned back around, awkwardly skirting past the Paxtons and William to retrieve his horse from the stables.

In a matter of minutes, he galloped away from the cottage once and for all.

"I daresay I've lost a friend in him," Hugh said, propping his hands on his hips as he watched him disappear down the road.

Mr. Paxton draped his arm across his son's shoulders. "Well, you may have lost a friend, but you've gained my respect. At least, in part."

Hugh eyed him, smirking at his father's words. The father and son, followed closely by Mrs. Paxton, wandered toward the house.

But William hesitated. There was only one thing he wanted to do right now, and it certainly wasn't joining the Paxtons inside.

He glanced to Amy, who smiled shyly up at him. His eyes settled on her pink lips.

"We'll expect to see the both of you in thirty minutes."

They turned at the sound of Mr. Paxton's voice, though he had already disappeared around the side of the cottage. In the next moment, the door closed behind the Paxtons, and William and Amy were finally left alone.

He stared down at Amy, *his* Amy, and she ducked her head. "I'm not sure what to say now."

William grinned. "I do believe that would be a first for you."

She dropped her mouth in feigned offense. "Is this what treatment I am to expect from you when we are married?"

He held out his hand to her which she took in an instant. "Not at all. What with the scolding I've seen you give Hugh and now Mr. Roberts, I wouldn't dare."

She playfully swatted him on the chest.

"In truth," he said, "you are to expect only the best from me. And if ever I treat you in a manner undeserving of you, I've no doubt you will let me know."

She laughed—that same laughter that had made him fall for her in the first place, that same laughter that had wrapped him up in that delicate ribbon and tied him directly to her.

"Although, I've not officially proposed, have I?"

She sobered instantly, looking up at him with hesitance. "No, you haven't."

He stared down at her glove, tugging at the finger of the fabric before looking at her. "May I?"

She swallowed, nodding all the same. Swiftly, he removed his own gloves, carelessly tossing them to the ground.

Then he moved to hers. One by one, he tugged the smooth fabric from her fingers, sliding the remaining silk down the length of her arm in a slow, deliberate movement. As he started with the next, his eyes found hers, unwavering as he worked.

Her breath shuddered as she breathed in, sending his heart in a frenzy. He slid his hand up the length of her glove, caressing her as he moved back down, pulling the fabric along with it. Her smooth flesh was soon covered in chills, and a smile tugged at his lips.

When he finished, he held both gloves in his hands, eying them before glancing to where his gloves lay in the dewy grass. He could not place the more delicate items on the ground to ruin them.

Amy reached for the gloves herself, tossing them directly to the ground without a care.

His heart skipped a beat with anticipation as she peered up at him.

Finally, he reached forth, taking her hands, now bare, in his. He held them for a moment before sliding his hands up and down her arms.

"I never knew what love was until I met you," he said. "I never knew what it felt like to smile, to laugh, to *feel* so much, until you came into my life." He stared into her eyes the color of Coniston Water in the morning. "I never wish to be without that again, I never wish to be without *you* again. So, my darling, my friend, my Amy, will you marry me?"

She drew in a shaking breath, smiling through trembling lips. "How could I ever say no to the man who encouraged me to shine? Yes, William. I will marry you."

He'd expected the answer—heavens, she'd already given him

one. But to hear the words leave her mouth, his heart was fully encompassed.

His breathing shallowed, and he raised a hand to caress her cheek with the barest hint of a touch. As his fingertips rested at the side of her neck, he leaned forward, her sweet breath on his lips, her nose brushing against his.

He wanted this moment to last, he wanted to remember it forever, so he paused just before their lips could touch, emblazoning every moment, every breath, every sweet smell in his memory before continuing.

Then finally, he leaned just enough for his lips to graze against hers. Pulses of energy swirled deep within him, and warmth cloaked his heart. He raised his lips from hers, only to return to them in a deeper, more fervent kiss.

This was everything a kiss ought to be. Soft, sweet, and shared with the woman he loved. But he could not be satisfied. He pulled away again, tipping his head to the side, hovering just above her lips. Their breath mingled warmly amidst the swiftly cooling autumn air until Amy's hands slid up his waistcoat, grasping his lapel and drawing him forward until their lips met in a firm, lingering kiss.

His smile begged to be released, to feel her own desire mixed with his, but he would do nothing to end the kiss he shared with the woman he loved—with the woman who loved him in return.

Amy had waited long enough for this kiss and was done with William's teasing. Of course, she'd hesitated pulling him in for a deeper kiss, but then, when had she ever hesitated being forward?

Certainly, this time, her forthright behavior had paid off.

A deep sigh, so deep it nearly sounded as a soft moan,

rumbled in William's chest. Her heart quickened, their lips moving against each other in perfect symmetry.

This was what she'd dreamt of for so long. This was what she'd longed for. Not just a kiss from the man she loved, but to feel his love for her in his affection. To feel his arms wrap around her, possessive and protective. To feel as if she was worth all the money in the world to this man who held her so comfortingly.

After a short time, their affection slowed, and they pulled apart, arms wrapped around each other as William rested his forehead against hers.

"I suppose we had better get inside before your father comes looking for us."

She nodded with a mumbled affirmation, though there was nothing she wanted to do in that moment more than kiss the man for the rest of her days.

There would be time enough for that later, though.

She pulled back, tracing his lower lip with her finger. "I love you."

He reached forward, placing a kiss to the tip of her nose before leaning back and taking her hand in his and leading her toward the cottage.

"Who would have ever thought a simple chicken being thrown in my face would have led to a marriage?" Amy said with a small curve of her lips.

He glanced toward her with a raised brow. "For the record, I did not throw the chicken at your face. She merely leapt from my hands."

"Because you were not—"

"Holding her properly, I know, I know."

They shared a smile.

"I just hope you will learn how to properly hold a child before we have any, otherwise I don't know how I would feel about one *leaping* from your hands."

He chuckled, stopping their progression to the cottage and sliding his arms under hers, wrapping his hands around her back. She linked her fingers at the back of his neck, smiling up at him.

"How many will we have, do you think?" he asked.

"Oh, ten, at the least."

His eyes rounded. "Children?"

She laughed. "Hens, silly. Children, we'll have a hearty dozen."

She winked, and he peered down at her, his green eyes holding the warmth of his love for her within them.

And as he leaned down to press his lips against hers once again, she was overcome with gratitude for where her life was, and for all that had occurred to get her to that point.

Thank heavens for William. Thank heavens for the cottage by Coniston. And thank heavens for hens.

EPILOGUE

*W*illiam stood in front of Birchwick Hall, clasping his hands behind his back as Amy came up to stand beside him, lacing her hand through his arm.

"They cannot be much longer, can they?" She peered down the long drive, standing on the tips of her toes.

William smiled, placing a kiss to the top of her head. After six years of marriage, her impatience still endeared her to him. "You know you cannot see farther down a straight road by being taller, do you not?"

She looked up at him, pursing her lips in feigned frustration. "I just cannot wait. It's been so very long since we've seen them last."

William nodded. They hadn't seen Mr. and Mrs. Paxton for months, and Hugh for nearly a year. Amy's parents still came every autumn—and occasionally in the spring—to the Lake District. Though William offered them rooms at Birchwick, they only ever requested to stay at the cottage.

"We have such fond memories there," Mr. Paxton often said. "It is where our Amy finally found her happiness."

William peered down at her, her smile beaming and eyes aglow. She certainly was happy. Just as he was.

Amy gasped, moving up and down on the tips of her toes. "I see them!"

William followed her gaze to where a carriage with two black horses rode toward them on the drive. The grass was no longer pristine, though it was still tidy, and a few of the trees had already begun to drop their leaves in the chilly, autumn temperatures. Grandfather had always required the leaves to be cleaned frequently so as not to hide the grass.

Amy, however, loved the leaves on the grounds and requested they be kept there as long as possible. She would often take the children on walks, crunching the leaves beneath their boots and jumping into piles.

Marrying her had been the best decision William had ever made, and for so many reasons—including improving the state of Birchwick's stilted air. In the six years they'd lived there together, her brilliance and vivacity for life had brightened every dreary corner and invigorated every lifeless room, until William had finally grown to love his home for the life he and Amy had created there.

Laughter and soft footsteps pattered behind them, drawing him back to the present.

"Mama! Papa!"

William turned around in time for their oldest son to barrel into William's hip. Philip, who had just turned five, staggered back with a laugh, wiggling his head back and forth with a silly expression.

"Are you all right, son?" William chuckled, steadying him.

"Yes," Philip said, moving toward him for a slower embrace. "Even after running into your large bott—"

"That is quite enough of that, Philip," Amy said with a raised brow, though her eyes twinkled.

She reached for the toddler in the nursemaid's arms, giving

her a grateful nod before the woman backed away. "And how are you today, John? My darling little boy." She kissed their younger son on his full, round cheek. "Excited to see your grandparents again?"

"Yes, yes!" John squealed, clapping his chubby fingers together. "An' gifts!"

"Oh, yes! Grandmother and Grandfather always bring the best gifts!" Philip added.

Amy gave William a look. "I suppose it is clear what makes the two of them happy."

William chuckled, resting one hand on Philip's head and wrapping the other arm round Amy's shoulder as the four of them turned to the carriage nearly upon them.

Gifts certainly did make their boys happy, but William couldn't blame them. Gifts made William happy, as well. And the greatest of all his gifts were standing right there beside him.

He didn't know what he'd done, being so blessed beyond measure with his wife and children. But Heaven knew he would do his best to always live worthily of their love.

Amy couldn't wait any longer. The moment the carriage door opened, she bounded forth, wrapping her arms around her mother. "I've decided you both need to relocate here permanently, Mama. I cannot bear only seeing you twice a year."

Mama laughed, pulling away so Father could embrace Amy next.

"How are you, cricket?" he asked, placing a warm kiss to her temple. He pulled back, leaning down to better see John, who was still in Amy's arms. "And how are *you*, my littler cricket?"

John reached forth, wrapping his little arms around his grandfather's neck.

As William greeted Mother and Father, Hugh stepped down

from the carriage, and Amy moved to embrace him next. She'd been so angry with him in the days leading up to William's proposal, but after he'd convinced Mr. Roberts to not go through with the duel, she'd managed to forgive him yet again. Now, she actually enjoyed his company. Not living in the same house as the man suited her very much, indeed, for there was less time for him to tease her.

"It is lovely to see you again, sister."

"And you, Hugh. Tell me, how is Bath? And our old friends?"

"Very much the same, I think. Miss Jones recently became engaged, and Mr. Tenney." He peered down at her. "And our Mr. Roberts has finally found himself a wife, too."

"Heavens." She never thought she'd see the day. The man had been trying for years now. "How did he manage that?"

"As a matter of fact, he fell in love—and somehow convinced the girl to love him, too."

Amy smiled. "Well, I am happy for him then. And I wish his poor betrothed all the luck in the world."

They shared a smile and turned to face the others, though Amy's mind wandered to where it always did at the thought of Mr. Roberts or their lives before she'd married William.

Charity.

Amy had had the opportunity to speak with her before the wedding years ago, and though the encounter had been tense and uncomfortable, Amy was able to apologize for hurting her. Charity had been more than gracious, though understandably uncomfortable, and a few weeks later, she and her mother had relocated permanently to Yorkshire.

However, only a year ago, Charity had sent a letter to them that brightened both of their hearts.

I wish you both to know that while I was hurt then, I have always been grateful for your honesty. Were it not for that, I would never have found the love of my life, nor have given

birth to my beautiful daughter. I truly hope you both are
happy, as I am now myself.

The letter had been a relief for Amy and William both, for
neither of them had wished to hurt the woman.

"Uncle Hugh!"

Amy blinked, coming out of her reverie and focusing on her
son as he barreled toward Hugh.

Hugh caught him in a wide embrace. "Philip! Look how
you've grown! You're nearly as tall as I am now."

"I'll be taller than you one day, Uncle Hugh," Philip said with
a sure nod. "But I won't be as silly as you are, because *I'm* going
to get married when I'm older."

Amy's eyes widened, her cheeks burning, and William stifled
a cough that sounded suspiciously like laughter.

Hugh glanced pointedly at Amy. "I see you've been listening
to your mother's opinions again, haven't you, Philip?"

"Yes! And Papa's, too."

"All right, son," William said with another chuckle. He leaned
toward Amy as he led the group forward. "He gets that blunt
trait from you, you know."

Amy waved a hand. "Nonsense." Though she shared an
amused look with her father.

Their small party headed indoors, Papa walking ahead with
Hugh, William, and the children. "Will your parents be joining
us soon, William?" Father asked.

"Yes, for dinner this evening."

"And are they enjoying living in the manor?"

"I believe so. I've never seen them so happy."

Amy couldn't help but agree. William had protested the idea
of his own parents moving out of the house that was rightfully
theirs, but his father had insisted.

"It is time we put this place behind us, Will," he'd said a few
months after their marriage. "Your mother has always wanted

to live in the manor, and now, I finally get to give her what she has always wished for, what she more than deserves."

William was gaining a better relationship with his parents daily as Mr. and Mrs. Eastwood finally grew into their own people—away from Grandfather's influence.

"I do hope Mrs. Rutledge will be joining us this evening, as well," Mama added as they moved through the corridors. "How I miss that woman each time we leave this place."

"Oh, of course," Amy said. "She is looking forward to seeing you, as well."

Amy and William called on Mrs. Rutledge twice a week, if not more. The woman now had a young lady living with her as a companion, and they both seemed quite content. Though, Mrs. Rutledge often spoke of how she missed her dearly departed Philip.

"I have faith we shall meet again," she'd say each time she mentioned his name.

Amy had learned a great deal from the woman, and she owed much of her happiness in Coniston to her. After all, had it not been for Mrs. Rutledge's public support of Amy and William's marriage, the village could very well still despise Amy.

She couldn't blame the members of town for being standoff-ish. They'd been expecting William and Charity to wed for years. But little by little, Mrs. Rutledge's goodness rubbed off on the others, and her vocal defense finally convinced the village to accept Amy as one of their own.

Amy would be forever grateful to Mrs. Rutledge for helping it come about.

With a deep, contented sigh, she trailed after her family as they made their way to the drawing room. How her life was so perfect was beyond her. She really could ask for nothing more.

Except, perhaps...another child.

She pressed a hand to her churning stomach, a secretive smile touching her lips.

"What are you smiling about?"

She glanced up, William falling back from the group to walk beside her. He offered her his arm, which she readily took.

"Merely how happy I am," she said with another sigh. She would tell him about his third child soon—especially the inkling she had that this one was a girl. But for right now, she wished to relish in how perfect everything was. "I do love my life."

"Is that just because your parents are here?" he asked with narrowed eyes.

She swatted his arm. "You know that is not the reason I am so happy."

"What is the reason then?"

She smiled up at him, holding his arm so they stopped alone in the corridor.

She rested a hand on his cheek and reached up to place a lingering kiss on his lips. After a moment, she pulled back, but he leaned closer, not yet ready to end their kiss. A smile crept across her lips, and he pulled back with a contended sigh.

"I love you," he whispered.

"I love you, too."

And after another shared smile, the two of them linked arms and followed their family into the drawing room.

How blessed they were to have each other. How blessed they were to share such a love, to have such a light between them. For they both knew their love and that light would only continue to grow all the brighter as the years moved on.

And what could be better than that?

THE END

Next in the Seasons of Change series
Book Six, A Haunting at Havenwood by Sally Britton

AUTHOR'S NOTE

Thank you so much for reading my book! I hope you enjoyed it! Writing about Coniston was a sheer delight. The Lake District is gorgeous—one of my British husband's favorite places to visit! My goal as an author is to transport my readers to new places—places that I love myself—so I hope I was able to do so with this book, as well!

If you enjoyed "The Cottage by Coniston," please consider leaving a review. And if you'd like to receive the latest news about my future novels, sign up for my newsletter. I always share newly released and discounted clean romance novels, as well as fun polls, quotes, and giveaways. My newsletter subscribers are also the first to see sneak peeks and cover reveals!

Make sure to follow me on Facebook (for more clean romance deals) and Instagram (for photos of my travels to the UK and more).

I hope to connect with you soon!

Deborah

ACKNOWLEDGEMENTS

This book, like every book, was a challenge to write. I couldn't have finished it without the help of so many wonderful people in my life.

Usually, I end the acknowledgments by thanking my husband, but for this book, he needs to come first. After all, he was the one who suggested I write about the Lake District in the first place. Thank you for always encouraging me and supporting me. I don't know how you have the patience to listen to me day in and day out, but I will always be grateful that you do! I love you. (Now for reals...tell me if this book is good enough to be dedicated to you...)

Next, I need to thank my wonderful friend, Kasey Stockton. Not only is she an amazing author, she's also one of my greatest friends. She listened to me when I first started plotting this book, she encouraged me to keep pushing through the hard days, and she dropped everything to help me edit, beta read, and improve my writing. Thank you! Now go reward yourself by listening to Sam Heughan's accent.

To the rest of you who helped me with this book—Martha Keyes, Jess Heileman, Joanna Barker, and Jennie Proctor—thank you all so much! Because of you, I was able to push past my insecurities and deliver this book on time.

And finally, I want to thank my lovely, wonderful readers. You are the reason I write. Receiving your reviews, hearing your kind words about my own written words, means more to me than you will ever know. It spurs me on to write and lifts me during my low points. Thank you, to each and every one of you!

THE SEASONS OF CHANGE SERIES*

Book One, The Road Through Rushbury by Martha Keyes
Book Two, A Forgiving Heart by Kasey Stockton
Book Three, The Last Eligible Bachelor by Ashtyn Newbold
Book Four, A Well-Trained Lady by Jess Heileman
Book Five, The Cottage by Coniston by Deborah M. Hathaway
Book Six, A Haunting at Havenwood by Sally Britton
Book Seven, His Disinclined Bride by Jennie Goutet

These books can be read in any order

BOOKS BY DEBORAH M. HATHAWAY

Stand Alone Novels
A Secret Fire
When Two Rivers Meet
To Warm a Wintered Heart

A Cornish Romance Series
On the Shores of Tregalwen, a Novella
Behind the Light of Golowduyn, Book One
For the Lady of Lowena, Book Two
Near the Ruins of Penharrow, Book Three

Belles of Christmas Multi-Author Series
Nine Ladies Dancing, Book Four
On the Second Day of Christmas, Book Four

Seasons of Change Multi-Author Series
The Cottage by Coniston, Book Five

ABOUT THE AUTHOR

Deborah M. Hathaway graduated from Utah State University with a BA in English, Creative Writing. As a young girl, she devoured Jane Austen's novels while watching and re-watching every adaptation of Pride & Prejudice she could, entirely captured by all things Regency and romance.

Throughout her early life, she wrote many short stories, poems, and essays, but it was not until after her marriage that she was finally able to complete her first romance novel, attributing the completion to her courtship with, and love of, her charming, English husband. Deborah finds her inspiration for her novels in her everyday experiences with her husband and children and during her travels to the United Kingdom, where she draws on the beauty of the country in such places as Ireland, Yorkshire, and her beloved Cornwall.

CPSIA information can be obtained
at www.ICGtesting.com
Printed in the USA
LVHW012348290920
667463LV00003B/896